WASTELAND BLUES

BY

SCOTT CHRISTIAN CARR
& ANDREW CONRY-MURRAY

DOG STAR
BOOKS

WASTELAND BLUES © 2014
by Scott Christian Carr & Andrew Conry-Murray

Published by Dog Star Books
Bowie, MD

First Edition

Cover Image: Bradley Sharp
Book Design: Jeremy Zerfoss

Printed in the United States of America

ISBN: 978-1-935738-59-6

Library of Congress Control Number: 2013956318

www.DogStarBooks.org

FOREWORD

Five years ago I edited my first anthology for Shroud Publishing—*Beneath the Surface, 13+ Shocking Tales of Terror*. I had acquired a chilling piece of cover art that depicted a Cthulu-esque creature submerged in the murky, virescent depths of some unknown sea. The image inspired the title, and although the anthology did not have a specifically-stated oceanic theme, one of the first stories I received was about a doomed submarine, *The Paramus*, and its lone suffering survivor stranded on the ocean floor. The story was *Thorguson*, and it was written by Scott Christian Carr.

So stricken by the tale, I accepted it immediately and made it the flagship of the anthology (which went on to receive a Bram Stoker nomination for "Best Anthology" by the Horror Writers Association). Thus began my relationship with Scott, which continued through our collaboration on the *Scandalous Misadventures of Hiram Grange*. It was Scott that truly captured the frenetic, tortured, drug-addled vision of Hiram in his book *Hiram Grange and the Twelve Little Hitlers*. Scott has gone on to write several more stories about Hiram, and I am always impressed by his wild imagination, uniqueness of voice, and dark, intelligent humor. I am both his friend and his fan.

In *Wasteland Blues*, Scott is joined by his college friend, Andrew Conry-Murray, in crafting an inventive post-apocalyptic adventure that features an array of deeply-realized characters, striking plot twists, and a wholly new vision of life after the fall of modern civilization. Andrew and Scott are effective in writing in a singular voice, where it seems that Scott's chaotic pacing is tempered by Andrew's sensibilities. This is mere speculation of course, but I believe it's bolstered by the fact that while Scott penned wild stories of diaper-clad Hitler clones, Andrew wrote *The Symantec Guide to Internet Security*.

Andrew is the editor of *Network Computing*, where he leads the site's reporting on technology issues. Technology plays a leading role in *Wasteland Blues*. Technology manifests as a lurking revenant in the shadows of the parched, and sand-covered towns that *Wasteland's* motley quartet of protagonists travel through. It is both sought after and cursed. It lies dead in the rusty, jagged piles of *The Heap* like a memory one begs to be forgotten; however, in the end, technology may also bring salvation...

It is no secret that Scott and Andrew are in some way inspired by T.S. Eliot's experimental poem, *The Waste Land*. Just as Eliot's poem reflected and refracted the dismal and dismantled conditions of post World War I Europe, *Wasteland Blues* similarly makes a statement about the violence and excess of the 21st century. Where Eliot creates an amalgam of voices and visions, both modern and ancient, Scott and Andrew congeal those voices and visions into a handful of unique points of view—each thirsty for the realization of their own hopes, and dreams of survival. In the end, both *The Waste Land* and *Wasteland Blues* deliver bleak, dry, landscapes populated with rich mythical images.

It's fitting, somehow, that five years after Thorguson haunted me deep below the surface of a vast ocean, *Wasteland Blues* would desiccate me and taunt me with the promise of water.

Tim Deal, 2013

CHAPTER ONE

The world had slid backward since Old Scratch pissed radioactive fire down on the righteous and unrighteous alike. Derek Cane, one of the unrighteous, understood this every time he gazed across The Heap—a hundred-acre dumpsite piled high with the detritus of another age.

Derek hunched in the cab of the wrecking crane, 150 feet above The Heap's auto yard. From this vantage he could see the warren of paths that a generation of scavengers had carved through the sprawling mounds of trash and rusting, motionless cars.

Derek and his younger brother, Teddy, had been coming to The Heap for as long as he could remember—playing in the auto graveyard, scaling the wrecking crane, and sifting through mountains of junk in search of salvage. Teddy loved the place.

The Heap was the economic center of San Muyamo, the tiny refugee village that, until today, the brothers had called home. The village had sprung up after the biotoxin cloud had blown in off the Pacific and draped itself like a funeral shroud over the coast.

San Muyamo's stock-in-trade was copper wire, car parts, batteries and other small components—washers, O-rings, gear heads, screws and belts, nuts and bolts. Things that meant the difference between scrap metal and a functioning machine. The village's clients were traders (Bedouins mostly, in their shrouded faces and covered wagons) that kept the rusty goods flowing among the struggling towns and villages as far north as Corvallis, Oregon and as far south as the fallout border near San Diego. Derek's father had laughed at the irony of the salvage trade. So much effort spent *'afore-The-War* in centralizing the waste, piling it all into one place, and now here they were scattering it all outward again, like seed pods blown from a clump of dandelions.

But the traders and caravans along the old road had grown fewer, of late. Derek's father, David Cane, had supposed that a better route to the coast had maybe opened up, but Derek thought otherwise. The elder Cane believed that over time the world would rebuild itself, each generation constructing on the foundations of the last. But Derek had been born after the Rendering, and he knew better—a new world couldn't be built from the junk of the old.

The cracked plastic of the crane's bucket seat stuck to his back. Derek toyed idly with his father's wedding band—he'd taken it before wrapping the dead man in a dirty white sheet. The sun rode high in the sky, a shard of angry light bouncing off the broken glass that littered The Heap like diamonds. It had been less than an hour since Derek had led Teddy down a seldom-used path to a moldering heap of mattresses, where they'd dumped the body of their murdered father near a nest of radar rats.

The cab shifted, rocking in a great creaking arc, pushed one way and then the other by slight breezes. Derek had only ever seen the crane in operation once, maybe nine or ten years ago, back when the tank still held muddy diesel and the engine hadn't been picked clean. He and Teddy had been halfway up the slope of a two-story mound of trash in the southeast corner of The Heap when they'd heard the engine bark and sputter. Derek had dropped the extension cord he'd been trying to free from an unseen snarl somewhere in the innards of The Heap and watched as the crane roared into life, lurching clumsily to the right and then to the left. A plexiglass window popped open in the crane's cab and they saw an older boy waving frantically.

"He musta found the key!" shouted Derek to his brother.

The boy had also found the lever that released the jaws that lifted cars into the crusher. The gaping metal mouth fell the length of its line and tore through the cab of a battered Toyota pickup with the joyful noise of destruction.

Derek pumped one fist into the air and shrieked with delight. Teddy thrust his hamfist toward the sky, emulating his brother. Ragged children scrambled over the heap toward the crane from all points of the dump. Derek pushed Teddy onto the round metal saucer they used to collect their haul and then leapt on himself. With a *whoosh* they slid down the side of the mountain of trash and nearly impaled themselves on the rusted end of an uprooted STOP sign at the base of the mound.

By the time they had clambered through the constellations of junk to join the others, who'd gathered a prudent distance from the machine, the boy in the cab had mastered the crane's basic operations. Again the huge jaws fell onto a car like a hawk dropping on a pheasant. Talons locked into the metal frame. With a grinding whine of motors and shriek of tearing metal, the car was lifted into the air. Rusty, threadbare cables strained as the boy drew it to the very top of its line, and then held it in a moment of shivering anticipation.

"Drop! Drop! Drop!" chanted the adolescent scavengers below, and, with a painful shriek, the crane's jaws sprang open. The car was released more than one hundred and twenty feet above a lot of tightly-packed vehicles that had been waiting nearly half a century to be scrapped. Teddy pressed his oversized hands to his ears and clenched his teeth—but Derek did no such thing. He wanted to hear the crash. Feel the punch of the impact in his scrotum and the bottoms of his feet. And for one wild moment he thought he might fling himself into the center of the bull's-eye, a fleshy wet target for a 2,000-pound gravity bomb.

The car landed squarely on the back of a minivan and obliterated it. Glass shards shotgunned outward as all its windows exploded. The noise was immeasurable and righteous, like the boot-heel of the Virgin crushing the head of the serpent.

And then the young scavengers were running for the base of the crane. Older kids shoved younger children aside in the mad scramble to mount the ladder and take a turn at the controls.

Derek had never gotten a chance. The crane had run out of fuel long before he was able to push and fight his way into the cab. That's the way it was in San Muyamo—the last bits of life got squeezed out of the relics of the past, got squeezed until nothing was left for you.

Derek's father had never understood this. To David Cane, The Heap was compost upon which to grow a new civilization, a map to circumvent the long ages of Bronze, Iron, and Steam and reclaim combustion engines and electricity. He'd pop open a cell phone and trace the printed circuitry of its guts and say, "We don't have to lose it all. We don't have to fall all the way back."

Derek knew better. The world had slid backward. The world was a corpse without the good sense to know it was dead.

Derek popped the window of the cab and took a last look at the only place he had ever known—the alluring filth of The Heap and the hovels of San Muyamo beyond, just over the hill. He looked down on his older brother, sitting at the wheel of his favorite car, a Cadillac El Dorado whose Mary-Kay-pink exterior had improbably rebuffed decades of blazing sun, acid rain and bird shit, and whose driver's seat could barely contain Teddy's muscle-bound girth. Derek couldn't hear his brother, but he knew that Teddy would be making *p-bbb-bb* noises as he pretended to drive.

Teddy. Weak in the head, strong in the body. Get him mad enough and he could probably flip the El Dorado without breaking a sweat. Get him mad enough, and with just two fingers he might snap his own father's neck.

Derek took his last look at the dump and climbed quickly down the rusting ladder. He and Teddy had to get on the road. Someone was likely to come across the body of their father because the good citizens of San Muyamo weren't above a little rat hunting to supplement their larders.

"Time to go," Derek said, interrupting Teddy's automotive fantasy.

"Go?" asked Teddy, looking up from the driver's seat. "We goin' home now, Der?"

"No. We're going away. But first we have to get someone."

They waited at the corroded aluminum picnic table that stood across from the Church of the Word, a doublewide construction trailer jacked up on concrete blocks. Derek knew John would be inside—John never missed Bible instruction.

The rusty door soon squeaked open and a dozen or so folks exited, John among them. John stood for a moment on the rickety steps chatting with Elder Hale.

Derek rose but didn't approach the church. His family was one of the few that didn't attend services. Neither he nor Teddy had been baptized—better to save what little kerosene they had for more practical purposes. Derek's father had tried to raise his boys to believe in technology, not an invisible spirit in the sky. God was not going to rebuild the world, but human ingenuity might.

"Those kids can quote the Bible front to back, but they can't do simple algebra!" This was one of David Cane's favorite complaints, and he had rehearsed it often.

Most of the churchgoing people of San Muyamo had little to do with the Canes—their infidelity hung about them like a cloud of fallout.

John saw the brothers and waved. Elder Hale turned to regard them, his wispy white hair a corona around his sun-scorched face. He frowned and put both hands on the boy's shoulders and spoke a in hushed, disapproving whisper, gesturing toward the brothers with a flick of his white cotton robe.

Derek guessed that Hale was exhorting John to bring them the Word of God, as was his duty.

Hale went back inside the church trailer and John strode across the dust to his friends. John was a scrawny young man with an awkward gait. He walked with his shoulders perpetually hunched, as if expecting a blow. He wore loose white robes in imitation of Elder Hale and had sandals made from old tires on his long feet.

Derek watched him approach, his argument ready on his tongue.

"Hi fellas," said John. "What are you doin' out here? You want to come inside? Elder Hale would be happy to see you."

"I had the vision again," said Derek. He put an arm around John's shoulders and steered him away from the trailer.

"The same one?" asked John.

"Yes," said Derek.

"And the angels? They spoke to you?"

Derek nodded. He wouldn't call the flying things in his dream "angels," but it was the right word to use on John.

"And they showed you the same thing? The buildings are still standing?"

"Yep. But there was more this time."

John was breathing a little more quickly now.

"I saw the road," said Derek. "Like I was floating above it—or maybe the angels were carrying me. And I saw shadows. Shadows of people walking, the sun at their backs...*Our* shadows...."

"You and Teddy?"

"Three shadows," said Derek. He looked at John, eyes flat and expressionless, letting John do the counting for himself. He let John digest his lie. There'd been more than three shadows, and Derek wasn't entirely sure the shadows were *theirs*, but John didn't need to know that. It was John he wanted.

John's hand trailed up to the celery stalk of his neck, one finger flicking absently at his Adam's apple.

"And you're sure," he asked quietly, "that it's *New York*?"

"What else could it be?" said Derek.

"The Third Prophet came from New York," said John. "He planted seeds—seeds that would bloom after the fire."

Derek said nothing. He'd heard all this before—the prophet who had predicted the destruction of the world and the believers who would renew the earth. The Church of the Word was built on two books: the Bible and the Book of Joseph. The latter was a collection of sermons from a man, Joseph Crier. Believers called him The Third Prophet. Derek had skimmed through the book. It was a bunch of nonsense, but John bought into the whole thing. Derek was willing to get what he wanted by using his friend's faith.

"You remember what the prophet said, don't you?" asked Derek.

"Sure I do," said John. He assumed his recitation posture, lifting one finger in the air. "I saw the angel, dressed in robes of white. And the angel stood above a great city to render the Word. And I recognized that city, the most famous of all cities, the city at the center of the world. After the days of fire, the angel said to come here and renew the city, remake its foundations to stand on faith, a foundation more secure than bedrock. And we shall lay the foundations for the New Jerusalem, here in this place."

"You believe those words?" asked Derek, though he already knew the answer.

"Course I do!"

"OK then. Let's go."

John thought for a long moment. "When are you leaving?"

"Today. Now."

John's eyes grew wide. "Now? Why?"

"It's time," said Derek, unable to stop himself from glancing over his shoulder toward the distant crane that rose up out of The Heap, looming in stark silhouette against the ultraviolet sun.

"Derek, I—" began John, but Derek cut him off.

"Look," he said. "Teddy and I are goin'. Today. And I think you should come with us. But if you won't, then that's fine. Walk away right now. We'll understand…the angels will understand." Derek didn't fail to notice the sharp pang of hurt in John's eyes. Without moving his lips, Derek smiled.

"What about your father? You're going to leave him all alone?"

Derek looked at the ground.

"I know you don't get along," began John, "but sons should honor—"

"He doesn't need us," said Derek sharply.

"Okay, okay," said John.

"Then it's decision time," Derek pressed. "Will you make up your own mind, or do you need to get permission from Daddy Hale? Sorry, I mean *Elder* Hale?"

John's parents had died when the boy was seven. He had been one of many orphans raised by the Elders, though he had spent nearly as much time living with Derek and Teddy, scavenging junk for David Cane, as he had in the common house.

"I've already spoken to him about it," John admitted, daring Derek to get angry with him. "I went to him the first time you told me about your vision."

"Huh," snorted Derek. "What'd he say?"

Teddy was twiddling his thumbs, bored and impatient. The conversation had transcended his ability to follow it.

"We goin' now, Der?" Teddy asked.

Derek ignored him. To John he asked, "So, what'd he say?"

Now it was John's turn to look at the ground. "He…he doesn't think you're telling the truth. He thinks you're making it up."

"Does he? Why?"

"Because," said John, "why would God speak to you?"

Good question, thought Derek.

"But I believe you," John quickly added. "I mean, if God would speak to Saul, why shouldn't He speak to you? No offense."

"None taken," Derek said.

He actually couldn't explain the dream—*the vision*, as he'd described it to John—but Derek was pretty sure it wasn't divine.

"So what if Hale says no?" asked Derek. "It's gonna be a Hell of a long journey. I mean, even if we make it, we'll probably never come back here again."

"I know," said John. "But if it's God's plan, how could I say no?"

Derek smiled. Things were always easier when you had God on your side. "Good. Meet us at the edge of town in fifteen minutes. After today, all roads lead east. To New York City."

Derek and Teddy snuck back home. They stood just outside the ramshackle RV that hadn't moved since Derek was five. The tires had long since rotted away, and the vehicle had settled onto its undercarriage in a roach-infested nest of dirt and filth. Derek looked over his shoulder. No one was looking their way. Returning here was risky, but he needed to collect a few things before they left.

He wanted to make it quick, but Teddy wouldn't step inside.

"C'mon," said Derek in his calmest, most soothing voice. He knew any hint of impatience would just set Teddy more firmly on his haunches. "C'mon, Ted—it's okay. The body isn't even here anymore. We tossed it, remember?"

"No," insisted Teddy. "There might be...spooks."

Derek sighed. Teddy'd been spending too much time listening to John. Spooks and angels. On the road, he'd have to watch that. "All right, fine. You wait out here. I'll be right out."

A meaty hand clutched Derek's arm in an iron grip. Teddy's fingers dug into Derek's bicep.

"Just one minute," said Derek firmly.

Teddy released him. "I sorry, Derek. I didn't mean to make him deaded." Teddy frowned, squeezed his eyes shut, and began to cry.

"Hush!" Derek hissed. "Just shut your fuckin' mouth!"

The Elders tolerated non-believers, barely, but not murderers. Justice would be swift and certain if they were discovered. The crane in The Heap transformed into a makeshift gallows. His and Teddy's bodies would be left to swing for a year and a day, food for crow and fly.

"You be quiet," hissed Derek. "What happened, happened. It wasn't your fault." He grabbed his brother's left wrist and pulled back the sleeve to reveal a trail of ugly red burns. "It wasn't your fault, see?"

Teddy yanked his arm away and pushed his sleeve down. He sniffled mightily and turned from his brother. "Go fast, Der-Der."

CHAPTER TWO

Derek and Teddy met John at noon, just as the village was settling in for siesta, when it was too hot to work, too hot to be swathed in the rags needed to protect the skin from the ultraviolet noonday sun. Derek didn't want anyone to see them leaving. There would be questions, and Teddy was a poor liar.

But Derek's hope to leave town unobserved was thwarted before the journey had begun in earnest. At the edge of town they ran into Leggy, the crippled, old village drunk. He was sitting in his wheelchair and urinating on a thorn bush. He zipped up as they passed.

"'Nother piss-ass day," he said. "How many more before I'm quit of this place?" The old man's legs had been sheared away at the knees by a bug, and the ugly, cauterized stumps poked from the dilapidated wheelchair like an accusation.

"All in God's time," muttered John.

"God's a cocksucker," said Leggy, inching forward on the battered rims of the chair—a wet patch stained the front of his pants where he'd hastily zipped them.

John ignored the blasphemies. The old man was famous for them. The Elders let him get away with it because they said he would have to reckon with the Lord when he passed. John reckoned that the Lord might be into more than He bargained for in trying to reckon with Leggy. Derek knew that the Elders let Leggy's colorful blasphemies slide, not just because he was the oldest man in the village, but because Leggy was the only one who could get the generator working—and keep it working. When they had fuel, that was.

"So where are you ladies off to this morning?" Leggy asked. "Headin' over to Sanger to catch yourselves some wives? Does this mean somebody's finally takin' my advice about not layin' with their sisters?"

"We're going to New York," said John proudly.

Derek stiffened. He hadn't wanted to broadcast their plans.

"Really now?" Leggy stroked his grizzled chin. "That's ambitious. Too bad you won't make it."

"We'll make it," said Derek.

"You won't. And so what if you do?" asked Leggy. "It ain't gonna be no different than here. Bound ta be a Helluva lot worse. If it's even still there, that is. Heh, heh."

"Derek believes there might be angels in New York," said John. He lifted up his copy of "The Book of Joseph," a gift from Elder Hale last season on his sixteenth birthday. "'And the angels came to the great cities of the world to render the Word, so that man might know his sin and repent.' The Book says New York was a great city. So maybe the angels are there. Derek thinks they are. He—"

"It was a great city," interrupted Leggy. "Till they nuked it. But don't let me piss on yer parade." He cackled and bugged his eyes out at them.

Leaving Leggy's biting laughter behind them, the boys hefted their meager gear and walked out of town. The disc of the sun hung lazily overhead. They had only gone a few yards past the scrabble of wild bramble and rusted tracks that marked San Muyamo's border—the path led into a decrepit forest of dead cacti, petrified signposts, leaning telephone spires, and long, thorny brambles—when the old man shouted after them, "When you get to the Wasteland, you'd better bottle your piss. You'll probably need it." He laughed again, turned his wheelchair back toward San Muyamo, and began to sing in a shrill, nasal voice. *"You are my sunshine, my only sunshine. You make me haaaaappy...."*

Then the land dipped, and their home was behind them.

Derek's face grew red and he trembled with rage as he turned the Legless Wonder's words over and over in his mind, "When you get to the Wasteland, you'd better bottle your piss. Too bad you won't make it."

Who did that old bastard think he was to cast doubt on *their* plans? And if that senile fuck told anyone else where they were headed, the villagers might track them down.

Derek waited until they had gone another mile or so into the bramble, then suddenly stopped and whispered "You hear that?"

He knew there was nothing out there, but was satisfied that the others had stopped.

"Could'a sworn I heard something," said Derek.

John squinted his eyes in concentration. After a second, Teddy mimicked this action, squeezing his own eyes shut and poking his huge purple tongue from the corner of his mouth.

"I don't hear anything," said John.

"I'm sure I heard something," Derek said. "You two wait here and I'll run back and take a look." He reached out and touched his brother lightly on the elbow. When there was no response, he poked harder. "Teddy, open your eyes," he commanded.

Teddy responded obediently. First one eye popped open and then the next. He grinned sheepishly and sucked in his tongue. "I wuz fallin' sleepy-sleep, Der."

"You stay here with John. Don't go nowhere." With that he turned and began to tread stealthily back in the direction from which they had come. "Don't move."

"But—" John began.

"I said stay put!" hissed Derek.

John sat down hard on the packed earth and the contract was sealed—Derek was giving the orders.

Derek crept back to the edge of town. Leggy was wheeling himself slowly along the road, still singing. *"Ooyyyy-yoouuuu yeeeeeeeee!!! Please don't take my sunshine awaaaaaay…"*

In a quick motion Derek pulled his father's bone-handled hunting knife from his belt and lunged. Leggy's voice cracked and his singing abruptly stopped as Derek grabbed a wheel of the chair with one hand and held the knife across the old man's throat with the other.

"Now listen to me, you legless old *fuck*," Derek hissed. "You don't tell anybody that you saw us goin', you got that?" He pressed the blade hard against the man's grizzled neck. "You don't say shit about this to no one!" He pulled the knife away and wheeled the old man roughly around to face him. A thin line of blood appeared on Leggy's neck. "One word about this and you're dead."

The old man blinked, but remained silent.

"You understand me?" Derek spat at him.

Leggy was nonplussed. "If you're really leavin', how are you gonna know if I told anyone I saw you go?"

Derek shook with fury. The knife trembled in his hand. He opened his mouth to speak, but could think of nothing to say.

Without a word he moved forward, gripped the chair by its tattered rubber handles, and wheeled the old man off into the scrubland.

The wheelchair bumped and rattled as Derek forced it over age-old remnants of cracked, sun-bleached pavement. He wasn't sure what he was going to do with the old cuss. He could roll him several miles outside of the village. By the time the old man wheeled himself back, Derek would be long gone.

Or he could finish the job he'd started with the knife.

Leggy cleared his throat. "I been across the Wasteland, you know," he said, his voice cool and calm. "Several times, actually—before my accident."

Derek stopped.

"What're you talkin' about you lying cocksucker?"

"No lie. I haven't always been a cripple. Back in the day I used to scout for traders. Led caravans all over the place—including through the Wasteland."

Derek smirked. "Well, shit! If you could do it, if you could cross the Wasteland, then why can't we?"

"Because I'm smarter than you," said Leggy.

A red flush crept into Derek's cheeks. He wanted to cuff the old man, a hard blow across the temple that would send him sprawling out of the chair and into the dust. "So maybe you want to share some of them smarts with us."

"With you lot?" laughed Leggy. "Why should I waste my breath?"

In a quick, fluid motion the hunting knife was back at Leggy's throat. "Tell me how to cross the Wasteland, or I'll kill you," said Derek.

"That's just what I mean about you not bein' too clever, boy. You cut my throat, and you'd be doing me a favor. And you'll still be no closer to crossin' the Wasteland."

Derek searched the old man's face. He saw fear, but he saw truth, too. He cursed himself. He wanted to cut up the old man for his disrespect, for his casual insults. For being ugly and crippled and old. For not being scared.

Derek's brain began to cloud over with hot rage, like a clump of flies on the carcass of a rat. It was the same feeling he used to get when his father tried to work him through a math problem. His breathing grew heavy and strained, his head begin to pound.

The voice of David Cane echoed in Derek's memory. "You have to learn this, Stoopid... Can't you see how important this is? You need to understand this if we're going to rebuild. Just put your mind to it! *Think!*"

But Derek's mind would never cooperate. David had been a teacher but, like his son, lacked patience. Lessons begun in hope invariably gave way to bitterness. "What're you, a stilbirth? Are you an idiot, boy? Like your brother? Good, then be a retard. Just like your brother. See where it gets you."

Inevitably Derek would fling the book onto the floor—his father's precious book. Inevitably, David would lose himself to rage, and try to *burn* the answers into his son with his cigarillo.

And now Derek had worked himself into another mental corner. He needed Leggy's knowledge, but he couldn't bully it out of him. A seeming no-win, a real bumfuckery. Then an idea came to him. He sheathed his knife and pulled a hank of twine from his knapsack. He roped it around Leggy's torso and pulled it tight.

"What the Hell are you doing?" demanded Leggy.

"Taking you with me," said Derek, removing the old man's head scarf.

"Am I being kidnapped? By a kid? I knew it was gonna be a fucked up day, but not like this."

"You won't tell us how to cross the Wasteland? Fine. You'll show us."

Derek gagged Leggy with the scarf, then forced the wheelchair around and headed back toward his waiting companions. It was rough going and the wheelchair seemed heavier with each passing minute, but Leggy was coming with them.

By the time he'd reached the tangled copse of acid-wood where he'd left John and Teddy, Derek was breathing hard and drenched with sweat. He felt dizzy. The wheels of the chair had lost their rubber ages ago, and while the steel frame was sturdy, it wasn't meant for dead roots and the cracked pavement of an old highway. Derek had to heave and shove with every step. *Leggy must have some strength in those scrawny arms,* he thought. But the old bastard wouldn't lend a hand. Derek grinned. He supposed it was unreasonable to expect his victim to cooperate.

John and Teddy were nowhere to be found.

Derek cursed under his breath. He left Leggy at the edge of the tanglewood and pushed his way into the thicket to find the others. He must've been more tired than he thought because he tripped on a root and went down hard. His sunshades skittering away into the dust. Behind him, he heard the muffled cackle of Leggy laughing behind his gag.

Derek's eyes were flooded with the dangerous rays of the violent afternoon sun. He blinked and raised a hand to shield them. A tall figure emerged from behind a clump of scrub—it was larger than life, too tall to be a man, and it seemed to be glowing from within, radiating a dazzling, preternatural light. The figure loomed over him and seemed to fill the world—golden flame seemed to envelope it, a pillar of holy fire stretching from the earth up toward the sky. Colors shifted into shadow, taking the blasphemous form of a man. Derek was still on his knees, cringing and backing away from the apparition.

It's an angel, he thought, wildly, *It's one of John's damned fucking angels come all the way from New York to kill me for my sins.*

He threw up his hands. The angel lumbered closer, reaching for him, a golden five-fingered aura. Derek closed his eyes to the burning light of the outstretched hand. Suddenly he felt his sunshades being put clumsily back over his eyes.

"You praying, Derek?" Teddy asked. "That why you kneeling? You getting ready for sleepy-sleep?" The behemoth kneeled down beside his brother, the sun less dazzling now behind him. Teddy clasped his own huge fists together. "Now I lay me down to sleep—"

Derek clipped him roughly on the side of the head. "I told you to stay put!" he said angrily.

The giant said nothing. Behind him, John emerged from the brush, another glowing silhouette eclipsing the hot sun. "You did," he said, "But you were gone a long time, so we went looking for you."

"Next time, stay put when I tell you," said Derek, rising to his feet. "Come on, I got something to show you."

The trio marched out of the copse. John blinked in surprise to see the old man, bound and gagged. He eyed Derek suspiciously. "What's up?"

"He's coming with us," said Derek. "He's going to help us."

"That old coyote? What's he going to help us with, our curse words?"

"He used to run the Wasteland. Back when he could run, that is. He knows how to get through. He wants to help us get to New York," said Derek.

"Him?" said John. "This trip is getting crazy."

"You want to go back?" asked Derek. "If you do, now's your chance." He pointed toward San Muyamo, knowing full well that John knew the direction.

"I'm going forward, not back," said John.

"Good. Then let's get this show on the road. Teddy, you push the chair."

The old cripple showed no signs of resistance, and after an hour of travel Derek removed Leggy's gag.

"I'd appreciate if you'd get this fucking twine off me too," the old man said. "It itches like Hell." Derek made no move to untie him.

"Look boy, I ain't going nowhere," said Leggy, nodding toward his legs, or lack-thereof.

"Bullshit," said Derek. "The second you get a chance you'll slip away."

"And do what? Wheel myself back to San Muyamo? It'd take me twice as long to get back without the help of Mr. Big here," he said, patting one of Teddy's meaty hands. "And believe me, that shithole ain't worth my effort."

Derek relented, but that night he bound the man's hands, just in case.

CHAPTER THREE

On the third day of the journey they came over a slight rise. The town of Sanger lay just ahead. Sanger served as a trading hub for all the villages and shanties for two-hundred miles around. A rough adobe wall encircled the town, and guards with old rifles stood at the gates. Beyond the walls, stunted apricot and olive groves dotted the hillside.

"We going in?" asked John.

"Yeah," said Derek. "We'll need extra water and food."

"I know," said John. "But how are we gonna pay for it? I didn't bring nothing for trade."

"Don't worry," Derek sneered. "The good Lord will provide."

The foursome passed through the gate just behind a scrawny herd of goats led by an even scrawnier shepherd. A pair of guards looked them over hard but let them pass.

Once inside they paused. Compared to San Muyamo, Sanger was a bustling metropolis with a handful of two- and three-story buildings from Before and an open-air market. They had all been to Sanger at one time or another to trade what they'd scavenged from The Heap, but as always, it took a moment to get oriented.

"Go over to The Atomic Cantina and get something to eat," Derek instructed the others. "I'll catch up with you later."

Derek made his way down the crooked and cracked pavestones of the central road that stretched from one end of the walled city to the other. He came to a wide dusty plaza with an ornate fountain in the center that had been bone-dry for as long as he could remember.

He crossed the plaza and headed for the largest building in Sanger. Another left-over from the Before Time, *Afore-the-War*, it had a granite face and stately columns and clean angular lines. His father had told him it was constructed in the *neo-Federalist style*. It loomed over the plaza—over Sanger—with an air of quiet authority. In the Before Times it had been a bank. Now it was the seat of government for the trade-town. The mayor, the tax collectors, and the marshals all had their offices here. But Derek wasn't interested in any of that. The building also housed a library.

As he ascended the wide stone stairs, he remembered his father explaining why the library was so important.

"This place is a storehouse," David Cane had said, impatient as always. "Not for grain, but for knowledge. The books in here hold secrets that we need to uncover if we ever mean to rebuild. Everything from animal husbandry to irrigation to stoneworking and smelting to physics and astronomy. Stuff you won't find in the Elders' bibles,' he spat. 'It took humans thousands and thousands of years to accumulate all that knowledge. And just a few days to nearly lose it. But if we can preserve it, save it, and begin to understand it again, maybe it won't take a thousand years to transform this wilderness. Maybe it'll only take a few generations. Just imagine, Derek—perhaps even your grandchildren will enjoy electric light. Just like my father did."

David had taught his boys reading, writing and mathematics since they were children—or tried to at least. Teddy had never got past eight in his numbers and F in his letters. David had focused especially on math, which he believed was essential for rebuilding. He had held out great hope that treasures could be stored up in Derek's brain.

But Derek had been good with language, not math. He'd been reading and writing since he was five, and by the time he was a teenager he'd read all of his father's books. That made him smarter, or at least more well-read, than just about everyone in San Muyamo, but that wasn't saying much—the Elders could read too, though they stuck to their Bible. Only once had he attempted, in front of Elder Craston, to tell John of all the books in Sanger other than the Bible. John said nothing, and the Elder berated him, threatened to beat him, and worse, made him feel stupid.

Derek never spoke of books or reading to anyone in San Muyamo again. The more his father had tried to encourage him, the more Derek had played the role of illiterate dummy.

When it came to mathematics, Derek's brain betrayed him. It was faulty. Weak. He could barely multiply, had to add larger numbers using his fingers and toes, and geometry, trigonometry, and calculus were black arts. And so David Cane despaired that the deeper studies of math would vanish from the earth, would have to be recovered painstakingly, eon over eon, by better people than his boys. Or perhaps lost forever, leaving the remnants of what passed for humanity to root in the ashes of the world like beasts for another millennia—no thanks to his idiot sons.

Derek made his way into the dim coolness of the building. His footsteps echoed in the vaulted ceiling. He knew his way to the library on the top floor. A few guards checked his progress, but allowed him to pass when he showed them the contents of his rucksack.

He ascended several flights of stairs, his footsteps echoing off the worn marble, the air cool and free of the ever-present dust of outdoors. At the top of the final landing he pushed open a heavy wooden door and stepped into a gated foyer. Light streamed in from large windows set along either side of the building, the only source of illumination—no lamps or torches were allowed up here.

Derek came to the gates of the library and rang a bell. A small man in librarian's robes came from within.

"Yes?"

"I've books for trade," said Derek.

The man ushered him in and led him through a warren of shelves. His eyes caught titles as they weaved their way into the inner sanctum of the place. Many farming books, some construction, some chemistry. A good history collection as well. Not a lot of math. Derek smiled. He would bargain well.

They came to a small counter nestled deep in the back. He rang a tiny bell. From a doorway behind the counter came a corpulent man in clean robes. His dark hair gleamed with oil and his face was clean shaven.

"Director, this one has books for trade," said the attendant.

"Well," said the director. He leaned his bulk against the counter and dismissed the attendant with a flick of his fingers. "Good day to you, lad."

"Good day, director."

"Shall we see what you're offering?"

Derek reached into his rucksack and removed a textbook: *Introduction to Algebra.*

The director's eyes widened. He reached forward and opened the book, flipping pages carefully. Then he looked into Derek's eyes.

"Where did you steal this?"

"It's my father's," said Derek.

"Really?" said the man. "Tell me truthfully, who's skull did you break to get this book?"

"No one's," said Derek, his anger rising. "It belonged…belongs to my father. Now it's mine. We've come to your library before. His name is David Cane."

"Cane?" said the director, searching his memory. "From San Muyamo?"

Derek nodded. The director frowned.

"And he's given you this book for trade?"

Derek nodded again. "We…we need the money."

"A book of this value…I must have some way to ascertain ownership," said the director.

"Then ask me a problem," said Derek. "I'll tell you truthfully that I didn't get far beyond chapter five of that book, but my father got at least a little into my hard skull."

The director looked at Derek for a long moment, then thumbed to an exercise in chapter two. He made Derek solve for X several times. Derek did so correctly. It was an old trick. He had fooled his father nearly as easily as the librarian—it had only been a matter of time and reprimands before Derek had taken it upon himself to memorize the answers to all the problems in the first five chapters of the book. His father had seemed pleased as Derek feigned consternation, pretending to puzzle over the slippery calculations and muddle over the tricky twists and turns of the mathematical riddles. It had been easy to memorize the answers, much easier than trying to figure them out fresh each time, a practice which seemed wasteful to Derek's mind.

And in a way Derek *had* learned a great lesson from his gambit—he had learned at a very young age that no one, not his father, not *anyone*, was privy to what was going on inside Derek's head. His mind was his own. An obvious lesson, in retrospect, but an important one. He had since cultivated that sense of concealment, practicing the talent of keeping his thoughts disguised and his intentions masked. The skill had gotten him out of a great many tight situations.

No one could see that inside he was rotten.

"Well then," said the director. "I can offer you…."

"I've another as well," said Derek, reaching into his rucksack. As he removed the second math textbook, a leather-bound edition fell out onto the counter. Before he could retrieve it, the director snatched it up and gasped.

"You are quite the traveling scholar, aren't you?" he said. "I haven't seen a copy of *Don Quixote* in twenty or thirty years. And what other treasure? Geometry? You're full of surprises lad. I'll give you seventy-five script for the lot. You can use it in the market."

Derek snatched the novel away. "That's not for sale. It belonged to my mother."

"And I suppose you can read as well," said the director.

Derek flipped open the book and read. "…he so immersed himself in those romances that he spent whole days and nights over his books; and thus with little sleeping and much reading his brains dried up to such a degree that he lost the use of his reason…"

The director blinked. "I misjudged you, indeed," he said, closing the book in Derek's hands. Then his eyes fluttered and he recited aloud from memory. "He was spurred on by the conviction that the world needed his immediate presence. But, Neither fraud, nor deceit, nor malice had yet interfered with truth and plain dealing."

The librarian opened his eyes and fixed them sternly on Derek. "Remember that, boy. If you're not going to part with that book, one hopes you might learn a thing or two."

Derek said nothing. He could read, but the Before Times language confounded him. He hadn't gotten beyond the first few pages of his mother's book.

"Well then. Thirty script for the textbooks?"

Derek sighed and placed Don Quixote on the table. "Seventy-five, then." He needed supplies more than he needed his mother's old book. And he would still have his memories of her. She had died when he was young, just six or seven, a cancer that had started in her womb and then spread through her whole body, a dark birth that took her life.

The librarian said nothing. For a moment he looked at Derek with mild amusement and then turned, cradling his newly purchased textbooks in his arms, and retreated to his office.

Derek pocketed his earnings and made for the exit, but stopped. His father's words resounded in his head, "This place is a storehouse. The books in here hold secrets that we need to uncover to rebuild. Everything from animal husbandry to irrigation to stoneworking and smelting to physics and astronomy."

Derek turned back to the desk. Behind it stood the card catalog. No one was allowed to remove books from the library—if you wanted a book, a librarian would look it up and then stand over you as you read it. But the director was nowhere to be seen. Probably shut himself in his office to drool over his new possessions. And the other librarian was still by the gate. So Derek leapt gracefully over the desk.

He yanked open the card catalog. To his dismay, Derek could only find a single listing for *Wasteland*. He frowned, and closed the file drawer. He jumped back over the counter and quickly located the appropriate aisle. After a few minutes search he found the book. It was not what he had expected.

Derek had hoped for a volume of maps and instructions, things that they could use to help navigate the great chemical wastes and radiation marshes. Instead, all he found was a slim chapbook. He flipped open to the first page, a section that apparently proposed to instruct on the proper burial of the dead. Perhaps there were added precautionary measures that needed to be taken in the Wasteland due to the profundity of radiation and great diversity of scavengers and wildlife.

April is the cruellest month, breeding
Lilacs out of the dead land, mixing
Memory and desire, stirring
Dull roots with spring rain.
Winter kept us warm, covering
Earth in forgetful snow, feeding
A little life with dried tubers.
Summer surprised us, coming over the Starnbergersee

Derek knew what a *tuber* was—a huge, snakelike worm that lived beneath the sand. A bug. They had been known to come up and swallow infants, carry children off, and exsanguinate adults and cattle in mere seconds, but he had no idea what a *Starnbergersee* might be. Something equally horrible, no doubt. Apparently the Wasteland was full of unknown dangers. They would have to be on guard. Someone would have to be awake and alert, on watch at all times. They would sleep in shifts. It would be difficult—Teddy could not be trusted as a guard, and Derek was unsure of Leggy's willingness to cooperate—but they would make do. Of that much he was certain.

He continued to read.

With a shower of rain; we stopped in the colonnade,
And went on in sunlight, into the Hofgarten
And drank coffee, and talked for an hour.

Apparently, this book chronicled the travels of an earlier group's journey through the Wasteland. Unfortunately, much of it seemed either to be anecdotal or just plain nonsensical. Derek wondered what in the world a *Hofgarten* might be, and he feared that by the time they found out, it would be too late.

He grunted. He doubted that the book would be of any use whatsoever, but still, the travelogue of Mr. T.S. Elliot and his companions might prove handy at some point. He resolved to study it later, in greater detail.

He looked cautiously about for spying librarians, and quickly dropped the small book into the folds of his jacket. Then he left the library, and never looked back.

Derek found his companions sitting at a small table at The Atomic Cantina, a dim and smoky old watering hole that boasted a corn-mash still and Friday night cock fights. Leggy nursed a small glass of something clear and potent from the still. Teddy was on his second steaming mug of goat milk and a plate of eggs and beans. John, who toyed nervously with the crucifix around his neck, had nothing.

Derek tossed the bundle of scrip onto the table.

"Christ Jesus," choked Leggy. He snatched up the bundle and stuffed it under his shirt. "You want to get our throats slit? Don't ever go flashing a wad like that out in the open."

"Make a list of what we need," said Derek. His cheeks turned red, but he refused to acknowledge that the old man had embarrassed him. "We'll stock up for the journey. Whatever's left over we'll split up and spend. That scrip's only good in Sanger."

"You make your own damn list of what we need," said Leggy, and then winked at John. "I got business to attend." He kept some of the scrip and carefully passed the rest to John under the table. "I'll meet you back here in two hours." With a shove he wheeled himself back away from the table and turned toward the batwing doors.

"I've gotten friendly with some of the ladies at the brothel on the other side of this dungheap of a town." He winked at Derek.

The old man didn't look back. He hoped that Derek would not resort to violence in such a public place, that he would let him go and trust that he'd come back. There was a semblance of law in Sanger, and like as not, Derek must know that kidnapping was a criminal offense. Leggy pushed his way closer to the door, the metal wheels of his chair grinding over the stone floor, his heart pounding in his chest.

It wasn't until he had reached the doors that Derek finally called after him. "If it's just a lay you're after, then we should be seein' you again in about half a minute."

Laughter resounded throughout the bar.

As Leggy passed through the doors, Derek offered a final warning. "Don't make me send Teddy out to find you."

Out in the bright midday sun, Leggy breathed a sigh of relief. He looked back and forth, up and down the street. All about him were tents and stands, buyers and sellers, peddlers and traders of almost every commodity the apocalypse had left to offer. A skinner carefully led his donkey, laden with panniers of goat cheese and jerky, toward a circle of trading caravans in the town's main square.

Leggy had no intention of visiting a whorehouse. He just wanted a few minutes to himself before the journey began in earnest. He wheeled himself into the market.

Nearby, an old woman stood behind an even older card table, hocking her meager vegetables—desiccated things that had struggled their way up through the sandy, irradiated soil only now to lay plucked and withering in the harsh desert sun. "Getch'yer taters!" she hollered, "Getch'yer greens! I got onions!"

It was good to be away from San Muyamo. Things had been getting bad there. They'd long since run out of diesel, and none of the traders that rolled through the village would accept anything from The Heap in trade for fuel. Without diesel, there was no need for the generator—and without the generator there was no need for old Leggy.

As he wheeled deeper into the maze of market stalls, he admitted to himself that he secretly welcomed his recent kidnapping. He'd become smaller during his convalescence in San Muyamo, sour and timid, too timid to do himself what the Elders would eventually do some day—roll his chair ten miles out of town and let the sun and the heat and the bugs finish the job they'd started when they took his legs at the knees.

Leggy turned to the west, the direction from which they'd come. People in desert gear milled about, all with hurried business of their own. Turbans and gas masks abounded. Bedouins. Travelers. Leggy smiled. And now he was one of them again.

Leggy looked east, past a stand of scrawny apricot trees, their meager fruit hanging like tumors from old bones, and could just make out the rise of the Black Hills. There were said to be uranium mines sunk throughout those hills, and other dangers too evil to be spoken aloud—or at least that's what men said when they really didn't know what lurked in a place. Still, those hills marked the true beginning of the wild territories, the unknown land, the great stretch of chemical wastes that, in these parts, was known as the precursor to the Wasteland.

Leggy reached into a secret pocket concealed in the seat of his wheelchair and removed a folded sheaf of papers. It was an old map, worn and creased. He unfolded it. Though San Muyamo wasn't marked on the map, he knew what it was near. The old man touched a tiny dot marked Fresno. Then he traced a finger from west to east across the long expanse of a country once known as the United States of America. From here to New York was a long road, longer than Derek and his friends could imagine. It would be a Hell of a trip. Leggy knew this journey would kill him—him and his three companions. They'd never see New York City. But that didn't matter. Better to die moving forward than to sit and wait for death to come to him.

John left Derek and Teddy in The Atomic Cantina and strolled out to the market. Sanger was the farthest he'd ever gone from San Muyamo and that only twice in his short life of seventeen years. Beyond Sanger was the great unknown, and eventually the Wasteland which only the mad ever tried to cross. He'd just heard rumor of two from San Muyamo who had been foolish enough to enter it, and none who had returned. And now he was trying, too. He was scared, but he drew comfort from his lessons—hadn't the Lord sent manna to the Hebrews in their wanderings? Hadn't Moses drawn water from stone? Hadn't He provided for his prophet Joseph when Joseph was in need?

Weren't the Angels calling to them from New York?

Of course, John also knew that the Lord helped those who helped themselves, so he would spend his scrip wisely, not waste it like Leggy on whores and who knew what else.

John filled his rucksack with dried apricots, goat jerky, and coffee. He outfitted himself with new boots, sturdy and tough, and a stout walking stick. He bought a second water skin, and filled it to the brim from a water-seller, tasting it first—it was oily and smelled of sulfur, but it was clean.

"No radiation," promised the seller.

When stocked to his satisfaction, John found a small chapel of the Prophet, its adobe walls smooth and white. He went inside. Shivering in the dank darkness he spent the last of his money to light a candle, then knelt on the hard wooden railing and bowed his head. Above him loomed a rough-hewn statue of the Blessed Mother, her arms open, blue eyes that pierced the heart, one bare foot crushing the head of a poisonous green serpent.

As John made his way back to the canteen, he found Derek and Teddy in the market. Derek was cinching a large pack to his brother's back. Teddy would be their mule. The pack bulged with supplies: dried foods, water skins, salt tablets, flint and tinder, signal mirror, and a few cook pots that clanked and rattled in time with Teddy's enormous stride.

"You all set?" asked Derek as John joined the brothers.

"I'm ready," said John, patting his own pack.

"Where's that wheelchair fuck?" asked Derek. "Figure he's still dipping his wick?"

"Can't we just leave him?" asked John, knowing the answer but asking anyway. "It doesn't sit right to be searching for angels with a fornicator. A legless one, at that."

"He knows the way," said Derek.

At that moment Leggy hove into view, though it took a moment for the boys to recognize him. He'd outfitted himself with a wide-brimmed gaucho hat and a broad wool serape that draped like a dress, hiding the stumps of his legs. The serape was woven in a mosaic of faded yellows, reds, and browns.

As Leggy moved toward them he seemed almost to float. He rolled to a stop. "Howdy boys. How you like the new duds?"

"You look like a fool," said Derek.

"Maybe so," said Leggy, "but it'll keep the sun off in the day and the chill out at night. This was the best purchase I coulda made."

He didn't tell them about the pair of throwing knives he'd also bought. They were tucked into the folds of his chair, secret-like, and with the flick of a wrist he could take a man in the throat at fifteen paces. At least, he could ten years ago. But even if he'd lost a bit of quickness or aim, he felt better knowing the steel was at hand.

Leggy eyed Teddy's new pack. "Hunker down here, boy, and let me see how you've outfitted us."

Teddy squatted by the chair while Leggy rifled through the pack. "Yup. Okay, that's good. Uh huh, good, good. All right then, boys," he said, tying it up again. "You did good. I think we've got about everything we need."

"So what now?" asked John.

"Now we go," said Derek. He turned to Leggy. "Well old man, which way?"

"Sanger is at what you'd call an axis," said Leggy. "Two roads run through here, one heading north-south, the other east-west. If you still want to aim for New York, then it's east-west."

Derek nodded. They made their way to the gate that would take them east, Teddy once again pushing Leggy's chair. As they exited the town, they found themselves behind four wagons of Bedouin traders that had formed up into a caravan and were taking the same road. Their faces were entirely hidden beneath turbans and gasmasks. Their long silks and robes lent them a ghostly air.

"How far until we get to the Wasteland?" asked John, who seemed worried they might come upon it at any moment.

"Oh, at least a week and several days, yet," said Leggy. "There's a few settlements and towns 'tween here and the edge. That's where them Bedouins are headed."

"Oh," said John with a mixture of relief and disappointment.

The road out of Sanger, though rough, was wide and clear, having been traveled so often by the pack mules and heavy carts of Bedouins, who made their living trading from settlement to settlement.

As they traveled behind the caravan, Teddy giggled to see two young boys leap out of the covered carriage ahead to scoop up the steaming dung that the donkeys left as they walked.

"Lookie, Derek," Teddy said. "They playin' with doo doo. They gonna get a smack for that."

"Don't think so, big fella," said Leggy. "Like as not, they'd get a smack for not collecting those donkey flops."

"Why's that?" asked John.

"You dry out those flops and they make good fuel. Come in handy when there's not a lot of brush for firewood. That's your first lesson in surviving the crossing— you don't waste a thing." He turned in his chair and lifted the brim of his wide hat to fix a grin on Derek.

"You think I was kiddin' about bottling your own piss?" Leggy asked.

Teddy scrunched up his face. "We gonna drink pee?"

"Let's hope it won't come to that," said Leggy.

"Amen," said John.

That night they camped in a shallow gully just off the road. In the distance ahead, they could see the wagons and cookfires of the caravan. The sounds of flute and tambourines drifted back to them, and voices lifted in a strangely somber wailing.

Derek found the Bedouin music irritating, but Leggy seemed to appreciate it, and Teddy looked damn near hypnotized. His jaw hung slack and his eyes were soft and empty. He didn't snap out of it until John sidled into camp a little later, a brace of small sand-dogs on a stick.

"Got 'em," said John, with a wide grin. He was the best among them with sling and stone and he knew it.

Leggy quickly skinned and cleaned the animals and soon had their carcasses roasting on a spit. They ate in silence, the strange music swirling all around them. Then the stars came out—a vast canopy magnified and distorted by the invisible layer of radiation in the atmosphere. They let the campfire die to its coals.

Before they drifted off to sleep, Leggy produced a section of plastic tarp. The boys watched as he stuck two sticks into the hard ground and attached the tarp to it as if he were constructing a lean-to. But it was far too small to cover any of them, even Leggy with his truncated frame. Then he weighted down the other end with a pair of rocks. When he finished, he wiped his hands and looked satisfactorily over his work.

"What's that?" asked Teddy. "A dolly house?"

"Dew catcher," said Leggy. "The change in temperature between night and day creates what we in the old days used to call "percipeetashun." This here tarp will gather up a good bit of moisture. You set the tarp at an angle so that it runs downward and gathers up here by the rocks."

"But we got our water bottles, and there's a stream not a hundred yards from here," said Derek.

"Sure," said Leggy, "but we're gonna need this eventually. Might as well get in the habit. Dew catchers have kept me from dyin' of thirst more than a few times. Tomorrow mornin' we drink what's in the dew catcher and save what's in the skins."

John swallowed hard. He didn't think the tiny dew catcher could collect more than one good mouthful of water. Suddenly the reality of what he'd done—running off into the night and desert—was coming home to him. He felt panic rise in his belly. With an effort and a silent prayer he shoved the panic down. He lay back in his bedroll and looked up at the stars. The night was nearly cloudless, a rare occasion. Heat lightning and static radiation bursts lit the horizon, but the air was still.

Leggy pointed out the constellations, naming them one by one for Teddy, who was enthralled by the game and was excitedly pointing out new constellations of his own. "There's the Ducky const'lashun." He thrust a meaty finger up toward the sky. "An' dat one dere's the Snail cons'lashun. An' dat one looks like a snake!"

Leggy laughed. "That one's called Orion." He patted the grinning giant on the shoulder. Teddy leaned back, using the large equipment pack as a pillow. They didn't have a blanket large enough to cover him, nor a bedroll wide enough to fit beneath him, but that mattered not. Teddy was used to hard beds, and he rarely grew cold beneath all his muscle and fat.

"Orion," he repeated. "O-rye-un."

Derek paid little attention to them, and, not having use for constellations, he contented himself with poking a stick at the dying embers of their small fire. John laid back on his bedroll and squinted his eyes to scan the skies. All at once he sat bolt upright. "Oh my gosh!"

"What is it?" asked Derek. "You got a scag in your sleeping bag?"

John pointed excitedly up at the sky. "They're out," he whispered breathlessly, "Look. Up there!"

The others followed the direction of his pointing finger. Derek saw nothing. But after a moment of staring silently at the night sky, it became obvious that one of the stars was actually moving against the flow of all the others around it, traveling almost imperceptibly eastward.

"Holy shit," muttered Derek. "What the Hell is that?"

"I don't see nothin'," said Teddy. "What ch'you lookin' at, Der?"

John licked his lips. "There's another one over there, by the horizon." He pointed. "They're angels. Don't you know nothing?" He turned to Derek. "You can see them sometimes when there's no clouds, like tonight. Not often, but sometimes you can. Elder Hale showed me once when I was little. Just look at it, gliding across the sky. But they never come down. Not ever—except in New York, maybe."

"Bullshit," said Leggy.

Derek and John both looked at him. Teddy had fallen asleep.

"Hate to break it to you, kiddo," Leggy said. "But those ain't angels."

"They are too," insisted John.

"Are not," answered Leggy, removing a silver flask from his shirt. He unscrewed the cap and took a long swallow. Then he offered the whisky to John, who shook his head.

Derek took the flask, swigged from it, and grimaced.

"If they're not angels then what are they?" challenged John.

"Well," said Leggy, reaching over and taking back the flask, "They're called sat lights. They're left over from Before."

John and Derek looked at him curiously. "What the Hell's a sat light?" asked Derek.

"They're sort of like…tin houses floating around in the sky," said Leggy.

"Houses? You mean they got people in them?" John was incredulous.

"Some of 'em do. Or did. They say that there might still be people alive in a few of 'em, trapped up there. Watching us, but unable to come back home. I don't know." Leggy shook his head.

"How do they stay up there?" John asked. "Why don't they fall?"

"That's easy," said Leggy. "They are falling. It's just that they're so high up that it takes a long, long time for 'em to fall all the way down."

"Ha!" said John. "Falling tin houses in space? You're the one talking B.S."

Leggy took a long swallow from the flask and passed it back to Derek. "Some people say that there's men trapped up on the Moon, too." The Moon was a thin sliver tonight that grinned sardonically at them from the horizon.

Derek nodded. "That's what my Dad said. Men on the Moon." He took another long swallow of the whisky mash, feeling it burn his throat.

"They say the sat lights used to let people all over Earth talk to each other," said Leggy. His eyes followed the bright dot moving slowly across the horizon. "Till the Chinese fired an EMP bomb into space and shut 'em all up, that is."

John frowned and turned his eyes away from the sky. Derek shrugged at Leggy, took a last pull from the flask, and then laid back in his own bedroll. The drink was churning in his gut. As the coals popped and sparked, the Bedouins took up their music again. Derek and his companions fell asleep with the strange, high-pitched wailing of unimaginable instruments and ghostly voices ringing in their ears.

That night, Derek dreamt of angels—cruel creatures filled with light and malice. They swept down from the Heavens on sulphurous feathers to mock him.

"New York!" laughed the creatures. *"Beyond You!"* and *"Why Bother?"* They swooped all around, diving and biting, laughing and spitting like harpies, spewing curses and hurling smelly white globules of shit. *"It's suicide!"* they cried.

These were John's damned angels that Derek dreamt. Merciless monsters full of hatred and biblical rage. Derek suddenly understood—these ushers to the kingdom of Heaven, these guardians of the gates of New York, had long ago gone mad. They were crazy with radiation and sickness, hunger and death.

As they continued to peck and to laugh and berate with their cold, sharp beaks, a calm realization swept over Derek—these monsters had long since fallen from grace. It was not just the Earth that had died, but it was God who had died, leaving his unholy wreck of a world to his orphaned children and his mad angels.

Any *Word* that these angels might have rendered, Derek knew, was nothing more than incoherent madness, despite what John might think. He could see that now—these creatures were incapable of anything more than pure animal violence. Anything else would just be nonsense, word salad, Babel.

Derek awoke with the burning taste of Leggy's moonshine in the back of his throat. *God damn*, he thought as he rolled off his bedroll, clawed his way across the dark ground away from the camp, and began to vomit. "God damn."

He retched for what seemed like hours before the constrictions in his gut passed. He crawled back into his sack and fell sickly to sleep.

Goddamn.

The angels were waiting for him.

CHAPTER FOUR

When the group awoke, just before daybreak, Teddy was gone.

"Fuck," muttered Derek, his eyes half-closed in bleary memory of the nightmares which refused to fade. His head pounded, his temples throbbed. He cracked open one eye and inspected the campsite.

All was quiet, only a harsh wind cut through the desert. The sun's fiery scalp was jutting over the horizon, casting long shadows and turning the sky a bruised purple.

"Teddy!" called Derek. He figured his brother had wandered off to take a piss. "Teddy!"

When his brother didn't answer, a cold fear slid up Derek's spine. The caravan ahead was gone. Their cookfires had been buried and the Bedouins were nowhere in sight.

"Sonofabitch." Derek cupped his hands to his mouth and hollered, "Teddy! Teddy, where you at? Get your ass back here, pronto. Teddy!" The sound of his own voice rang in his ears, making his splitting headache worse. "Teddy!"

His brother couldn't have gone far. Hell, Derek could hardly believe that he had taken even a step away from the camp of his own volition. It just wasn't like him. Teddy didn't do anything without express orders from his brother.

"Maybe he's taking a pee," Leggy offered, massaging his stumps as he sat up in his bedroll.

"Teddy don't breathe unless I tell him," Derek answered. "And he sure as Hell don't wander off."

"He's gotta be around here somewhere," John said.

The land was flat for miles all around, except to the east where the Black Hills jutted like sore teeth over the horizon.

"Maybe he—"

"Maybe those fucking scavengers took him is what's maybe!" Derek spat. "Fucking Bedouins! Thieves is what they are, nothing but thieves. Most of them's mutants, anyhow. Fucking Bedouins!" he hollered eastward at the top of his lungs.

32

"Well," said Leggy, looking around, "If that's the case, we can easily catch up to them. We're traveling light, they're not. We're in a hurry, and as far as we know, they're not."

"And they can't have that much of a head start," added John, rubbing his chin.

Derek looked around again. Suppose Teddy had decided to head back to San Muyamo? He squinted his eyes and looked to the west, but could find no sign of the colossal youth.

Leggy seemed to read his thoughts. "You think he got homesick?"

Derek shook his head. "I'm his home. It's the Bedouins or nothing."

Suddenly Derek spun and kicked the dew catcher, spraying droplets of moisture into the air. "Fuck!" he cried.

Leggy frowned but said nothing. He scanned the camp. "Look," he said. "Teddy's boot marks. They lead up to the road."

Derek quickly began to climb the side of the shallow gully where they'd camped. As he climbed Leggy and John hurriedly packed.

Derek went to the road and peered east. Far off in the distance he could just make out the dust of the caravan's trail. It was miles away.

"They must've started off hours ago," he yelled to the others.

"Then let's go catch 'em," yelled Leggy.

"That's what I aim to do," said Derek. He took off down the road, leaving Leggy and John behind.

Hours later, Leggy and John saw the caravan far in the distance. Their march had been tedious and tiring. They had been running what they believed to be a losing race—Leggy with the enormous supply pack balanced precariously on his lap and John heaving and pushing, fighting for every inch, behind the weighted-down wheelchair.

At times, John had thought about simply ditching the pack and turning back to San Muyamo, but these thoughts had gone unspoken. They had not turned back. And thus, even in his absence, Derek's authority pulled them forward, like a dangerous magnet.

And now they could actually see the caravan. The faint outline of Bedouin wagons stood against the horizon and shimmered in the heat haze. John stopped pushing and Leggy lowered the pack to the ground.

"What do you suppose they're doing?" John asked. "It looks like they've stopped."

"It sure does," said Leggy, chewing at his lip.

"Maybe one of them's sick? Maybe they've found a spring and are filling their skins?" John offered.

"Maybe Teddy decided he wanted to turn around." Leggy smirked.

"Maybe Derek caught up with them."

"A lot of maybes," Leggy said, "But all's we know is that we won't know until we know. Now get back there and start pushin', boy!" Leggy hefted the pack back up onto his lap.

John wiped the sweat from his forehead, took a long swallow from his canteen, and began once again to force the chair forward, lurching over the cracked and broken road.

Thirty minutes later they saw the birds. The caravan had not moved in the entire time that John had watched it. He grew more and more wary as they drew closer. Finally, when they were well within earshot they stopped and listened. Nothing.

Leggy pointed. "Those are vultures."

John squinted his eyes against the rapidly darkening sky. He could barely discern the circling forms of the scavenger birds. "What does that mean?" he asked, "Do you think...?"

Leggy shook his head and motioned for John to continue pushing. "We'll know soon enough," he said.

CHAPTER FIVE

John and Leggy rolled into the Bedouin camp just before dusk. Sitting across from one another around a fire were the unmistakable forms of Derek and Teddy. All about them lay the ruins of the Bedouin's caravan—two of the wagons had been overturned, their goods flung across the desert floor. Scraps of cloth and canvas flapped in the ragged breeze. The ground was red with blood. Just outside the ring of firelight, John watched scavenger birds alight on a prone shape, their cruel beaks hooking and tearing into dead flesh.

Leggy gaped, and as John rolled him closer they could see, in the fire's unearthly glow, that the giant's hands and shirt were soaked and black.

Derek smiled that evil, innocent smile that had so scared John when they were young. "What kept you ladies?"

"What the Hell happened here?" demanded Leggy.

Derek scratched his chin. He'd been pondering how to answer that question ever since John and the old man hove into view over the horizon. A part of him wanted to take credit for the destruction that lay all about them. He could see from John's horrified expression that John just might believe it, too, and that would be good. But Leggy was a clever old poke. He'd spotted Teddy's tracks this morning, and sure as shit he'd be able to read the signs around the ruin of the Beduoin caravan once the shock wore off. So Derek told the truth.

"Bugs," he said. "The caravan ran into a sand-hive."

Leggy's face went pale.

"We gotta get out of here," John said, his voice shaking. "We gotta get out of here before they come back to get us."

"Cool it," said Derek. "You forget what you know about bugs? They've gorged. They'll be sleepin' it off for a week."

John turned away from his companions and puked onto the blood-caked ground.

Derek grinned. He turned to the old man. "How's your guts?" he asked.

Leggy's hands trembled on the hard wheels of his chair, but he kept his voice steady. "What happened? And why didn't they get you?"

"Pull up a seat," invited Derek. He sat on the hard carapace of a dead bug. Its head had been smashed in. "These gypsies were hauling a bit of coffee, so I had Teddy brew up a pot."

Leggy shuddered at the sight of the creature, but wheeled himself forward.

"I caught up to these sons of bitches just before noon," Derek said. "They were still a few hundred yards ahead of me, but I could see Teddy. He was tied to one of their pack mules—*behind* the donkey. Not even riding. Those cunts made him walk the whole way."

"But how did they get him?" asked Leggy.

Derek turned to his brother.

"Da music." Teddy frowned. "I wanted to hear more music. I got up in the night to sit by their fires. They played for me and gived me a drink. It make me so sleepy-sleepy."

"So how'd you get him back?" asked John.

"That's what I was tryin' to figure out," said Derek. "I could see him, but there was no way I could sneak up on the caravan, and no way Teddy and me could fight off the whole caravan. I thought maybe I could bargain for him with some of the gear we picked up in Sanger. But seein' Teddy roped up behind that donkey, it occurred to me that they would just take my gear and tie me up too. I was still figurin' what to do when all Hell broke loose."

Derek paused, remembering the bug attack. "The creatures, each nearly as big as a man, had boiled out of the sand like a plague, hissing and whistling," he said. "There couldn't have been more than a dozen of them, but it seemed like the sky went black. They tore through the first wagon, shredding and slashing with their pincers, their chitinous armor rattling. Men and mules screamed in terror before they were gutted. Bedouins leapt from the other wagons, some armed with clubs and spears, some trying to flee into the desert. One man had a rifle, but even the boom of gunfire couldn't drown out the cries of terror and pain.

"Teddy's donkey bolted. He ran off the road and into the desert, dragging Teddy right behind. I screamed his name but he couldn't hear me, so I ran after him. By the time I caught up to them, Teddy and the donkey were having a tug-o-war. I cut his ropes, and we went back to see what had happened.

"The fight was over. The bugs were…" Derek's voice hitched a bit, "…were draggin' bodies—people and mules—back down into their nests. Then one of 'em spotted us."

Derek remembered how fast it had moved, scuttling like a sand-colored nightmare across the brown desert, hissing with greed, bony legs clinking, mandibles alive and dripping blood.

"Teddy snatched up one of the Bedouin's clubs and beat its brains in," said Derek. "This fucker right here," he said, tapping the carapace on which he sat. He himself had picked up a spear, ramming it into the soft shell of the bug's underbelly, screaming in triumph over the creature's agony. But it was Teddy who'd made the kill.

"Them other bugs looked us over," said Derek, a hideous grin on his face. "Guess they decided they got enough. Huh, Ted?"

Teddy nodded gravely. He'd been proud to stand on the edge of ruin with his brother, to have bashed the monster, to chase the other insects back into their ugly holes.

"They slunk off with a few more corpses," said Derek, "and that was that. We've just been going through what's left of their goods and waitin' on you slow-pokes."

The group was silent for a while. Leggy spiked his coffee with a healthy measure from his silver flask. His hands trembled in the firelight. "Good thing the Bedouins…good thing they were ahead of us. Otherwise we might've…" He couldn't finish.

John turned to Derek. "Where's the nest?"

"About fifty yards that way," said Derek, pointing north of the road.

They sat in silence for a time, watching sparks from the fire rise into the night air.

"This is bad," said Leggy. "The road used to be kept clear of bugs, at least between Sanger and Moses Springs. We're gonna have to be careful."

John cleared his throat. "I guess…I guess we gotta destroy the nest, right?"

"*What?*" said Derek.

"It's the law," said John. "All bugs and nests are to be destroyed on sight."

"Fuck the law," said Leggy. "There's no Elders here."

John turned to Leggy. "Just because no one can see you doesn't make it okay to break the law."

Leggy rolled his eyes.

Derek said "We don't know how big that nest is. I saw a dozen bugs, at least. But there could be fifty more down in there. A hundred. You wanna go poking around and find out?"

John frowned.

"If it makes you feel better," said Leggy, "we'll report it when we get to Moses Springs."

"Report it to who?" asked John.

Leggy started to speak, but stopped. He looked back and forth between the boys. "Used to be, you could report these things," he said. "These days, I'm not so sure. But still—there'll be somebody there we can tell."

"But we're days away," said John. "What if...what if there are other travelers? They'll walk right into—"

"That's their fucking problem," said Derek.

"But—" started John

"No." said Derek. "There's only four of us, and one doesn't even have legs. How the Hell are we supposed do anything about this?"

A tense hush fell over the group.

Leggy spat into the fire. He'd be damned if his legs, or lack thereof, were going to be the deciding factor in this. And he didn't like the fact that Derek seemed to have the final word on everything.

"Of course," said Leggy, "now that I think about it, old Teddy there is probably worth three men himself, ain't you fella?"

The big man grinned and wrung his hands together. "Oh yeah. I kill lotsa bugs, Der. You see."

Derek looked up at Leggy. "What are you saying?"

"I take it you've searched the wagons," said Leggy.

"Course," said Derek.

"Bedouins usually carry a bit o' fuel with 'em."

Derek's face grew flush in the firelight. "Yeah...."

"We could burn those fuckers out." He let his suggestion hang in the air for a moment, and then gave the group an appraising look. "Nah. On second thought, we better just let it lie. Course, if you can't handle a few half-domesticated bugs, you're gonna love the Wasteland."

Derek stood up. "Those things could have a twenty-mile warren. You try and burn 'em out and we might find ourselves up to our assholes in creepy-crawlies."

Leggy didn't think so. A large colony wouldn't leave prey, no matter how good a fight it put up. And the one Teddy had squashed was still a juvenile. This was a new nest, still small in number.

"Is there gas, Derek?" asked John.

"Guess we'll have to find out, won't we?" said Leggy. He wheeled away from the fire to root through the supplies that Teddy had arranged into piles.

"We gonna burn bugs?" asked Teddy.

Derek, his face pinched, said nothing.

"Looky here," said Leggy, hoisting a pair of bright red jerrycans. They gurgled when he shook them.

John looked at Derek. "Well?"

Derek's eyes slid from John to Leggy and back.

"Go ahead then," he said, his voice quiet but laced with menace. "Obey your stupid law. Have your little bonfire. And if those bugs get you? Well, I guess I'll see you in Hell."

"Then it's settled," said Leggy. "We'll pay that nest a little visit come sunrise."

He replaced the jerrycans and then rummaged through another pile. "You find anything to eat?"

"That reminds me," said Derek. He stood and walked over to the only wagon that remained standing. A donkey was hitched nearby, flanks still trembling in fear. The wagon, like all Bedouin wagons, was covered, tent-like, in a dusky gray cloth, serving both as transportation and shelter for the traders.

Leggy looked at John, who shrugged. They moved behind Derek. Derek undid the snaps that held the gray cloth closed at one end and threw the flaps aside.

Inside the wagon tent were two bound figures, laying prone on a homespun rug. Their faces were swaddled in burnooses, but Leggy judged them to be an adult and a child by their size.

"Are they alive?" asked John.

"Yup," said Derek. He climbed into the wagon and unwound the burnoose from the adult. Dark hair cascaded from the white cloth. It was a woman. She regarded the strangers carefully with coal-black eyes.

John stared in disbelief. He'd never seen a Beduoin uncovered. Everyone said that's because they were muties, permanently disfigured from chemical fallout, radiation sickness and inbreeding. But the woman's face was well-formed, her caramel skin free of scabs and scars.

Derek unwound the burnoose on the smaller figure to reveal the face of a boy, no more than eight years of age, also free of blemish.

"She says her name is Raina," said Derek. "And that's her son, Tariq. They were the only ones the bugs didn't get—thanks to Teddy and me."

"Why are they tied up?" asked Leggy.

"Because they kidnapped my brother, that's why! And because they owe us," hissed Derek. "If Teddy and me hadn't smashed that bug and chased off the rest, these two would be underground right now with the rest of 'em. I tied them up to make sure they didn't slip away while I was waitin' for you two to show up."

"That was unnecessary," said Raina. Her voice was husky, and cracked with thirst, but otherwise strong and clear. "We know our debt to you and we would honor it."

"Sure," said Derek. "I'll trust kidnappers and slave traders to keep their word."

Raina shrugged. "The man-child came to us."

Derek struck her across the face. Tariq shouted in his own language and struggled against the ropes to get to his feet. Derek put a boot on the boy's chest and forced him back to the floor.

"He's feeble," snarled Derek. "You lured him with your music. You tied him up and dragged him like a goat. You'd have sold him in the market at Moses Springs."

Raina looked up at him impassively. It was true.

"I should cut your throats right now and leave you for the vultures. Or the bugs." Derek's right hand hovered over the hilt of his knife. "Leave your bodies and take your wagon myself. Sell it and everything in it at Moses Springs."

"You could," said Raina, "but if you rolled into Moses Springs in a Bedouin wagon without us, or came upon another caravan, my people would kill you. If you leave us alive, Tariq and I will transport you to Moses Springs and pay you what you've earned."

"Or I could burn your wagon down with you in it," said Derek.

"You could," agreed Raina, "but that would be foolish. Are you a fool?"

"I'd be a fool to trust you," said Derek.

"No," said Raina. "Understand that my people are opportunists. Yes, we took the man-child to sell. It's business, eh? But once we give our word, we keep it. We must, because who would trade with us if it were otherwise?"

Derek glared at the woman for a moment, then he spun on his companions.

"Leggy, you're a man of the world. Is she a lying whore?"

"Who can say?" said Leggy. "But I'll tell you this—I've never known a Bedouin to welsh on a deal. And another thing, on foot it's a ten-day journey to Moses Springs. By wagon, it's three. After Moses Springs come the mountains. There won't be any more wagons. I say ride while we can."

"Me too," said John.

"Yeah Der-Der!" said Teddy excitedly. "Wanna ride in the tent! My feetsies hurts."

Derek glared at his companions. "Fine," he said quietly. He turned to the bound traders. "But if I catch you tryin' to fuck with us, I'll kill you." He stalked out of the wagon and into the darkness, leaving Leggy and John to deal with the Bedouins. John undid the ropes and Leggy fetched them some water.

That night, after Raina cooked a strange-tasting stew over the fire, the crew threw themselves willingly into their bed rolls. All except Derek. He watched the sleeping figures of Raina and Tariq and scratched at the ground with his knife until a harsh red light touched the eastern rim of the horizon. Then he got up and poked at Leggy's side with his boot.

"C'mon, old man. Get up. Let's kill them bugs and get the Hell out of here."

CHAPTER SIX

John's eyes popped open and he sat up. Something was wrong. The fat sun was just poking over the horizon. An acrid stench hit his nostrils and he was suddenly aware of a rushing, roaring sound in the distance. His first thought was of bugs, boiling from their nest to drag them all down into darkness.

"Oh, Lord," he shrieked rolling over and pounding on Teddy's chest. "Wake up! Wake up. Teddy, wake up!" John pounded on the giant's shoulder—Good Lord, he was as solid as a rock.

Climbing to his knees, John peered into the distance toward the strange rushing sound, just as the enormous man-child began to stir. The rumble grew louder. There was a rustling from the Bedouin wagon and the woman and her boy poked their heads outside of the canvas cover, speaking rapidly in their own language.

Now Teddy sat up.

"Wakey time, Der?" The giant rubbed his eyes and looked around. He was as startled as John to discover that his brother was nowhere in sight. Neither was Leggy.

John stood up just as the harsh, bright light of fire suddenly filled the camp. A hot wind caressed his cheeks and ruffled his hair. He squinted his eyes and peered into the distance just as the world quickly grew to unbelievable brightness—without warning the sky was filled with flame and the smell of burning. Hot ash and fiery debris began to rain down all around them. An explosive thunder pounded his ears.

John was dazzled. Had the angels returned to once again render the Word and purge the land? Had he and his companions proven unworthy?

He clutched the cross at his neck and fell to his knees. The ground began to tremble and shake. One of the caravan wheels buckled and slipped off its block, causing the wagon to tilt. The wood creaked and moaned as the wind built to a gale.

Suddenly a plume of fire erupted from the ground not a hundred yards from the camp, a blazing tongue screaming toward the sky. It grew to an impossible height, until John thought that it would lick the bottoms of the thick, low clouds

42

that filled the morning sky. The plume twisted and writhed, a giant, fiery snake thrusting itself out of the ground and into the world. It grew in length and intensity, burning more and more brightly with every passing second.

John held his cross on its chain out in front of him, as if to ward off an unknowable evil, or to identify himself to the Rapturers as a true believer, as one of the Saved. He opened his mouth to utter a prayer of repentance and humility, but only gagged and coughed as a concussive blast drove a wall of thick, black smoke directly over him, enveloping the camp, enveloping the world. John was blinded. His breath was robbed from him and his lungs filled with a foul acrid burn. Bathed in heat, he felt his hair singe and his skin shrivel.

Teddy cried in the suffocating swell.

And then the thick of it was past. The air cleared until John could just make out the shadow of the caravan and the staggering, flailing giant. He could hear the cries of the woman and child inside the listing, tented wagon. He gagged and choked, retching onto the ground, as the smoke continued to clear.

The plume of fire still reached up toward the sky, but now it seemed somehow diminished—either that, or it was merely dulled by the still lingering banks of smoke and haze.

John stood up, still retching—long dry heaves that reeked of the toxicity of the cloud.

When he looked up he saw the unmistakable silhouette of a figure rushing toward him, seemingly from out of the plume itself. It was as wide as it was tall and appeared to be winged. It did not so much run as it seemed to *glide* over the ground toward the camp. Closer and closer, faster and faster.

John watched and within moments the blurry silhouette took form. He discerned its dark shape—two dark shapes, really—from the black smoke and fiery glare behind them: It was Leggy in his wheelchair, hanging on for dear life, long hair and singed serape billowing in the wind. And Derek was behind him, gripping the chair by its rusty handles, leaning forward and pushing, running, *charging* for all he was worth. He was on fire—small flames danced upon his shoulders, licked at his cheeks and played along the lengths of his arms.

"Whooooooo-hooooooooo-wheeeeeeeeeee!" cried Leggy, his mouth open and his face turned up toward the blazing sky. He gasped and gulped for air and hollered defiantly to the Heavens. "Yeeeeeeee-haw!"

Derek let go of the chair and dropped to the ground, rolling and sliding, desperately smothering the flames that were trying to devour his back and reach for his hair. The wheelchair continued to roll forward until Leggy brought it to a skidding halt in front of John.

"Whoopie! Just like old times," he shrieked. "You missed all the excitement, Johnny-boy. Heh, heh. Now help me find some water. I'm parched. Oh, and we gotta put out Derek." The old man hitched his thumb and pointed back toward his comrade, who by now was standing and brushing the dust and char from his smoldering clothes.

Derek's hair was singed and his cheeks covered with dark, oily ash. Smoke rose from his clothes and patches of his army jacket smoldered. He opened his mouth to speak, but was cut off as Teddy tackled him, smothering his brother in a terrified embrace.

"Der-Der! Fire and smoke...Burned my eyes...Couldn't see...."

Derek patted his brother on the back and tried to escape his worried bear hug. "It's okay now, Teddy. The fire's all gone."

"To tell the truth," said Leggy, cracking an egg into the pan suspended over the campfire, "I don't rightly know *what* happened." He paused and cracked several more eggs into the pan, added some salt, some Bedouin spices, and gave the concoction a brisk stir.

Then he reached back and removed a large, flat steel plate that had been fastened to the back of his chair. He held it in front of him like a shield. "It was this that saved us, though. I'll tell ya *that* fer sure," he smirked, holding up the metal plate and lowering his head to demonstrate how he had used it to shield him and Derek from the flames.

The face of the plate was badly charred, and before that it had been weathered and rusted, but John could just make out the vague remnants of red lettering across its surface:

TEXACO

"Found it by the entrance to the nest," Leggy continued. "And good thing we did, too. We'd've been roasted alive without it. I don't know what it could mean, though—we ain't nowhere near Texas."

"But what about the nest?" asked John.

"We never even saw a bug," said Derek. "We creeped right up to the hole—"

"More of a crack," offered Leggy.

"And did the deed," said Derek.

"How?" demanded John.

"Well, back in the day there used to be these things called IEDs," said Leggy, tending the eggs. "Improvised Explosive Devices. It's a fancy way to say we soaked rags with gas, then stuffed 'em into the jerrycans, lit 'em, and kicked 'em down the hole."

"Then we ran like sons of bitches," said Derek.

"There's no way two cans of gas would blow like that," said John.

"No sir," said Leggy, spooning out eggs all around. "The bugs must've dug their nest over an oil well or something—or maybe the nest was just full of bug farts."

Teddy laughed. "Bug farts!" He made a gassy noise with his lips and tongue. Tariq, the young Bedouin boy, giggled. Raina silenced the boy with a hard look.

"Anyway," said Leggy, "the nest is dead. Now we can turn our attention back to the road. I'd say we eat, pack up, and get rollin'."

"How many mules survived the attack?" Derek asked.

"Just one," said John, "wandering over there past those cacti."

"Must've been the one Teddy was tied to," suggested Leggy. "We'll use him."

John frowned. "One donkey to pull an entire wagon?"

The group was silent. After a time, Teddy spoke. "I want to ride in the tent, Der."

Leggy rubbed his chin. "That donkey'll have enough strength to get us to Moses Spring, maybe," he said. "If we're lucky. If we take it slow. Once we get there, I doubt that he'll ever be good for anything again. But I think he just might be able to get us there. Or at least close. And then, if it comes to it...." The old man glanced at Teddy. "But it won't come to it. We can always abandon the wagon."

Tariq started to protest but Raina put out a hand to stifle her son.

"That ass'll make it to Moses," Derek said grimly, "if we beat him hard enough."

Leggy nodded. They spent another hour or two discussing giant insects, high explosives, and the potential endurance of one lowly donkey.

Raina and Tariq sat between Teddy and John the entire time, saying little. They had not protested when Derek had rummaged through the wagon and discovered a caged hen and her eggs. And Raina had held a hand to quiet her son as Derek had plucked the hen itself from its cage and broken its scrawny neck.

These men were dangerous, Raina had explained to her child the night before. Although they had rescued them from the bugs, they were still not to be trusted. It was best to remain silent, to let them have their way until the remains of the caravan reached Moses Spring. There, they would find other Bedouins who would be willing and obligated to come to the aid of their kidnapped clan-cousins.

CHAPTER SEVEN

By mid-morning they loaded the wagon with just enough supplies to get them to Moses Springs. Everything else had to be left to the desert—there was no way the donkey could carry it all.

All that morning, Raina and Tariq had worked. First, they constructed a simple pyre. They gathered the bodies of their caravan-mates and burned them. Then they set about emptying the wagon. They buried most valuable items—some jewelry, tools, and strange gadgets that none of the boys could identify. Everything else they heaped into a pile away from the road and planted a small flag with their tribe's crest next to it.

They wished to one day reclaim their goods, but Raina didn't hold out much hope. Any Bedouin who came across the goods would honor the flag and leave the wares unmolested, or even return them to Moses Springs. But there were other desert wanderers—scavengers, thieves, nomads—who would make off with everything they could carry. At least the buried items might go undiscovered until they could return.

"Mother," said Tariq, "I will walk beside the wagon. That way we can store a few more goods, yes?"

She stroked her boy's cheek. "Thank you my brave son, but I want you near me. Your life is more valuable than a few extra pots and blankets." She crouched down to look into his eyes. "Remember this—don't ever let your possessions encumber you. A man who can't cast his goods aside to save his own life is a man enslaved. Do you understand?"

"Yes, Mother."

"Good. Now, how will we remember where we've hidden these things?"

"They are one hundred paces from where the road bends," said Tariq. "From here I can see a rock formation that looks like the face of an old man with a big nose. And we have marked the spot with a stone the size of a water jug, and scratched our sign onto its underside."

"Well done. Now we'll return to the wagon. Stay near me and keep alert. Soon we'll be with our family again."

When they returned, Raina invited each of the men to choose items from the pile.

"It is the least form of repayment," said Raina.

"Don't go crazy, fellas," said Leggy as the boys made for the pile. "We're supposed to be travelin' light." For himself he took only a whetstone and a mirror. The mirror was slightly bigger than a playing card, and fit inside a leather pouch that could be worn around the neck.

"What the Hell you want to look at yourself for?" asked Derek.

"For when I want to remember what handsome is," said Leggy. "It's easy for a man to forget when all he sees is your pokes."

John fished through the pile until he found a new bedroll and a container of matches. Teddy chose a large blanket with intricate patterns weaved in red, gold, and black thread. He also found a flute-shaped instrument. It produced a reedy wail that Derek found instantly annoying, but Teddy wouldn't give it up.

Derek found a silver bracelet, fashioned like a serpent swallowing its own tail. As he put it on his wrist, his eye caught site of a smooth cylinder, perhaps eight inches long. He bent to pick it up, thinking it was another musical instrument. Maybe it made a better sound than the one Teddy had fixed his heart on. But he was surprised by its weight. It was hollow, and it was made of brass, not wood. As he picked it up, a smaller cylinder slid out so that the whole tube was now a foot long. One end was stopped with glass, and the other end had a strange, cup-like fixture attached to it.

"Ho now," said Leggy, wheeling over to Derek. "Is that what I think it is?"

"Don't know," said Derek. "What do you think it is?"

Leggy took it and put the cup to his eye. "Lord a'mighty," he said. "It's a spyglass. Come and see, boys."

They crowded around him. "This here is a device for making things far away seem closer. You set your eye on this end and point the other end at whatever it is you want to see. Go ahead and give it a try."

One by one the boys put the device to their eyes. Each gasped in amazement as distant objects suddenly sprang into clear view.

"Hallelujah!" said John. "I can see prickles on that cactus, and it must be three or four hundred yards from here."

"How's it work?" asked Derek.

Leggy scratched his head. "Don't quite know," he said. "It's got pieces of glass in it called lenses, sort of like spectacles. You fellas know what spectacles are, don't ya?"

"Sure," said Derek. "My father had specs. It made the words seem bigger on the page."

"Well, that's it then," said Leggy. "It's in the way they shape the lenses. But that's a powerful tool you got. Take good care of it."

"I will," said Derek, snatching it from Teddy, who wanted to see how far up the donkey's nostril he could look.

They set off at a slow pace, but still faster than they could've traveled on foot. The boys stayed in the shadow of the tent, happy to let the donkey do all the work. Raina steered the wagon, her son at her side. They had both swaddled themselves against the sun. The landscape rolled past with dreary regularity.

"I don't think them Bedouins have to worry about too many people makin' off with their stuff," said John, scanning the baked, blasted earth and dry hills in the distance. "Who on earth could live out here?"

"You'd be surprised," said Leggy, swigging water from a fat, gurgling skin. "This place is a damn garden compared to the Wasteland. I'll wager that pile'll be picked clean by sundown."

No one said much as they traveled. They halted briefly at midday to water the donkey and eat a sparse meal, then rolled on again. All that day they met no one on the road. They halted again just after sundown. Raina steered the wagon into a small copse of Joshua trees. She hobbled the donkey and then rubbed the beast down. Tariq gathered brushwood for a fire. John helped, but the rest of the group stayed put.

Raina poked her head into the tent. "There's a cistern near here. Will you help?"

Derek clapped Teddy on the back. "Go haul us some water, okay, Ted?" They loaded the boy with skins and a few pots. Tariq led him to the cistern.

Once the fire was going, Derek and Leggy got out of the wagon. They let Raina cook their meal, and lay back and looked into the night sky. The evening was less clear than the night before, but stars were scattered across the horizon. Without the Bedouin's strange music, it was eerily silent.

John read quietly from the Book of Exodus.

Tariq taught Teddy how to play a song on the pipe. The reedy wailing filled the quiet and seemed to fit somehow with the somber mood of the night. The shrill, hollow notes undulated upward into the darkness, like the smoke from the campfire.

For the first time in a long while, Derek felt something like peace in his heart. The scene was downright…domestic. There was food, and fire, and companionship. He remembered that sometimes it had been like this with his mother and father, that once upon a time he had felt safe and content.

Suddenly an overwhelming feeling of loss welled up in him—not for that San Muyamo shithole, but for the early days of his life. He'd been a bright child, beloved by his mother and older brother, and the hope of his father. Before he'd proven himself to be a failure in his father's eyes, before the knot of resentment had been looped and tied into his guts, growing tighter each year. Before his mother had gotten so sick that she withdrew into delirium and violent seizures. A time when Teddy's childishness had been appropriate and not an embarrassment, before Derek's hands had turned to fists, first to beat anyone who mocked his brother, and then to beat his brother for being so mockable.

Derek stifled a sob. He stood up, eyes bleary, and stumbled away from the fire. "Gotta piss," he mumbled, and fled into the darkness.

CHAPTER EIGHT

The next morning Derek took a turn at the reins, sending Raina and her son into the wagon. The woman was too easy on the beast, and Derek aimed to remedy that. He'd fashioned a switch from the peeling husk of a Joshua tree and applied it liberally to the back of the donkey, forcing it slowly closer to Moses Spring, one haggard step at a time.

And so the day passed, with no sound other than the swish and thwack of Derek's goad—that is until near dusk, when Leggy called for quiet.

"Hold off," said the old man, pulling on the rein. The wagon rolled to a halt. The donkey stood dumbly in the road. Its eyes had long since taken on a glassy, myopic stare, and its breath came in struggled gasps and foamy heaves.

"What is it?" demanded Derek.

"Listen," said Leggy.

Derek reached back into the wagon for his spyglass and raised it to his eyes. By now they could all hear the sound—a low rumble like distant thunder, continual, and marked with higher-pitched whines that reminded Derek of the constantly overheating generator that had been Leggy's charge back in San Muyamo, before the fuel had run out.

"What do you see?" Leggy asked, but Derek only shook his head.

"It's like…I can't tell," he frowned. "Horses? A caravan?" He lowered the spyglass and handed it to the old man. "Whatever it is, it's kicking up a lot of dust."

"Not horses," said Leggy, who had taken the spyglass. His jaw dropped, and his face went white. "Not horses," he repeated, "Motorcycles. At least two of 'em, maybe more. Fuck!"

John poked his head from the tent. "Motorcycles? Really? Can I see?"

"No time," snapped Leggy. "We've got to move before they spot us. If they haven't already. Damn!"

They scrambled out of the caravan and off the side of the road. Teddy pushed Leggy's chair with such speed that the two front wheels lifted from the ground

50

and the old man's hair blew back in the breeze. They ran toward a collection of large, dung-colored rocks about thirty yards from the road.

When they reached the rocks they dropped to the ground and did their best to remain out of sight.

"What about the caravan?" asked John. "They'll see it."

"Too late for that now," hissed Leggy. "With any luck they'll just take it with them and not bother to look around for whoever might've been in it."

"Who are they?" asked John. "And where'd they get motorcycles?"

"I don't know and shut the fuck up!" said Leggy.

John lowered his head just as the motorcycles hove into view. There were two of them—Leggy's ears had been correct. John's jaw dropped. He'd seen rusted, stripped motorcycles in the salvage yard at The Heap, but never working specimens.

And the riders.

John could not tell where the machines ended and the riders began. They were dressed entirely in black leather, with shiny patches of metal and mesh adorning their shoulders and chests. Their faces were covered in black masks with thin slits for eyes. Large round bulbs of scuffed and dented steel covered their heads and came down low over their brows and the backs of their necks. On the left shoulder, each rider wore the only bit of color on them—three small ribbons, one blue, one red, and one white that dangled nearly to elbow length. Holding the ribbons to the shoulder, and pointing dangerously up into the air was a long, shining metal spike. The ribbons billowed in the wind behind them as they cruised to a halt a few yards from the caravan. The donkey raised its tired head and regarded the men with rheumy eyes.

The riders dismounted, and John was relieved to see that they were indeed men, after all. They wore high leather riding boots and—John could not believe it—each had, not one but *two* rifles strapped to his back. John's heart skipped a beat as one of the men climbed into the caravan and the other shielded his eyes to the sun and peered off into the desert, directly where the group lay huddled.

The first man emerged from the caravan shaking his head. His friend pointed to the ground, and then moved his finger up to point directly toward the hiding group. With a shock, John realized they had left tracks in the dust as they hurried off the side of the road—that the wheelchair's rusty rims had dug ruts in the earth as Teddy had forced it forward. With desperate fear, John turned to look at Leggy, and was amazed to see that the old man was smiling.

Not only was he smiling, but his arms were actually maneuvering his chair out from behind the rocks.

"Hey there!" he called, cupping his hands to his mouth. The men drew rifles and pointed them at Leggy. He raised his hands and shouted, "Ukmuk, Uk-hey!" Leggy waved his arms side to side.

John was certain that the old man had gone mad or suffered a heatstroke.

"Uglooooo. Mooka-mooka, deeeeka, moooka," Leggy said.

"Nick?" said the man pointing his finger at their hiding place. "Nicodemus? Holy Christ on a half-shell, is that you? We thought you, we thought…." The man stopped hollering and sprinted over the baked ground toward Leggy. The rider was surprisingly fast for all the armor and leather he wore, and did not appear even to break a sweat. Muscles rippled beneath leather, and his strong legs, as big around as timber, propelled him forward in leaps and bounds. He was tall and broad-shouldered, the biggest man—other than Teddy—that John had ever seen.

The man reached Leggy and stopped, while his friend remained back by the caravan watching. He looked at the old man's stumps, and his face grew pale. He opened his mouth to speak, but no sound came out. Then he shook his head and scooped Leggy up out of the chair, embraced him in a bear hug and began spinning around and around in circles.

"We thought you was…we thought we lost you, old man!"

"Easy there, Silas, easy," said Leggy. He patted the huge man on the back. "Now you put me down and introduce me to your friend."

Silas gripped the old man in one more bear hug and held him for a moment before placing him carefully back into his chair. The he wheeled him toward the caravan.

Leggy turned back and regarded Derek and John. "You boys stay put."

"What's going on here?" demanded Derek. He stopped short as the ominous *chock* of a rifle being cocked carried across the still air.

Silas's companion sighted down the barrel of his weapon. Derek's cheeks burned red with a blush of anger, but he stayed put.

Leggy spoke with the two men for nearly an hour, laughing and hooting and hollering. Eventually, one of the men untied the donkey, while the other fixed the caravan's reigns to the motorcycles. Finally, Leggy waved for the group to come and join them.

As they approached the caravan, Silas looked over at them. "You're mighty lucky to have Nicodemus for a leader," he said.

Leader? Derek opened his mouth to correct him, but was cut off by Leggy—the old man spoke in a commanding tone that Derek would not have thought him capable of. "Don't speak to them," he said. "Get in the wagon."

Silas grinned at Derek and winked. Derek bit his tongue and climbed into the wagon.

Silas's friend, who had not introduced himself, shooed the donkey off the side of the road, and tossed a bacon rind into the desert after letting the animal sniff it. After a moment, the tired, stubborn animal got the idea and followed. Then the two climbed onto their motorcycles, started them up, and they were off.

At first the sound of the motorcycles was deafening, but once they began to move and the reigns had stretched out giving them some distance, they were able to speak.

Leggy spoke first, cutting off the questions that rose to everyone's lips. "They're friends of mine," he said, "at least Silas is. Never met Corrin, but he seems able-bodied. They're good people, friends, but they're serious and don't take kindly to tribals. You boys would do well to mind your Ps and Qs around them."

"Tribals?" screeched Derek. "Who the Hell do they think—"

"I'm not joking," Leggy said. "You got a beef about it, go ahead, take it up with them. See if I didn't warn you."

"But who are they?" asked John, without taking his eyes from the motorcycles.

"And how the Hell do *you* know them?" added Derek.

"Well, used to be they called themselves Paladins. But that was a long time ago. I didn't think they were around any more these days. They were heading out this way to take care of that bug nest. Seems folks in Moses Springs already knew about it."

"But how do they know *you*?" John pressed.

"It's getting late," Leggy said quietly, and yawned. "We'll talk more about it tomorrow." The others protested, but the old man would divulge no more on the topic. "Tomorrow," he said and closed his eyes. "I've gotta think this thing through." Waving off any further questions, he made himself comfortable beneath a blanket and closed his eyes.

Teddy, John, and Tariq moved to the front of the wagon to watch the Paladins. Derek stayed in the rear of the caravan, sulking as the sun dipped beneath the horizon. The intoxicating smell of exhaust drifted back to them from the powerful engines of the bikes.

The Paladins drove all night, pulling the caravan behind them, and didn't stop until the sun peeked above the eastern hills.

CHAPTER NINE

They stopped for breakfast at sunrise, but the motorcycle men sat apart from the others and ate alone. Leggy refused to speak and ate his breakfast in silence, hushing the others when they tried to provoke a conversation.

The next day was uneventful. The wagon, hitched behind the motorcycles, rolled forward, and the landscape zipped past more quickly than John had thought possible. The hard-packed desert was littered with twisted foliage and the occasional crumbling remains of some long-forgotten *Afore-the-War* structure. The road seemed to be making for some distant low foothills. Derek spied a small band of scavengers with his glass, but when they heard the motorcycles they backed off and let the wagon pass unmolested.

The foothills grew closer as they traveled, and that night they camped at the base of a small hill. After the evening meal, John urged Leggy to talk more about the Wasteland—how long ago he'd traveled there, and why. He hoped eventually to steer the conversation back to the Paladins. The two men had made their own small fire on the other side of the road and sat astride their motorcycles, eating and smoking.

Raina and Tariq, who'd spent much of their time in the wagon, came and sat near Leggy, drawn by the sound of his voice. John suspected it was Tariq's idea—the boy had taken to Teddy, and regarded the rest of the crew as irresistible curiosities, wild and strange and dangerous. The boy crept closer to the fire and Teddy, but a sharp word from Raina brought him back to her side, where she wrapped him in a fold of her robe.

Leggy took a nip from his flask, lit a pipe he'd purchased in Sanger, and settled into the work of storytelling.

"Back in the day, when I weren't much older than you all, I took work with *Rasham's Recovery*. Old Rasham was big, fat, and as rich as Midas. He ran salvage operations all over the place, from up and down the coast to deep into the Wasteland."

"Recovery of what?" asked John.

"Just about anything we could get our hands on," said Leggy. "Food, water, fuel, mechanical parts, 'lectronics. And weapons. In those days gas was somewhat easier to come by and Rasham had a small fleet of vehicles. That's where I learned about motors and such. You could count on at least one break-down on your route.

"I got my start on the Santa Cruz-Kettleman City line. See, Santa Cruz hadn't been hit as bad as some of the other cities. Rasham said San Diego, San Fran and Los Angeles got the nukes but not Santa Cruz. Just the tox clouds for ole SC, and the half-life on that shit ain't too bad.

"A crew would drive in, search around for stuff, load up whatever we could, and drive back out again."

Leggy paused, lost in a memory.

"Boys, you wouldn't believe how they lived in the Before Times. Had these places—buildings—so big you could fit a thousand double-wides inside and still have room to spare. These places had shelves fifteen, twenty feet high stocked with stuff. More stuff than you could imagine."

"What kind of stuff?" asked Derek.

"Food. Clothes. Books. Mechanical items."

"It was all still there?" asked John.

"Well, no," said Leggy. "Most places had been picked over pretty good by survivors, scavengers, other recovery crews. Now and then you'd find a cache someone missed. But damn, boys, those places used to make my head spin. It didn't seem possible that the world could make so many things. They must've lived life fat in the old days."

"What was your job?" asked John.

"Job? I was a guard, son. If any bandits rode up to steal the haulage, I was supposed to chase 'em off. I had me a big old sawed-off shotgun. I rode right up front with the driver."

"A shotgun." Derek whistled. "Did it work?"

"Sure did," said Leggy. "Muties tried to jump our rig once. I let fly, and it sounded like thunder. Mutie practically disintegrated, and the rest took off like hens in a rainstorm. Guns are rarer now than they used to be, bullets even more so. Wish the same could be said for muties. But even then, a good firearm was hard to come by. Rasham had hisself a pretty fair arsenal—shotguns, rifles, pistols, grenades, even shoulder-fired rockets. Took me a while to figure out where he was getting 'em from…but, hey, I'm getting ahead of myself.

"See boys, I was young. Full of ambition, and bein' a gunner ain't no job for a man of ambition. After a couple of Santa Cruz-to-KC, runs I asked the road boss for a new assignment. I was possessed of pretty good eyesight, so he apprenticed me to a couple of scouts. That was more to my liking. Scouts rode out ahead of the caravan to check for danger—bug nests, ambushes, road blocks, downed bridges, things like that. That's where I learned the art of spyglassin'. Well, pretty soon I was scoutin' up and down and all over. Sacramento, Reno, San Bernardino, and a hundred towns in between. Most them towns're now either dried up, disappeared or blown away.

"The scouts taught me a heap of things, like how to find food and water, how to read a landscape, how to follow a track, how to kill a man quick. How to find trouble afore it finds you. I took to scoutin' pretty good—good enough that I started running the Wasteland. Rasham only put his best boys on Wasteland runs."

"But what would anybody want with the Wasteland?" asked John. "There's nobody there to trade with 'cept muties and bugs, and they don't trade. They just eat you."

"Clever boy," said Leggy. "Most scavengers don't bother with the Wasteland for just those reasons. But Rasham didn't go to there to trade. He went there to recover."

Derek frowned. "You mean like recuperate?"

"Hell no." Leggy laughed. "You think a fat cat like Rasham's gonna vacation in the desert? They say he had a castle by the seaside—used to belong to some old guy named Hearst from Before."

"Then what did he want in the Wasteland?" demanded Derek.

Leggy smoked his pipe thoughtfully for a few moments, pleased to have a captive audience.

"The Wasteland has always been a desert," he said, "even in the Before Times, or so they told me. But the people who lived in the Before Times were clever enough to make the desert livable. I've seen the ruins of whole cities out there, smack dab in what must've been the harshest, hottest, driest places you could think of."

"Was that what Rasham was after?" asked John. "Goin' to the cities to scavenge?"

"Sometimes for salvage, yes," said Leggy, "but them places are overrun with bugs and muties. The haul you get usually ain't worth all the trouble gettin' it. The bigger prize was somethin' else."

"What's that?" asked Derek. "Sand to pound up his ass?"

Teddy giggled at the profanity.

"Weapons," said Leggy. "Seems that in the Before Times, the desert was a popular place for army bases. And private compounds. And personal bunkers. *Afore-the-War*, many folks had a sense that bad times were coming and took to fortifying themselves away, usually underground, or in caves, mountains and valleys.

"I don't know how Rasham found these places, but he did. Had a sixth sense for it. Some people said he could sniff 'em out. Those army bases were something. Built deep down into the ground. And not just like a root cellar, but sometimes as much as like a small town, with streets and passages and living quarters and warehouses."

"That's where you got the guns," said Derek. He'd only seen a gun once before the Paladins had arrived, when a dangerous-looking man had passed through San Muyamo with a pair of pearl-handled pistols laced across his hips. Derek had longed to hold one of them, feel it, maybe even shoot it, but he didn't dare speak to the stranger, who didn't say a word and didn't stay in San Muyamo long.

"That's right," said Leggy. "Weapons were Rasham's specialty. That's how he got rich. Folks would trade just about anything for a firearm. I remember one time, a small band of people holed up in a compound traded a thirteen-year-old girl for two rifles and ten bullets.

"I made at least a dozen runs into the Wasteland to root through old army bases—twice as lead scout. You boys keep that in mind after we cross the mountains. If you listen to me, and we have some luck, we'll make it through."

"Will we pass any of these bases on the way?" asked Derek.

"Maybe," said Leggy casually. "But I don't suspect there's much left these days."

"Can't hurt to look," said Derek. "Can it?"

Leggy shrugged.

"How come you stopped runnin' the Wasteland?" asked John.

"Things got hairy," said Leggy, sucking on the pipe. "A few other recovery gangs found out about the bases, started running their own scavenging operations. Now you got armed competitors in addition to the bugs, muties, and the desert."

Leggy leaned back into his blanket. "Like I told you boys, there's at least a hunnerd easier ways to make a living. I liked working for Rasham, but not enough to get killed for him. Bugs and muties is one thing. Armed men is entirely another. That's about the time I decided to seek employment elsewhere."

"Doin' what?" asked John.

"Shit, son, you want to hear me jaw all night?" laughed Leggy.

John shrugged.

"Maybe another time," said Leggy. "I've heard my own voice enough for one night. I'm turnin' in."

With that, Leggy extinguished his pipe, wrapped himself in his bedroll, and was soon snoring.

The others followed his lead, not bothering to set a watch. They figured that the Paladins would take care of it.

CHAPTER TEN

The troop rolled on toward Moses Springs. As night fell, John sat at the front of the wagon. The motorcycles had lights on them, white in front and red in back, and he'd spent hours watching the desert flit past in the wash of their glare. The motorcycle men had completely captivated his imagination, and he was determined to take in as much of them as he could. He admired their casual boldness, the surety with which they moved, and the easy confidence that seemed to course through them, even as they sat upright on their machines, as still as statues but moving faster than jackrabbits. To think that Leggy—Nicodemus—had once been one of them, a captain no less. The old coot had risen considerably in John's estimation.

Ever since John was a boy he'd known Leggy only as a foulmouthed drunk, mocked by children and spurned by adults. In John's mind, it was hard to imagine that that wasn't all Leggy had ever been. But now these bits and pieces of his past emerged like old bones in the sand, and the shape they made spoke of hidden capabilities and marvelous experience.

John would not have believed a word of Leggy's talk about being a scout, about traipsing the Wasteland not once, but several times, if the legless alcoholic told his stories back in San Muyamo. Yet here was proof, in metal and leather and human flesh, not twenty yards ahead. The big man, Silas, had called Leggy a teacher, a leader. And John wasn't about to call Silas a liar, even without the guns and the strength he so flagrantly possessed. Something in Silas's grim countenance spoke that this was a man who told it like it was. Whatever his sins might be, deception wasn't one of them.

John could tell Derek didn't like the Paladins. The appearance of the motorcycle men had added some steel to Leggy, and that meant Derek's authority would no longer go unchallenged. Derek glared at the driving men rolling ever forward into the desert night. John wondered if Derek was plotting something, a way to strike down the Paladins. Teddy could probably take one of them, but not two, and not when they had guns. Even Teddy couldn't survive a shotgun blast.

John offered a silent prayer that the Paladins would let them on their way soon, before Derek's anger stirred up something more than resentment.

At full dark, John noticed campfires in the distance. He motioned to Derek, who stuck his head out of the tent.

"Shit," he said. He disappeared, and reappeared a moment later, Raina firmly in tow, Derek's hand on the scruff of her neck.

"Them your people?" asked Derek, pointing her toward the campfires.

"Yes," said Raina. "Our settlement is just outside the town."

Derek pursed his lips. "Hey, old man," he shouted back inside the tent. "If there's trouble, which side are your boys gonna be on?"

Leggy inched himself forward and surveyed the scene. Then he grinned. "If you're thinkin' an ambush, I expect they'll be on my side."

Derek scowled.

"Your side?" asked John.

"Don't worry, son," said Leggy, patting John's shoulder. "Just stay close to me. But I wouldn't worry too much. I 'spect the Bedouins will have some questions, but I'm sure this pretty lady here is as good as her word, yes?"

"Of course," said Raina. "I've already pledged your safe passage."

"Still though," said Leggy, eyeing the distant fires, "it won't hurt to have Silas and Corrin around. Not one bit." He winked at Derek.

They hit the outskirts of the Bedouin camp at speed. Tented wagons were drawn up in circles around bright cookfires. Shadowy faces peered out of the night at the strange scene—Paladins carting a battered Bedouin wagon home.

Tariq poked his head from the tent and began to shout happily in his own language. Soon young boys were chasing the wagon, shouting in return. Then the motorcycles began to slow.

"Get on that brake, quick," ordered Leggy as the wagon caught up to the slowing motorcycles. "Shit! Pay attention!"

Derek slid into the wagon seat next to John, clutched a wooden lever and eased it forward. The caravan rolled to a halt.

The glare of the motorcycles' headlights starkly illuminated a crowd of robed figures. Some of the group bore spears, others short clubs. John thought he might've caught a glimpse of an old rifle among the robes of one of the men, the rusty barrel pointed at the ground…for now.

Then one Bedouin, the oldest of the group—a frail, wrinkled man with weathered eyes, wispy hair and sunbaked skin—stepped forward. He raised a hand. Silas regarded the dry, cracked skin of his palm and returned the gesture.

"What is this riddle?" asked the Bedouin elder, studying the spectacle of the wagon. "That one of our wagons should return to us in such a fashion? I see by the markings that this is the train of the family Caliph." The old man turned to regard Raina and her son. "Where is your husband? Or your father or brothers?"

"Killed," said Raina, stepping down from wagon, Tariq in tow. She did not meet the elder's eyes. "There was a nest before Storum's Basin. Bugs killed all my kinsmen."

A murmur of horror trilled through the crowd.

"How is it that you have lived?" asked the elder.

"These men," she said, gesturing to the group in the caravan. "They chased off the bugs before they found me and my son. And they burned the nest."

Figures crept from the shadows toward them. Derek eased the knife from his sheath.

"Steady," whispered Leggy. "They ain't done nothin' yet."

"Might be too late when they do," said Derek, but he left his knife undrawn.

Raina now stood before the men who had blocked the road. She spoke to them quickly, in her own tongue.

John held his breath. He squeezed his thighs together, afraid he might wet himself. He could see that the night was full of robed figures, lurking in the shadows all around them. Surrounding them. They could swarm the wagon in seconds, Paladins or no, and spirit them all away into the inky darkness of their camp. Their fate rested with Raina now.

John wished Derek hadn't been so cruel to her since that day they discovered the ruins of the caravan. Elder Hale had told terrible stories about what the Godless Bedouins did to those who trespassed against them. John didn't want to wake in the Heavenly Kingdom to find that his pecker had been cut off and stuffed in his mouth—surely the Lord could understand that and see fit to be merciful. John crossed his legs tighter, clenched his teeth, and waited.

The discussion lasted two, maybe three minutes. Several men spoke to Raina, questioning her closely. The Paladins sat, unmoving, their machines idling, headlights burning a path in the darkness toward the gate to the town. The steady rumble of the bikes' engines cut into the babble of the Bedouins.

Then three men approached the wagon, Raina following. They stopped several feet away and looked closely at the travelers. Derek's body was rigid. If they moved he would spring, taking as many as he could with his knife before they brought him down, screaming all the while for Teddy to kill as many as he could.

The three men did move, but slowly. They bent, first one knee, and then a second, then bowed until their foreheads touched the dust. They put their faces in the dirt three times, then stood. The leader spoke.

"This woman says you have been rewarded with goods from the caravan. But what you have done cannot be measured in goods. Her debt to you is too great for any one person to pay. Therefore, the whole people must pay."

He reached into his robe and tore four strips of cloth from an intricately woven undergarment. "This is the token of the house of Caliph. If you show it to any of our people, on this side of the mountain or the other, they will come to your aid. So say I, Amit, of the house of Caliph."

He tied a strip around each of their wrists, and then embraced them one by one. The figures who had been surrounding them had melted back into the darkness. Only Amit, Raina, and Tariq stood before them.

"Peace," said Raina, bowing to them.

"Bye Teddy," said Tariq. And then they too stepped into the darkness, and were gone.

The Paladins killed their engines, dismounted, and walked the bikes over to the travelers.

"Now what?" asked Derek.

John sidled away to relieve himself into the darkness at the side of the road.

"Let's get our gear out of the wagon and get into town," said Leggy.

"How far is it?" asked Derek.

"Not far," said Silas. "Maybe a mile. We'll ride ahead and tell the gatekeepers you're coming."

The motorcycles roared to life and flew on before them. The travelers hitched their gear on their backs. Teddy took up his old station behind Leggy's chair. They pushed forward.

"Shit," said Derek after they'd gone a few hundred yards. "All that trouble and what do we get out of it? A smelly rag from some gypsy's underwear. I was expecting serious loot."

"No, Der Der. This is a good present," said Teddy. "We got a family again."

CHAPTER ELEVEN

Moses Springs sat nestled among the foothills at the base of the Sierra Nevada mountain range. The outskirts of the town supported stingy groves of apricot trees, date palms, and a few ranches that herded handfuls of bony cattle.

Like Sanger, Moses Springs was a gated town and a center of trade and commerce for a surrounding web of homesteads and small villages. At night it buttoned itself up tight against the perils of the desert.

The Paladins were waiting for them at the gates, which were constructed from thick wooden posts on creaking metal hinges. A quartet of guards eyed the travelers curiously. Their party didn't seem like much, certainly not enough to warrant the attention of the Paladins, but there it was.

The travelers passed through the gates, which swung quietly shut behind them. The Paladins led them a short way to a two-story wooden building, their headquarters and barracks. Derek noticed a man patrolling the roof of the Paladins' home. Moonlight glinted off a rifle barrel.

"Home sweet home," said Silas. "We can give you supper and a few cots, if that'll suit."

"Sure will." Leggy smiled. "We been sleepin' out for quite a bit. Won't mind a roof over my head for a night."

They came into a large common room warmed by a wood stove. A rough-hewn table stood in the middle of the floor. The good smell of cooking meat came from a room on their left. On the right was a cloakroom.

"Stow your gear in there," said Silas, "then go 'round back and have a wash. I'll see what Champer has on the pot."

They tucked their bags into large cubbies and found a door leading outside to a hand pump. Teddy worked the pump while the others soaked their heads and washed the road grime from their hands and faces. The water smelled slightly of sulphur and was metallic-tasting, but it flushed the road dust from their mouths and faces. They came back to the common room dripping a bit but feeling refreshed.

"You recognize this place?" asked Derek, his eyes shifting right and left, getting the layout of the rooms.

"Nah," said Leggy. "Back when I was with the Paladins, we operated out of an old barn in the hills. Looks like these fellows are doin' a bit better."

At that moment a large, red-faced man tramped into the common room from what must have been the kitchen. His hair was pulled back in a greasy kerchief and he was decked out in sweat-stained, homespun wool. One meaty arm strangled a wide-mouthed cook pot, the other balanced a tray of bowls, spoons, and a fresh-baked loaf of sourdough.

"If you fuckers weren't friends of Silas I'd give you a kick in the ass," he said. "I just washed every goddamn dish and plate in this place. Supper's at six o'clock, not half past midnight. But Silas says I gotta feed ya. Well sit down, goddamnit."

The group approached the table sheepishly. The red-faced man slopped thick stew into the bowls with great sweeps of his arm, nearly knocking John in the face with his elbow as he did so. Silas and Corrin joined them at the table.

"Eat up, but don't blame me if you get nightmares or gotta use the shithouse at two a.m.," said the man. He dropped the cook pot on the table and disappeared again.

The group fell to eating without much talk. The stew was a concoction of meat, potatoes, beans, and stringy carrots in a thick gravy. They ate to the bottom of the first bowl and sopped up the juices with the bread, then ladled in more stew. The fat man appeared with another tray, this one sporting mugs full of drink.

Leggy sipped his. His eyes widened. "Sweet Jesus, I'll be damned if that's a beer."

"Sure is," said Silas. "Champer got his own works out back and kegs in the root cellar. You work miracles with a little hops and barley, don't you, Champ?"

"And I could work a hundred more if you bug humpers just kept to the shittin' schedule and let a man get some goddamn work done."

Silas grinned. "Champer doesn't need firewood to cook. He curses so hot he can sizzle a horse-steak just by talkin' to it."

"Bah," muttered Champer, disappearing into the kitchen again.

When they finished eating, Silas motioned to the fireplace at the far end of the hall. "You can bunk down there, if you don't mind. All the rooms upstairs are filled. We got two spare cots, so you'll have to draw straws to see who gets the floor."

Leggy and Teddy won the draw. Silas and Corrin went off to bring in the cots. John stacked the dirty bowls and empty mugs onto the tray and carried them into the kitchen, which was large and spotless. Champer was in the corner, stacking firewood for his stove.

"Can we help you clean up?" asked John sheepishly.

"Help? How's a rabbit turd like you gonna help? Just get the fuck out of my kitchen. Breakfast's at six a.m. Beans, bacon, and biscuits. If you sleep through it, you can ask your momma for a bag of farts. Now piss off."

John fled.

They bedded down next to the fireplace, which was fading to embers. Teddy, far too large for the cot offered him, surrendered it to Derek. Corrin had disappeared, but Silas sat with them a bit.

"Nicodemus says you're going over the mountains and into the Wasteland. Can't say I'm thrilled with the idea, but it's your necks," said Silas. "We, that is the Paladins, don't operate on the other side of the mountains. The trails are too rough on the bikes, and we got enough to do running the roads around here. The Bedouins carry on some trade, but they don't send caravans up that way too often. You're gonna be on your own."

"I prefer it that way," said Derek.

"What's it like in the mountains?" asked John.

Silas shrugged. "There's a few settlements up there, a ranch or two, but they don't take to strangers. Plenty of bandits, some hermits and loners. And wildlife, bears and mountain cats. Sometimes they come down to Moses Springs to hunt. A mountain cat killed three cattle and an old herdsman two weeks ago. I saw its paw tracks myself." He held his hands apart to show the size of the creature's print. "One swipe would take your face off."

Silas cracked his knuckles and frowned at his old running-mate. "You're heading into rough terrain, Nicodemus. I ain't sure about that chair of yours. You might want to think about trading in your wheels for a good pack donkey. That's what the Bedouins use to haul goods over to the other side. You can trade for one at the bazaar in town."

Leggy scratched his chin. "I don't know if I'm too keen on riding a donkey."

"Well then, how about a proposal?" asked Silas, leaning forward. "Don't cross the mountains. Stay here and join up with us."

"Join up?" asked Leggy. "You mean be a Paladin again?"

"That's right," said Silas.

Leggy looked down at his wheelchair. "I can't see how that's gonna happen."

"Shouldn't be too hard," said Silas. "We could fix up a sidecar to one of the bikes. Think about it, Nick. Back on the road, running with the Paladins, fighting bugs and bandits. It'd be beautiful."

"Silas, I'm just a broken down old man. What help could I possibly be to you?"

"You were my best teacher," said Silas, "and that's no lie. You still got a lot of knowledge to pass on. I'm sure of it. You could train a whole new generation of Paladins."

Leggy stared into the fire. His days of running with the Paladins had been some of the best of his life. Could he recapture them? Just maybe he could. It'd be nice to be respected again, to be a man that other men looked up to.

Then he looked over at his traveling companions. He could see the worry in John's eyes, and the coldness in Derek's. Would those boys go on without him? Probably. And they'd end up dead in the Wasteland, too. But was that his concern? Derek had forced him on this crazy march at knifepoint. Kidnapped him. He didn't owe these boys a thing.

Or did he?

"I think," said Leggy quietly, "I better sleep on it."

"Fair enough," said Silas. He rose, shook Leggy's hand, and asked the others if there was anything else they needed.

No one spoke.

Silas bid them goodnight, blew out the oil lamps that lit the room, and tromped upstairs to his own quarters.

Derek lay on the hard cot, staring into the darkness of the rafters above. Though the bunkhouse was quiet, he couldn't sleep. His mind was clenched like a fist. That asshole Silas wanted to steal one of his band away, and he tried to do it right out in the open.

And so what if Leggy did choose to stay with his old companions? He was an ornery cuss, and harder to boss around than John or Teddy. After their encounter with the Paladins, he'd be harder still. If Leggy left, Derek wouldn't have to put up with the old man's back-talk. So why not let him stay? Good riddance!

But Leggy had proven his value. He had a cache of unexpected resources, not the least of which was his knowledge of the Wasteland. Without Leggy, Derek knew their chances of survival beyond the mountains would be slim. And then there were the army cities that Leggy had talked about. The ones with the weapons. Derek had no idea where such places might be hidden, but Leggy could lead them right there.

Derek hated to admit to himself that he wanted—needed—Leggy to make the journey with them. And he hated even more that Leggy might abandon them. He gripped the shaft of his knife. It would be easy to cut Leggy's throat right now, so that everybody lost. Derek would prefer that to seeing Leggy choose the Paladins and send the three of them packing. He lay on the cot, nursing his spite, waiting to see which direction his heart pushed him.

Leggy didn't sleep. He pondered Silas's offer. This should have been an easy decision. Rejoin the Paladins. He would be Nicodemus again, not an old feeb whose name itself was a mockery. The Paladins would be a much better choice than riding into the blasted nightmare beyond the mountains with a sociopath, a brute, and a religious fanatic.

He'd joined up with the Paladins about a year after turning in his guns to one of Rasham's road bosses in Santa Cruz. His tenure with the recovery crews had been instructive, and it put a bit of silver in his pocket, but he'd been tired of putting his ass on the line only to make Rasham richer. Sure, he could've demanded a bigger piece of the pie for himself, and Rasham was sensible enough to give ambitious types an opportunity to pick up more of the take, but it would've meant staking his own money, outfitting a caravan, training his own team... Nicodemus wasn't interested.

He'd spent the next year wandering the coast, north as far as Corvallis where the acid storms had given everything a glazed and melted appearance, where the buildings were crumbling and the people were, more often than not, burned and scarred.

Then he headed back south.

He stayed awhile in Santa Cruz, bunked out on the boardwalk beneath the rusting skeleton of a roller coaster. It was there he'd shacked up with a lady named Betsy.

If scouting for a hauler was a frenetic nightmare of heat and dryness and violence, Santa Cruz was a slow, soupy dream of quiescence. His thirsty pores had lapped up the damp air coming off the briny ocean, and he could feel his skin softening and loosening around his brow and on his cracked palms. He'd wiggled his toes in the sand and raised his hands in salutation to the hot ultraviolet sun.

He and Betsy ate fish and wild dog, and smoked a weed that Betsy had called *shemp*, which grew like kudzu in the hillsides.

But as weeks turned to months, Nicodemus was surprised to find himself uneasy. The damp sea air made him moldy. The *shemp* made him slow. When a trio of itinerant bikers nearly got the jump on him and Betsy one evening, Nicodemus knew it was time to go. He tried to persuade Betsy to come inland with him, but they both knew she wouldn't. And so he left her, and when he found himself in Moses Springs with no money and no fuel, he'd signed on with the Paladins.

Leggy sighed as he remembered those days. The Paladins were paid by a consortium of trading hubs to keep the roads passable, which meant trying to stay a step ahead of the bugs, muties, bandits that fed off travelers and traders. In short time he'd risen to the rank of captain, leading men on long missions, negotiating deals with new villages, extending the Paladins' circle of influence. Could he have that again?

He shifted in the cot. Something in his heart held him back from accepting Silas's offer, and it took many hours before he could unknot it. At first, he'd told himself that he didn't owe these boys anything. They'd dragged him along at knifepoint, for Chrissakes. But the more he thought about it, the more he realized that he *did* owe them something.

As the stars outside the windows twinkled in their mad, radioactive dance beyond the polluted atmosphere, Leggy was forced to admit that if they hadn't dragged him along, he would've lived out his last days as the town fool in that dung heap of a village. These boys hadn't kidnapped him, they'd rescued him. And for that, he owed them more than he could ever repay.

And then there was the journey itself. It was so wild, so improbable, so impossible…yet the idea of it had kindled his heart, set his enthusiasm ablaze. Sure, running with the Paladins would have a stock of adventures. Patrolling the roads wasn't for the faint of heart. But crossing the continent? Traveling from West to East, as far as a man could go before he ran up against the other ocean? *Searching for New York City?* Even the Paladins wouldn't dare that. Not in their wildest dreams.

He made his decision just as the sky shifted from black to cobalt. He would stick with the kids, and take them as far as he could. At that moment, he heard the soft hiss of a knife slipping from its sheath. He cracked open one eye to see Derek rise from his cot and come toward him.

He's gonna stab me in the heart, thought Leggy. *Sunnofabitch!* He tried to get his mouth to work, to tell Derek of his decision, but his throat wouldn't cooperate. Derek glided on cat feet, the blade picking up the first hints of dawn.

Then there was a crash from the kitchen, and Champer trundled into the room with an armload of firewood.

"Wake up, fuckers. Any of you turds know how to get a fire going?"

Teddy sat bolt upright. "Wake up, fuckers," he shouted.

Champer brushed past Derek, who still had his knife in his hand, and piled the wood next to the fireplace.

"Kindling's in the box," Champer said. "Flint's on the mantle. Build a good one or I'll piss in your eggs. Goddamn late sleepers, but you'll shit yourself if breakfast ain't on time, is that right?"

The big man went back to his kitchen, cursing all the way. John and Teddy got up and worked on the fire.

"I'm going with you," said Leggy quietly.

Derek looked down at the old man, then at the knife in his hand. His knuckles had gone white around the haft. He stood for a moment, then tucked the knife back into its sheath. "I'm gonna take a piss," he said, and strode outside.

Leggy sighed. It would be a Hell of a trip, that was for sure.

A dozen or so men made their way to the breakfast table. Leggy knew only a few of the older ones, but they'd all heard of him and wanted to shake his hand. Then he told Silas he'd be moving on. Silas nodded

"I'm sorry to see you go," he said.

"Me too," said Leggy, "but I want to do this."

"I understand," said Silas. He looked at the travelers. "You've got a good man here. You're lucky. I expect he'll see you through some tough scrapes."

After breakfast, they gathered up their gear and thanked the Paladins, especially Silas and Corrin. Silas walked them outside and pointed them in the direction of the market, where they could buy a pack mule for the mountain journey. Then the Paladin mounted his bike. His engine barked to life, and they watched the plume of dust he left in his wake rise up into the morning sky.

Teddy turned back to the Paladin house, surprised to see Champer watching them from the kitchen window. The grizzled man winked at the oversized boy, and smiled.

"So long, fuckers," called Teddy, smiling back at him.

CHAPTER TWELVE

As they made their way to the market and its stables, Leggy gathered the boys around him. "Now listen fellas, you let me do the buyin'. Bedouins are sharp traders, and I don't care how much cloth from the house of Caliph we have tied round our wrists, they'll fleece us if they can."

"So what are we supposed to do?" asked Derek.

"Watch and learn."

But it turned out Leggy's bargaining skills weren't needed, for when they arrived at the stables they found Tariq waiting for them.

Teddy greeted the young boy with a glad cry, and scooped him into his massive arms. Tariq hugged him, then motioned to be put down.

Once on the ground, he bowed formally and said, "Please accept this gift, which we offer humbly as brother to brother."

"What gift?" asked John.

Tariq grinned, and ran inside the stable. When he returned, he had a pair of mules in tow.

"This is Minna," he said, "and this is Afha. We trust they will serve you well."

"How'd you know we needed a donkey?" asked John.

Tariq shrugged. "You said you were going over the mountains and into the wastes." He pointed to Leggy's wheelchair. "That strange chair would never make it. You must ride, or be left behind. You will also need to carry extra rations. These mules can bear a great burden. They are small, but strong. Like me!"

Derek advanced on the mules and examined them. "This one looks all right," he said, pointing to Minna, and stroking her white mane. "But this one's a fucking mutie." He pointed to Ahfa's forehead, where a small third eye had grown. It had no lid, and no pupil, just a milky gray cataract that seemed to swirl like clouds in a wind, nestled into the brown fur of the animal's brow.

"Please," said Tariq, stroking Afha's nose. "This is a very fortunate marking. It is good luck to travel with such a beast."

"Sure," said Derek, bending to examine Minna's teeth. "If it's such a good luck charm, why're you giving it away?"

Leggy looked at Afha closely, then turned to Tariq. "Look kid, we appreciate the gesture, but I think one's enough. I ain't even sure how we're going to feed and water this one, let alone two of them."

Tariq furrowed his brow. "But these are desert asses. They can go days without drink or food. They are tough and canny. And they can smell moisture from miles away. They may be watering you, sir!"

Leggy laughed, stroking his chin. "You're quite the salesman, kid. You're a Bedouin, that's for sure."

But the kid was right. It made sense to have a pair of mules. For one, they could carry more water. And for another…an idea popped into Leggy's head. With a pair of beasts, perhaps one of them could haul his chair. He never thought he'd want to cart the damn thing around with him, but now it came time to leave it behind, he'd grown accustomed to it. And it seemed infinitely more preferable than having to spend the rest of his life on the hard spine of a donkey.

He turned back to Tariq. "Okay, we'll take 'em both."

Tariq grinned. "I am very pleased. These beasts will serve you well."

The travelers moved on to the market, where they outfitted themselves with extra food and water, which they split between Minna and Afha. Tariq had also given them a saddle for Afha, but Leggy wasn't ready to mount up.

"Figure I'll wait until the road runs out before I get on that donkey."

They left Moses Springs at mid-morning, passing between the eastern gates with a nod to the guards, who regarded them curiously.

They followed the road up into the foothills. It was well-maintained and clearly marked, which led Leggy to believe that the Bedouins ventured into the Sierras more often than they let on.

For a time they thought that they'd heard the distant sound of engines behind them, whenever the wind turned. None of them had mentioned it, and assumed that the Paladins must patrol the roads leading up to the foothills. But eventually even the faraway rumble of the motorcycles was lost as they put Moses Springs farther and farther behind them.

The Paladins maintained a watch tower on Moses Peak, a small hill that rose up from the desert surrounding the town. It was from here that Silas watched the travelers slowly make their way through the foothills. He'd sent Corrin to shadow the band for half a day. It was a courtesy more than a necessity. The real dangers would start in the mountains proper and beyond, in the Wasteland.

How in the world had Nicodemus fallen in with this crew? Silas was unsure of it all. Unsure of those three untried souls so determinedly heading east. Unsure of his old teacher. Silas didn't pretend to understand them or their reasons for this half-baked journey.

The one called John was scared of his own shadow but so devout he'd asked the Paladins if he could say a blessing over breakfast. Silas didn't hold much to the boy's religion—the Church of the Word was an old cult that clung on in the backward shanty towns and tribal villages. Still, he'd allowed the blessing because there was something saintly about the boy. Silas could see it, even if he wasn't sure if that was necessarily a *good* thing or if it would be much help in the Wasteland.

And Teddy, the simpleton. His strength was to be admired. Silas had seen his share of strong men, but he couldn't think of three combined that could match the dimwit's might. He had no doubt that it would be one of their greatest assets in the unforgiving east. But beyond his muscles, the man-child seemed free of the gritty survival instinct that made self-preservation the first, and sometimes *only*, law.

But Derek...now there was a cause for worry. The boy was so full of anger, hatred, and rage that it genuinely frightened the Paladin. The fire that drove him could easily consume the whole band of travelers. And yet there was more than rage to him. He was crafty, observant, patient even.

Silas didn't want to admit it to himself, but there was a dark glimmer to Derek, like the fire that draws the desert moths. Clearly he commanded the allegiance of John and Teddy. Maybe Nicodemus had been drawn in too. There would be a great many tests for them all in the desert, but Silas sensed that Derek had the most at stake. The boy had a troubled soul.

Then there was Nicodemus. His old teacher. A man whom Silas had believed to be more than twenty years dead. Resurfaced as a vagabond and a cripple, but still a teacher, a guardian...an adventurer. A man to be respected, yet his companions called him Leggy. It was a bad joke of a name. Why not just spit in his face? But Nicodemus just took it. Silas didn't know what to think. Why had Nicodemus turned down the offer? Surely, this was a fool's errand. Or a suicide mission.

But, "to each his own path." That was something that Nicodemus had drilled into him. *Leggy.* He called himself Leggy now.

Silas put a pair of old binoculars to his eyes. He searched the foothills until he could make out a hint of movement among the brown peaks. The misfit band marched slowly forward, away from the setting sun. The teacher, the saint, the innocent, and the hero. The cripple, the fanatic, the retard, and the maniac.

Silas climbed down from the tower and mounted his bike. He stepped hard on the clutch, swung his roadhog around, and roared off back toward Moses Springs.

CHAPTER THIRTEEN

At dusk the travelers made camp in the lee of several huge boulders. Teddy, who had taken a liking to the mules, relieved Minna and Afha of their packs and then patted them down with his strong hands. Derek walked a wide circle around their small campsite, scouting the perimeter. He found no signs of bug nests and no signs that anyone had been here in a long time.

When he returned to camp, he found Teddy nearly hysterical with excitement. Leggy and John had already gathered around his brother and Afha the mule, which Derek took to be the cause of Teddy's animation.

"Look, Der! Look at this," shouted Teddy.

He showed his brother a pebble in one great hand. Then he put both hands behind his back, then made a show of bringing them out front again, fists closed. The guessing stone. Teddy could be amused for hours with the game. Derek remembered Teddy playing the game with his mother when he was still a child. His brother shrieked with delight whenever he'd guessed the right hand. Now Derek thought Teddy wanted to play with him, but he was wrong. Teddy was holding both fists out to the mutant donkey.

"Which hand, horsey? Which hand?" asked Teddy, his face nearly split in two with a grin.

"Jesus H. Christ, Teddy," said Derek. "Are you getting stupider on me?" He raised a hand to cuff his brother, but John tugged at his sleeve.

"No wait," he said. "Watch."

Derek watched. Afha stared at Teddy's meaty fists, the milky cataract of his superfluous eye roiling. Then the donkey reached out and nuzzled Teddy's right hand.

"Hee hee hee," shrieked Teddy. He opened his right hand. The pebble was on his palm.

"Come on," scoffed Derek. "It's just luck."

"I don't know," said Leggy, stroking his beard. "Your brother's done it ten times already, and the donkey's got it right every time."

"Oh bullshit," said Derek. "Did you all just get radiation poisoning?"

"See for y'self," said Leggy.

Teddy played several more times, and each time Afha chose the hand that held the pebble.

Then Teddy said, "Okay horsey, last time now. Okay? Last time." He put both hands behind his back, and fixed his face with a look of exaggerated seriousness.

Derek instantly recognized the look—it was Teddy's "I'm trying to fool you" face. Derek sighed. Teddy never understood that if he really wanted to trick someone, he should keep up that shit-eating grin.

With his hands still behind his back, Teddy leaned over to his brother and stage-whispered in his ear.

"I put the stone in my pants, Der," he said, the veneer of his serious face nearly cracking. He composed himself and brought both fists out from behind his back.

Afha stood and stared at Teddy, blowing through his nostrils. Then he backed away two paces, shook his head, and whinnied.

"Pick, horsey. Pick a hand," sang Teddy. He waggled each fist enticingly, but the donkey would not pick a hand.

Finally Teddy opened his hands. They were both empty. Afha brayed, and Teddy clapped.

"He knew! He knew I played sneaky," shouted Teddy. "Smart horsey!"

"I'll be damned," said Leggy.

"The Lord be praised," said John.

"Get straight," said Derek. "The Bedouins probably taught it how to play games. Or maybe the stone smells funny."

"It does now," said Leggy, watching Teddy fish in his drawers for the pebble.

Then Leggy looked up. The sky above was gradually being hidden by a thick gauze of gray haze, and the sun was going down fast.

"We better see about a fire. Looks like it's going to be a dark night."

Leggy was right. The darkness fell fast, and a haze above them hid the stars and moon. They were terribly glad when orange flames began to eat greedily at the deadwood they'd gathered.

The scraggly remains of dead, twisted trees provided copious firewood, and they stacked a supply that would keep the fire hot and bright all night long if they wanted it to.

Nights had grown steadily colder as they ascended the foothills, and they huddled close around the fire, glad for the boulders that threw back the warmth of the flames. The darkness was utterly complete outside the small ring of light—no moon, no stars, only an invisible landscape hidden behind a black curtain.

"I gotta piss," said John, "but I'm afraid if I go too far, I'll never find you all again."

"Sidle on up to the edge of the firelight and aim yourself away from us," said Leggy. "You'll be all right. Just don't piss on the mules."

As John urinated, he stared into the darkness, straining to see anything at all in the void. He seemed to pee for hours, and he didn't like the way his urine just vanished into the night. He felt as if he were standing at the very edge of a chasm, that if he stepped forward he'd tumble from a high precipice and fall headfirst into the darkness and never stop.

"The Lord is my shepherd, I shall not want," he whispered, trying to calm himself. But the words died on his lips as he detected movement in the distance, fluttery and uneven. He rubbed his eyes, thinking perhaps he was imagining it. But then he heard a sound, a soft chuffing sound, and it was getting closer. His bladder clenched closed with fear.

"Something's coming," he whispered breathlessly. He hurriedly buttoned himself into his pants again and scooted toward the fire. "Something's coming outta that darkness."

"Huh?" said Derek.

"What'd you see?" asked Leggy.

"Not sure I *saw* anything," said John. "But I heard something. Sounds like, like wind."

"Get this fire out," said Leggy, his voice urgent.

"Are you crazy?" said Derek. "We'll be blind out here."

"Yeah, but so will whatever's comin' for us," said Leggy. He removed his heavy serape to beat out the fire, but then stopped.

Suddenly they heard the noise. It sounded like wind. Or like sheets hung to dry on a line, snapping and cracking in a gust.

Leggy lifted his serape, but at that instant wings exploded out of the darkness all around them, beating and flapping madly over the fire. Musty, cobwebby tendrils brushed against their necks and faces.

Teddy howled in fear, throwing his hands up over his head. Minna and Ahfa joined in, braying with terror. John watched in gape-eyed horror and wonder as a dozen or more of the creatures swooped and dove around them.

The creatures were nearly man-sized, with large, papery wings marked in swirling patterns of black and gray. Their faces were oval, with almond-shaped eyes and small mouths. Their cylindrical bodies looked like elongated infants wrapped in swaddling blankets. Six slender, jointed legs sprouted from wrinkled abdomens and writhed manically. Their wings beat the air as they swooped, turned and hovered over the fire.

"Angels," whispered John in awe. "Are they angels?"

"No, you dumb shit," shouted Derek. "They're bugs!"

"Moths," shouted Leggy. "Put out the goddamn fire! They're attracted to the light." He tried again to flip his serape over the campfire, but one of the swooping creatures knocked it aside.

Derek snatched a blazing branch from the fire, leapt to his feet, and smashed one of the creatures to the ground. It shrieked in agony as its papery wings ignited in flame. Derek beat down another with wild swings.

The creature fell at John's feet, and he watched in horror as the thing writhed in the dirt, its almond eyes wide with pain, its wrinkled torso flaring like a match. It locked its eyes on John, its mouth moving pathetically. John could feel the pain and confusion in the creature's death gaze, but he did nothing, merely watched as fire engulfed its face and head, reducing its body quickly to black ash.

Derek killed three more before the creatures, still swooping and diving toward the camp fire, lifted themselves out of reach.

Leggy tumbled out of his chair, recovered his serape and finally smothered the blaze. Derek scattered the hot coals and ash with several savage kicks. Darkness engulfed them, broken only by the orange glow of scattered bits of smoldering wood, which winked out one by one as they cooled. They could hear the creatures still troubling the air above them, but soon the noise of beating wings died away as the things moved off.

"Everybody all right?" asked Leggy in the stillness.

"I'm okay," said Derek.

"Me too," said Teddy, his fear gone now that the bugs had departed.

"I…I'm here," said John, his voice hoarse.

The half-charred corpse of the moth was lost to the darkness, but he could still see it in his mind. No creature deserved to die as horribly as these had. It just wasn't right. And what if they were more than just bugs? Their resemblance to angels—at least what John imagined angels to look like—disturbed him. Surely their poor treatment of these creatures would come back to them somehow. Not just to Derek, but all of them.

"I expect the mules bolted," said Leggy. "I didn't hobble them very securely."

"No," said Teddy. "Horsies are still here. They don't run away."

From the darkness, Ahfa snorted as if in affirmation.

"Well that's one good bit of news," Leggy said. "Fellas, we're gonna have to do without a fire for the rest of the night. I hope you all ain't afraid of the dark."

"I'm not," said Teddy, but they could all hear the lie in his voice.

"The dark doesn't worry me, but what about the cold?" asked John. "I can already feel a chill creeping into my bones."

"That we can do somethin' about," said Leggy. "Let's all gather up close, fellas. Just follow the sound of my voice."

Leggy hummed a creaky old tune as Teddy, John, and Derek clambered blindly toward him. There were a few moments of stumbling about. Teddy stepped on John's foot hard enough to bring tears to his eyes, and Derek tripped over Leggy's wheelchair with a curse, but soon they were close enough to hold hands, even if they couldn't see each other.

"Okay now," said Leggy, "we just lie down back to front and use each other's body heat to stay warm. I done it a few times before when I was runnin' freight and got into a spot where we couldn't light any fires. I'd rather be bunkin' down with a nice full-figured gal than you smelly lot, but it beats freezin'."

And so they bundled themselves together on the hard ground, with Derek and John bookended by Teddy and Leggy.

"Who's teeth are chatterin'?" asked Leggy.

"Me," said Derek. "I don't think this is workin'."

"Just give it a minute," said Leggy. "You'll warm up, and you'll probably fall asleep before you know it."

"Shit," said Derek. "It's so goddamn dark I could probably sleep with my eyes open."

Teddy and Leggy laughed, but John was silent. The episode with the moths troubled him, and he too thought he'd never get warm. But within a few minutes he realized that Leggy was right about body heat. Teddy was practically a blast furnace, and soon John felt drowsy. He desperately wanted to fall asleep and not wake up until daylight, so that he could forget this strange, dark night.

But sleep eluded him, and he lay in a restless despair while his companions snored around him. His long vigil was finally broken as the sky lightened, and the first fingers of dawn reached slowly over the Sierras.

They marched farther into the foothills that day, watching the landscape around them slowly transform. Gone were the brown sagebrush and the desiccated tumbleweeds that rolled like bony fingers across the cracked earth. The desert plain gradually transformed to rocky soil, from which grew sparse clumps of grass and low shrubs that Leggy called gorseberry. Rocks and boulders poked up from the earth, their hard faces crusted with pale white and blue lichen. Now and then they passed through stands of scraggly pine. The trees stood no higher than ten or twelve feet, but they were a wonder to the boys, for whom a tree meant the gnarled and stunted Joshuas.

They spotted numerous creatures in the brush and stones all around them—

scampering brown lizards, brown-furred rodents, and flights of small birds. Teddy spotted a hawk high overhead, gracefully hovering on an updraft.

In the late afternoon, Leggy suggested they set up camp early, to try and bag some of the wildlife scurrying about. Derek set out traps while the others gathered brushwood and hunted up water. Then they rested. Leggy put his pipe in his mouth but didn't light it. He felt content to sit in his chair and just be. A soothing bliss had fallen over him, better than anything he'd ever poured out of a bottle, and he wanted to fill himself up with it, to brim with it, because he knew what lay on the other side of the mountains.

A blasted waste, a nightmare territory.

Thoughts of what was to come crowded his mind, but with an effort he shoved them aside. That was for another time. Now, he would simply sit and watch the light change, and feel cool, moist air kissing his cheeks.

Derek checked his traps at dusk, but they were empty. "May not get anything till morning," he said. "May not get anything at all."

"No matter," said Leggy. "We still got rations."

They made supper over a hot, bright fire, then sat back to watch the flames.

The night was clear, and a brilliant moon held court over a thousand bright stars strewn across the sky. The group drifted off to sleep without bothering to set a watch.

Near midnight, Leggy roused his companions from sleep.

"Look," he said, pointing up toward the moon.

They could see, on the horizon, a strange fluttering cloud, which slowly resolved itself. It was the moths, dozens of them, an indeterminate distance away. The creatures were high up in the sky, and seemed to be straining to reach the moon itself, their papery wings beating inexhaustibly in the thin air.

John watched the creatures. From a distance they looked even more like angels. It looked like they were trying to fly back to Heaven. Something stirred in him, a mixture of sadness and joy.

Back home, the Elders had spoken longingly of Heaven. They said Heaven should be the goal of every man, woman, and child. In Heaven there would be no more pain, no more hurt, no more desperation. Only milk and honey in plenty, and white light, and cool days that went on forever. And these angels were trying to reach it.

"What are they doing?" asked Derek.

"Don't know," said Leggy. "But it looks like they're attracted to the light of the moon. Like they're trying to fly to it."

"Dumb bugs," said Derek. "Even if they could, they'd die as soon as they got there."

"Why, Der-Der?" asked Teddy.

"Cause there's no air on the moon. They'd choke to death."

"Oh," said Teddy.

"How do you know?" asked John, his voice sullen. He didn't like Derek's dismissive tone.

"What'd you mean, how do I know?" asked Derek.

"You ever been to the moon?"

"Course not."

"Then how do you know?"

"My father told me."

"You mean your father went to the moon, then he came back and told you about it?"

"What the Hell's wrong with you, John?" asked Derek, turning on him. "It was something he read about from the Before Times. One of the damn things he was always tellin' me about."

"But Leggy said there were men on the moon," said John. "If there's no air, how'd the men stay alive?"

Everyone turned to Leggy.

He coughed. "Well, I'm not too keen on the details, but I believe they had special suits. Special suits that helped them breathe."

John shook his head. "You don't know any better, either." He rolled over and went to sleep.

The next day, Leggy had to abandon his wheelchair. The going had been getting steadily rougher. The land was sloping upward, and the ground was growing more tangled with brush and roots that snagged the wheels. In addition to gorse bush and stands of pine, the hills were alive with a profusion of greenery that was beyond even Leggy's ability to indentify.

Thus far, Teddy had been able to manhandle Leggy over every obstacle, but even his great strength was waning, and the group's progress was slowing.

Before mid-day, Derek called a halt. Teddy and Leggy were several hundred yards behind—again. Teddy was wrestling the chair through a particularly malicious tangle of trailing vine. The metal wheels of Leggy's chair looked like a strange bouquet of green leaves and stems.

Derek strode back to meet them. "Time to pack up the chair, old man."

Leggy looked up from the ground, where he'd been trying to search out a clearer path. Teddy stood behind him, panting and blowing.

"You're slowin' us up," said Derek.

Leggy knew there was no argument.

"Ah, shit," said the old man. He found himself reluctant to give up his chair, a feeling that surprised him. He'd never particularly cared for his wheelchair. It had always been cumbersome and uncomfortable, and in the last year or so strange bits of metal had begun to poke him in odd places, a sign that its frame was coming unaligned.

But now that the time had come to pack it up, he didn't want to get out. And he certainly wasn't looking forward to its replacement, the hard spine of a braying donkey.

"Time's a wastin'," said Derek.

"All right, all right," said Leggy crossly. "Get them mules back here and let's saddle up."

Leggy watched from his wheelchair as the boys transferred Afha's baggage to Minna, and then inexpertly applied the saddle to Afha.

"Tighten it up good," said Leggy. "I don't want to slip off on some steep mountain pass."

Derek kneed Afha in the belly. The donkey brayed and exhaled, and Derek cinched the saddle an extra notch.

"Okay cowboy," said Derek with a mocking grin, "mount up."

Leggy motioned to Teddy, who lifted the man from the wheelchair and placed him gingerly on Afha's back. The donkey took Leggy's weight easily and didn't seem to mind the rider.

Teddy handed Leggy his serape and a tattered old satchel that had hung behind the wheelchair to hold Leggy's possessions, his whisky flask, pipe and tobacco, matches, and a pocketknife.

"How's it feel?" asked John, as Leggy settled in to his new ride.

"Ain't too bad, I guess," said Leggy, "though I expect by the end of the day I'll be singin' a different tune." He looked around for a moment and then asked Teddy to fold up the wheelchair and pack it on Minna's back.

"What for?" asked Derek.

"What do you mean what for?" asked Leggy. "That's my chair."

"Yeah," said Derek, "but we can't take it."

"Not take it? You expect me to spend the rest of my life on the back of a three-eyed donkey?"

Derek shrugged. "Don't know. But look at it."

Teddy had tried his best to collapse the chair, but it was rusted in sections and wouldn't cooperate. Derek took it from his brother and approached Minna. "This one's already got all the baggage. You expect her to carry this too? It's heavy as shit, Leggy. And awkward to boot."

Leggy licked his lips. He could see that Derek was right, though the son of a bitch didn't have to enjoy it so much.

"Maybe we can hitch it up and wheel it along behind us," said Leggy, already knowing it wouldn't work.

Derek shook his head. "Sorry, Hoss. Either we leave the chair, or we leave you. Which is it gonna be?"

"Fuck," shouted Leggy.

Afha shied a bit. John reached out and grabbed the donkey's bridle, spoke soothingly to calm the animal.

"Fellas..." started Leggy, then stopped again.

Derek smirked. "You want us to leave you alone for a minute so you can say goodbye?"

Leggy said nothing. He wanted to punch the boy in the mouth. He yanked Afha's bridle. "Let's get this goddamn show on the road."

And so they set off again, trudging higher into the hills, the mountains above them beckoning.

"Bye d'bye chair," said Teddy with a wave.

Soon they had passed out of sight, and the metal wheelchair stood alone in the stubby undergrowth, where it would pass through the seasons one by one, a mystery for any who might come across it.

CHAPTER FOURTEEN

The next day they topped a high ridge and found themselves on a wide plateau, a natural border that signaled the end of the foothills and the start of the mountains in earnest. Their eyes boggled at the sight that greeted them. Green grass undulated in a slight breeze, and in the distance, vast stretches of pine and oak sat astride the mountains.

What they knew as grass in San Muyamo was brown and bristly and grew in scattered tufts. Here, knee-high green blades carpeted the plateau in unbroken waves. Derek reached down and plucked a blade. He stuck the shoot in his mouth.

"Beautiful," said Leggy. "Let's sit for a minute, boys."

Teddy lifted him off Afha, and they sat in a circle, plucking at the grass and letting it caress them. The mules bent their nuzzles to the ground and ate, snorting with pleasure. The grass was a welcome change from the thistles and sour underbrush that had been their diet thus far.

John couldn't appreciate the beauty of the landscape; his heart was still troubled. Life had been almost idyllic these past few days—plenty of clean water to drink, sweet cool air to breathe, fresh game turning up more and more often in their snares. But still he felt that their treatment of the angels—or moths, or whatever—had been a bad omen and would come back to them. He gnawed nervously on a bitter shoot, then spit it out.

"Let's keep going," he said.

He stood up and began to walk. The others followed. They hadn't gone more than ten yards when Afha, who was being led by Teddy, pulled to a stop. The donkey brayed and shied. Teddy tugged at the guide rope. "C'mon, horsey, c'mon!" But the donkey would not be budged.

"Take it easy," admonished Leggy, who was mounted on the donkey's back. Minna stopped next to Afha.

Derek, who'd been bringing up the rear, came forward.

"Now what?" he asked.

81

"Horsey won't go," said Teddy with a shrug.

"The Hell it won't," said Derek. He bent to the grass and picked up a stout stick.

"Now wait a goddamn second," said Leggy, his eyes wide. "You hit this donkey and it bolts, it's my neck that gets broke."

"Take him down," said Derek, motioning to Teddy to lift Leggy off the donkey.

"Please," said John. "Please don't hit him. I'll get him to come."

He began to walk away from the group, trying to coax Afha forward with coos and whistles. Afha screeched and shook his head in agitation. The milky cataract of his third eye swirled.

"Come, Afha, come," said John, striding forward in the high grass, snapping his fingers and whistling.

Suddenly John screamed and fell to the ground. Derek rushed forward and saw a flash of brown slithering through the grass.

"Snake," he shouted. He bent to John, who was clutching his calf.

Teddy ran forward and stamped in a wide semicircle around his brother and John, hoping to kill, or at least scare off, any other snakes that might be in the grass. Leggy urged Afha forward. The donkey now cooperated.

"Lift me down," Leggy said.

Teddy placed him next to John, whose face was pale and twisted with pain. Derek had already begun to cut away at John's pants leg. Two puncture wounds were clearly visible in the scant meat of John's calf, and blood trickled from them, bright red against John's pale skin. Leggy unslung his water flask and poured water to clear away the blood.

He put his mouth over the puncture marks, then sucked and spat, hoping to remove any venom. He repeated the process several times, then tied a bandanna tightly around John's leg, just above the wound.

"Anybody get a look at the varmint?" asked Leggy.

John shook his head. "Didn't see it," he said weakly.

"Brown," said Derek, after rinsing his mouth with water from Leggy's waterskin. "That's all I saw. Didn't look like any snakes back home, so I don't know if it's poisonous."

Leggy removed his whiskey flask. He passed it to John, but John wouldn't take it.

"Might help with the pain," said Leggy.

John shook his head no.

Leggy shrugged, then poured a dose over the puncture marks. "I've got clean cloth in my pack," he said. "Tear it into strips and let's bandage this."

Derek did so, and then eased John into a sitting position.

"How you doin'?" he asked.

"I...my leg. Feels like it's burnin'," said John. "The ground...spinning."

Derek looked at Leggy.

Leggy stroked his chin. "He'll hafta ride."

"What about you?"

"I think that donkey can bear us both," said Leggy.

"Okay, but where we goin'?" asked Derek. "He's not fit for much travel."

"I agree," said Leggy, "but I want to get out of here. There might be more snakes around in all this grass. And I want a better place to camp. Let's head to that tree line. It ain't too far."

They got John on Afha's back. The young man was muttering to himself, and alternatively sweating and shivering. His calf had swollen to twice its normal girth.

"Let's go," said Leggy. "Keep your eyes peeled for a good campsite."

They had been traveling for less than an hour across the plateau when Leggy spotted a rocky outcropping near a stand of dwarf pines. The air was sweet with the scent of their needles.

"That might be a good spot," he said, pointing the party toward the outcropping.

As they drew nearer they were surprised to see a dog come at them through the tall grass. It was large and fast, and it growled menacingly. It stopped twenty yards from them, barking and baring its teeth. Short brown fur bristled along its back, and it slobbered as its beady eyes dared them to take another step. The party halted. Minna brayed nervously.

"Step aside," said Derek, unholstering the sawed-off shotgun that he'd gotten from the Paladins. "I'll blow its goddamn teeth out."

The shotgun was an American Eagle smoothbore. Silas had wanted to give it to Leggy, but Leggy had seen the gleam of desire in Derek's eyes, and he knew he'd save himself some trouble if he just gave it to the boy outright. Corrin had reluctantly helped Derek clean off the rust which was threatening to set into the hammer, had showed him how to break down, clean, and oil the weapon. He'd even helped him saw ten inches off the barrel, making the gun easier to manage, more maneuverable, and deadlier at close range. Now Derek carried it in a holster on his back, a belt of nearly a dozen precious shells around his waist.

"Wait," said Leggy. "I believe that dog belongs to someone."

A leather harness was strapped across the dog's chest and back. It looked as if it were designed either to hook the dog to something or for holding the dog as you walked.

"I don't care," said Derek. "Feral or not, we don't have time to return stray dogs to their owners."

"He's not stray," said a high, clear voice.

A woman stood on a boulder near the copse of trees. She had long white hair, and wore a homespun shirt and breeches. She also cradled a long-barreled rifle in her arms.

Derek regarded the woman. There was something odd about her face. She didn't look like a mutie, but something wasn't right. He put that thought aside and considered the shotgun in his hands. She was a good thirty or forty yards away, well out of his range. He might get the dog, but she'd have a clear shot at him if she were any good with a rifle. He wasn't ready to find out.

"Call him off then," said Derek roughly. "We're in a hurry."

"Where are you going?" she asked.

"What's it to you?" called Derek.

"This land belongs to my mother, and strangers aren't allowed to pass without her say."

Derek opened his mouth to tell her where she could stick her say, but Leggy cut him off.

"Our friend's snakebit," he said. "We're trying to find a place to camp, so we can treat him."

The woman frowned. "How long ago was he bitten?"

"Not long. But fever's set in, and he's getting delirious."

"Did you see what kind of snake it was?" she asked.

"Not a good look. But we think it was a brown one."

"Do you have medicine?" she asked.

"We have aspirin, for the fever," said Leggy. "And whiskey for the wound. But nothing for the bite. We need to make a fire, keep him warm, let him rest. Give his body a chance to fight the venom."

"He'd be dead before morning," said the woman. "You'd better come with me."

"Where?" asked Derek.

"To see my mother. She's a wise woman and good with medicines."

Derek scowled at the woman and her dog. Who the hell was she? What if this was a trick? But he could feel John shivering behind him, the fever-heat coming off him like a clay oven.

Derek spat into the grass. "How far is your place?"

"Not far," said the woman. "Just over the next rise."

"Your dog," said Derek, nodding toward the animal.

The woman whistled, high and piercing. The dog, which hadn't taken its eyes off the strangers, turned and ran toward her. He bounded onto the rocky outcropping and then stood by his master. The woman reached down and took the handle of the harness. Derek watched as the dog led her down to the grass, picking the easiest route through the pines. Suddenly Derek realized what had bothered him about her. When she was standing on the stone, the setting sun had been shining directly into her face, but she had made no move to shade her eyes. Why should she? She was blind.

She came forward, led by the dog, and walked right to Ahfa's side. She placed her rifle in Leggy's arms, then reached up a hand and stroked John's cheek. He murmured incoherently. She stroked him with her hands, running her palms and fingers across the contours of his face, then came to rest with one hand on his forehead, the other on the back of his neck.

"His fever's bad," she said, finally taking her hands away and retrieving her rifle. "Follow me." She moved off into the grass, lightly holding the dog's harness.

They followed her through a clever hidden trail of pathways and hills and soon found themselves amidst a small herd of goats. The woman clucked and cooed to them, and the goats pooled in around her, matching her stride. Another dog, larger than the first, bounded into view. Its long gray hair was knotted, making the beast resemble a wet mop. It ignored the strangers, instead patrolling the herd. It nipped at lagging goats and dashed back and forth, defining a perimeter for the herd to remain in.

The group crested a low rise. The grass had been cleared for a homestead—a simple, solidly built cabin with a stone chimney, a large pen for the goats, and a shed. Leggy noted firewood stacked in neat cords, a small kitchen garden, and several fowl patrolling the front yard. The homestead itself was nestled against a rocky hillside that ascended at a nearly vertical angle for hundreds of feet. He watched as the sheepdog drove the goats into the pen. The guide dog led the woman to the gate, and she closed it and fastened it, then turned to the travelers.

"One of you bring your friend inside," she said, gesturing to the cabin. "You can hitch your mules around the back of the house. There's a post and a trough there."

Derek took John from Ahfa's back and carried him to the dooryard. "You two take care of the mules and then come inside," he said to Teddy and Leggy. "And make it quick."

Teddy and Leggy did as they were told. Then Teddy lifted Leggy and carried him around to the front, and only, door. Teddy had to stoop as he went inside.

It took a moment for their eyes to adjust to the darkness of the one-room cabin. When they did, they saw the stone fireplace at one end of the room, a small fire burning in the hearth. A cast-iron kettle bubbled over the flame. Dried herbs hung in bunches from the roof, giving the cabin a pleasant odor.

John lay stretched across a rough wooden table that dominated the middle of the cabin, and a wrinkled crone unwound the bandage from his calf. She probed the wound with her fingers, and laid a gnarled hand on John's brow. She nodded to herself.

"You're not too late," she said. "It was a brown snake, wasn't it?"

"Think so," said Derek.

"Yes. The venom from a brownie's bite moves slow. It wants to get at the heart, to *squeeze* it, but it takes its time. He's lucky, your friend. If it was a greenie or a diamondback?" She fixed them with a sharp eye, "Best you could do is check his pockets and start digging." She mimed working a shovel, then cackled.

"So you can help him?" asked Leggy, feeling foolish being held in Teddy's arms.

"I can. But can you?" asked the crone.

"Can we?" asked Derek.

The old woman rubbed the tips of her fingers together. "What's his life worth to you?"

"Mother," said the blind woman.

"Hush daughter," said the crone. "I'm doin' business. What's the coin of your realm, eh?" she asked Derek.

Derek pulled his father's wedding band from his finger. He held it in his palm for a moment, the last token of his old life, the final link to his parents. Then he tossed it to the crone. She snatched it from the air like a bird of prey, and examined it closely, even more closely than she'd examined John.

"Will that do?" asked Derek.

"Bring me my pestle," said the crone to her daughter, "and the kettle, and clean strips of cloth." Then, to the visitors, "You call me Mother Morgan. That skinny thing is Magdalena."

Soon the cabin was a bustle of activity. The crone worked with practiced ease, creating a smelly concoction from the various plants hanging above their heads, fermenting in bottles, or scraped from old pots in one corner of the room. She was assisted by her daughter, who moved with quiet efficiency about the room, never once stumbling or tripping over anything, even the travelers' bags that had been dropped unceremoniously on the floor. The young woman fetched up a chair for Leggy, so that he could sit without being cradled by Teddy.

"Did you treat the bite at all?" asked the old woman.

Derek explained about sucking out the poison and applying a tourniquet.

"Hmph. We need to drain this wound." She produced a small knife from her belt, held the blade in the flame of a candle for a count of thirty, and then made a series of thin incisions just above each puncture. Blood and pus began to seep from the cuts. John moaned.

Mother Morgan applied a sticky paste to several strips of clean cloth, and bound up John's wound. "This will draw the poison out," she said. "Now, take him off the table and put him over by the fire."

Magdalena spread a blanket near the hearth, and they laid John on the floor.

"What's his name?" asked Mother Morgan.

"John," said Leggy.

"Sit him up," said the old woman to Magdalena, who obeyed.

Mother Morgan bent and pressed a cup into his hands. "Hear me, John. This is Mother speakin'. Drink this. It will help your insides."

John did as he was told. When he'd drained the cup, he lay back on the blanket, his eyes fluttering. He caught sight of Magdalena and tried to lift himself up, but then settled weakly back to the floor, muttering under his breath. In a moment he was asleep.

The crone rubbed her hands. "Sleep, boy. Sleep and my poultice will be your best cure." Then she turned to her visitors. "And now that my table is free again, we'll set out some supper."

David Cane's ring hung loosely on her bony finger.

As Magdalena set out the supper, Mother Morgan sat in a high-backed chair, smoked a thin pipe, and listened to Leggy explain their journey, occasionally casting a critical remark at the girl's preparations.

Soon enough supper was ready—goat's milk cheese, wild rabbit stew with carrots, and green beans from the kitchen garden. Leggy watched as the boys set to. He was hungry, and the food looked so good it almost hurt, but something wasn't setting right with him. The old woman noticed.

"No appetite, eh? This good-for-nothing girl's a terrible cook. I've tried to teach her, but she doesn't take to learning, do you daughter?"

Magdalena said nothing.

"No," said Leggy. "It's fine." He bent and began to eat in earnest, hoping to spare the girl from the old woman's sharp tongue.

When they had finished, Magdalena cleared the table with a brisk efficiency, then stood near her mother, hands clasped in front of her.

"Go on," said the old woman, gesturing to a corner of the cabin. "Up to the loft with you. I expect our guests want to talk a spell, and then get some rest."

"Goodnight," said Magdalena, nodding her head toward the guests.

Leggy couldn't help but return the gesture, even though he knew she wouldn't see. She went to the far corner of the cabin and scurried up a small ladder. They heard her shuffling around above them for a minute, and then it was quiet.

Mother Morgan lit her pipe, and then held the travelers in her gaze. "So you plan to cross these mountains, eh? Into the Wasteland?"

"That's right," said Derek.

"You know the way?" she asked.

"He says he does," said Derek, nodding toward Leggy.

The crone raised an eyebrow.

"I been over these mountains before," said Leggy.

"Before you lost your gams," said Mother Morgan with a malicious cackle.

Leggy merely nodded.

"Well," she said, "I've roamed these mountains for more than fifty years, ever since my wretched husband settled us here." She turned and spat on the floor. "Might be, I could point out a shortcut or two, if you're interested."

"Hell, yeah!" said Derek.

The woman showed her yellowed teeth. "You're an eager one. Are you that anxious to die?"

"The sooner we leave, the sooner we get where we're going," said Derek.

Mother Morgan sucked her pipe for a moment, then pointed at Teddy. He'd gorged himself on the fresh food, and now, in the warm, dim closeness of the cabin, his great head lolled down toward his chest.

"I see I'm keeping my guests from their slumber," she said. "Let's blow out the candles and say goodnight."

"What about the shortcut?" asked Derek.

"Patience, boy. Your friend will be on his back for at least two days. You'll hear of your shortcut soon enough. Though I'll tell you right now, and for nothing, that your best shortcut is to turn around, go back home to suckle your mamma's teats." She cackled and drew closer to the table. "In the meantime," she said, her eyes alight with avarice, "might you princelings be interested in a poke before sleep?" She looked at the ring on her finger. "This bit of gold would do for the three of you."

"You mean…go and lay with the girl upstairs?" asked Leggy.

"Of course," said the crone. "Unless you happen to fancy me?" With a laugh she pulled open her bodice to reveal a pair of withered dugs. Teddy awoke with a start. Seeing the old woman with her dress pulled open, he launched into a fit of laughter. He pounded the table with one meaty fist and cried "Looky, Derek! She got wrinkly boobies! Wrinkly boobies!"

The crone closed her dress, her eyes bright with a wild light.

"But," said Leggy, his mouth dry, "but…she's your daughter, ain't she?"

"So she is, and a good-for-nothing girl. Well, at least she's good for one thing."

Leggy shook his head.

"What's the matter?" asked the crone. "Did the bug that took your legs get your pecker too?" She made a snipping motion with two fingers.

Leggy said nothing, so the crone turned to Teddy and Derek.

"How about you young bucks? Fancy a poke? One at a time or both at once. Whatever's yer fancy—"

"Not Teddy," said Derek. "He wouldn't know what to do with a girl."

Red blush crept up Teddy's cheeks, and he turned away from the table.

"But you know what to do with a girl, don't you?" Mother Morgan said, eyeing Derek from top to bottom. "Oh, yessiree, I can see lust in yer eyes, boy."

Derek stared at the ring on her finger. It was thin, but it was gold—he'd taken it from his father's cold hand just before Teddy had tossed him to the radar rats. He'd paid for John's life, and apparently for more than that. He glanced at Leggy, who slowly shook his head. That decided it.

"Not just one night," he said. "For as long as we're here." He held Mother Morgan's eyes until she nodded. He stood up.

"Guess I'll see you fellas at breakfast," he said, climbing the ladder that led to the loft.

"Glad to see one of you's got something in yer pants." Mother Morgan laughed. As Derek disappeared into the loft, she snuffed the candles between her callused fingertips and cast the room into darkness.

The loft was tucked among the bare beams of the ceiling, and Derek had to crouch as he came through the trap door in the floor. The musty space was dark, save for a single candle. He could make out the shape of the young woman, sitting up in bed. She pushed a blanket aside, and Derek could see that she wore a light shift. He suddenly found himself breathing heavily, his head and groin throbbing.

Magdalena began to lift her shift, exposing milky thighs.

"Is your friend resting all right?" she asked.

Derek stumbled forward, kicking off his boots and shrugging out of his trousers. He lay on the mattress, which was lumpy and smelled of hay. Up close he could see the girl's eyes. Pink pupils with no irises stared up emptily at him.

Then he got on top of her. He felt her body beneath his, taut as a wire. A sudden urgency consumed him, and he took her quickly. Then weariness overcame him, profound and irresistible, and he rolled off her, already plunging into deep sleep.

As he fell, he heard the girl ask, "Will the others be coming up?"

Leggy awoke the next morning beside John, who lay unconscious by the hearth. Magdalena removed his bandages. The wrappings were yellowed with pus, and the skin around the bite marks was spiked through with angry red lines. She bathed the wound, applied more poultice, and wrapped John's leg in clean bandages. He groaned and his eyes fluttered open. Magdalena stroked his face and spoke soothingly. John stared at her in fevered fascination for a long moment before he fell back into unconsciousness.

"He's still sick," said Magdalena, turning to look at Leggy with her dead eyes.

"Will he live?" asked Leggy.

"Who can say?" said Magdalena. Then she rose and went out to attend to the goats.

Leggy pressed his own palm to John's forehead. Still hot, but not as bad as yesterday. Maybe he'd make it.

In the meantime, Leggy had his own bodily concerns—he needed to pee, and badly. He thought about waking Teddy, still slumbering beneath the table where they'd supped, to lug him outside and prop him up behind the shed. He didn't want to have to be carted everywhere like an infant, but his other option, walking on his hands and his stumps, was just as distasteful. He felt there was something undignified in getting around on his hands, as if he were an ape. And Derek, or Mother Morgan, was sure to have some smart remark if they saw him do it. Dammit, he missed his chair!

Clenching his teeth against the rising urgency of his bladder, he scanned the cabin. Derek was still up in the loft. Who knew where that old hag was? Reckoning that wetting himself would be more embarrassing, Leggy propelled himself forward by pressing his palms against the floor and swinging his hips out in front of him. As his stumps touched the ground he brought his arms forward again. In this manner he moved steadily and with good speed. The door was just a few strides away. Suddenly, just as he reached it, it flew open. Mother Morgan stood in the doorway, bearing eggs in her apron. She looked down at Leggy and smirked.

"Well, don't you scoot along nice and proper. Calls to mind a three-legged dog I once had. My husband wanted to shoot the thing, but I told him that dog would get along just fine. And so do you."

Leggy brushed past her and out into the daylight.

"Don't piss in the well," she called. "That's all I ask."

Leggy didn't piss in the well. He pissed on her tomatoes instead.

The day passed quietly. Teddy, once he awoke, made fast friends with the dogs and goats and spent the morning with the herd. Derek and Leggy earned their keep doing chores—Derek chopping wood and fixing small holes in the roof, Leggy weeding the garden.

In the afternoon, Magdalena returned to the cabin. She squatted down beside John, who still lay unconscious, and checked his bandages. As she did, she addressed the old woman. "I thought I'd go out to the salt lick and see if I can get a buck."

"What about them goats?" asked Mother Morgan.

"The big one's watching 'em."

"The feeb?" she shrieked, unconcerned that Derek stood nearby, plugging wattle into a small hole in the wall.

"He's good with them," said Magdalena, shrinking into herself. "And the dogs are there."

"Girl—" began Mother Morgan, raising her clawed fist, but Magdalena interrupted. "I thought he could go with me, to carry the body back," she said, tilting her head toward Derek. "It's our chance to get fresh venison. We can lay up most of the meat for winter."

Mother Morgan looked closely at Derek, and then back to Magdalena. "Is this some excuse to get his pecker between your legs again? That the meat you want?"

The young woman blushed, and her palms flitted over John's ears. "No."

Mother Morgan scowled. "I suppose some deer meat would be worth a lay. Don't come back till you shoot something. I'll fetch in them goats myself."

Mother Morgan turned to Derek. "And don't you be thinkin' this is a freebie. You'll pay all right. Everyone pays Mother."

Derek stood and opened his mouth to speak, but she cut him off.

"G'won then. She moves quick on the trails."

Magdalena stood up quickly, grabbed the rifle and fled from the cabin.

The old woman was right—Magdalena moved fast. As Derek came around the back of the house, he saw her disappear over the rise of a rocky slope that led into the forest. He caught up to her at the edge of a thick wood. She had a stick in one hand that she held in front of her, tapping the ground as she went. The long rifle was slung over her shoulders.

Derek fell in step beside her. He was breathing hard, partly from exertion, and partly in anticipation. He looked at her bosom. Her breasts were small, but firm and round. He'd gone too fast the night before to pay them much attention, but he thought he might remedy that oversight now.

"We're not going to do it in the woods," said Magdalena.

"No?" asked Derek.

She said nothing.

"S'all right. I paid in advance for tonight. And tomorrow night, if we're still here."

"We're here for venison."

"Fine," said Derek. He put his lust aside and looked around as they crossed over the threshold into the woods. The air was cool enough to make him shiver. He'd never seen this much plant matter in his life—trees, bushes, flowering shrubs, all bursting up out of the ground in a riot of life. All that growth pressed in on him, branches snatching, vines wrapping round his ankles. He fixed his eyes to the ground. If there was a path here, he couldn't see it anymore. He wondered if he'd gone insane, following a blind girl into the forest. Maybe she'd lose them both or maybe she'd abandon him here, slip away and leave him to wander helpless as the sun went down and night crept out of the roots and branches.

He stumbled and fell, landing face first in a patch of bushes dotted with white flowers and yellow faces. He stood and found his hands sticky with resin. Magdalena stopped, turned, and sniffed.

"Mountain Misery," she said. "You can grind the leaves to make pitch. I'd recommend you don't touch your hands to your eyes until you've washed."

"How much farther?" grumbled Derek.

"Not far." She strode ahead, leaving Derek no choice but to follow.

They walked perhaps another quarter hour when they came to the trunk of an old oak that had been toppled in a storm before Derek was even born. Magdalena crouched down and motioned for Derek to do the same. She pointed over the trunk to a stand of trees about fifty yards away.

"There's a deer trail over there. We put a salt lick up here at the beginning of spring," said Magdalena.

Derek squinted through the dappled light and thought he could make out a lumped shape at the base of the trees.

"I get it," said Derek. "We wait till a deer comes for a taste and then shoot it. Well, hand over the rifle and get comfortable."

"You aren't shooting," said Magdalena. "I am."

"Bullshit," said Derek.

"Hush," she said. "Just be silent and wait." She laid the barrel of the rifle across the trunk, threaded her index finger gently through the trigger guard, and then seemed to withdraw into herself.

Derek frowned. He hunched down beside her and waited. Magdalena was so silent beside him that he became aware of how loudly he was breathing. As he quieted himself, a stillness trickled into the spaces where his breathing had been. It seeped up out of the ground like a spring, pooling around his ankles, rising up to cover him until he was immersed. Woodland sounds flitted across the surface of the stillness above him.

He drifted for an unknown time until he was startled by the loud crack of a snapping twig. He popped his head up over the log to see a large horned creature at the salt lick. It raised its great neck and fixed its eyes directly on Derek's. In an instant it gathered itself to spring away.

Thunder boomed inside Derek's head.

He leaped over the fallen oak and into the open. Derek saw a flash of tawny skin as two other animals vanished into the woods. He sprinted to the salt lick. The buck had collapsed in the brush. It was dead.

He turned back to their hiding place. Magdalena had come over the trunk and was using her stick to feel her way across the clearing, her broken eyes fixed perpetually on the middle distance, as if she were looking at something beyond Derek. Smoke rose lazily from the barrel of her rifle.

When she reached Derek and the dead buck, she squatted and ran her hands over the length of its coat, and then up and down the branches of its horns.

"Big one," she said, smiling to herself. She unwound a hank of rope from her waist. "Find a good long stick. We'll truss him and carry him home on our shoulders."

"How'd you do that?" demanded Derek. He didn't believe in witches or bruja, but he felt strange, as if this girl had enchanted him.

She ignored his question and instead bent and began the grueling process of dressing the buck. Derek stood over her for a long moment, watching her quick hands working the blood and guts. Already the parasites were abandoning their host in droves—ticks and fleas swarmed from the deer's fur, seeking better fortune in the tall grass. Derek headed off to hunt up a stick.

They returned to the cabin after dusk to find John sitting at the table, flanked by Leggy and Teddy. His face was sallow and his eyes bleary, but he smiled as Derek and Magdalena came inside.

"Look, Der-Der! Johhny's all better," squeaked Teddy.

Derek strode over to John and put a hand on his shoulder. "I knew you'd come through."

John smiled and nodded.

"How you feelin'?"

"A little weak," he said, "and lightheaded. But there's no more pain." John's eyes slid past Derek to Magdalena, who was hanging the rifle over the fireplace. When she turned around he saw her damaged eyes and blanched for a moment, then cleared his throat.

Magdalena came toward him and put a palm on his forehead.

"You're through the worst of it," she said. She put a small jar in his hand. "Be sure to apply this poultice every morning, and wrap your leg in clean bandages. Now you just need to get your strength back. Please eat something."

John prodded his calf gently, and looked up at the blind girl.

"I dreamed of you," he said.

She smiled.

"You put your hands on me," said John. "There was healing in your hands."

She turned her head away. "Not in me. In the medicine."

"What's your name?"

"Magdalena," she said softly.

At that moment Mother Morgan poked her head from the loft. "About damn time you got back," she said, scuttling down the ladder. "It's getting dark and still no supper on the table." She leered at Derek. "Get what you were after?"

"We got a buck," said Magdalena quickly, a red flush creeping up her throat.

"Get to your pots. I'll take care of Mr. Buck."

That evening, Magdalena doted over John, helping him eat and changing the dressing on his wound. "Would you like to step outside and look at the stars?" she asked. "The fresh air will do you good."

John stood up from the table and limped toward the door, leaning into Magdalena. Derek watched the pair step outside, then turned to Mother Morgan.

"You think he'll be well enough to travel tomorrow?"

"Could be." The old woman sparked her pipe and fixed Derek with a grin. "Seems ready for a trip upstairs, I'll wager." She pointed her pipe to the loft overhead.

"What's that supposed to mean?" asked Derek.

"Ain't you got eyes, son? You may be rentin' that girl, but it's your friend that's a lookin' ta buy. Har, har, har."

Derek laughed, but his eyes were cold. "He wants a mama to coddle him, not a woman." He pushed his plate away and strode to the ladder of the loft. When he was halfway up, he turned and looked at Mother Morgan.

"You send her on up when she's done her chores and kissed the baby goodnight."

"Derek," said Leggy.

Mother Morgan sucked her pipe and then blew a ring of stinking blue smoke at Leggy. "That's interestin' company you keep," she said.

Derek ignored them and disappeared into the loft.

Leggy awoke to the sound of eggs sizzling in a skillet. He sat up and rubbed his eyes. Magdalena worked at the cookfire, John beside her. Mother Morgan cackled to her hens outside. Teddy was still asleep, snoring beneath the great table where they'd eaten dinner.

"Mornin'," said the old man. "How's the leg?"

John turned and stood up. "Just about good as new." He winced, then smiled and looked at Magdalena.

"Good," said Derek, coming down from the loft. "Then we can get out of here today."

Magdalena turned her head away.

Derek strode over to Teddy's inert form and kicked one of his brother's great feet. "Wake up, lazy bones. Wake up!"

Teddy sat up and cracked his head on the underside of the table. Derek laughed. Teddy crawled out, rubbing his head, his face still wrinkled with sleep.

"Let's go take a piss before you wet yourself," said Derek. He put a hand under one of Teddy's arms and urged him to his feet.

After a breakfast of eggs and biscuits, Magdalena excused herself to go and tend her goats.

"Perhaps," she said to John, "you'd like to come with me into the field. It'll be good to stretch your leg, get the blood pumping. It's not a long walk, and we can rest along the way."

"Yes," said John. "I'd like that."

"Take Afha and Minna with you," said Leggy. "Let 'em graze a bit before we head out."

"And don't wander too far," said Derek. "I want to be back on the trail before mid-morning."

When they had gone, Derek turned to Mother Morgan.

"Now what about this short cut?" he asked.

"There's lots of ways to get over the mountain," she said. "Some are safe, others are short." She cackled. "Some are faster, but a bit more dangerous."

"Dangerous how?" asked Leggy.

The crone winked. "Sometimes the path is bad. Treacherous slopes, sudden precipices, unsure footing, rock slides. And sometimes it's the folks who live up here that are bad."

"Can't be that bad," said Derek. "They leave you alone."

"They don't bother Mother because I birth their babies and mend their bones. I tell them when to plant and when the storms will come. Fix their snake bites. But you? You're a stranger. They'd fall on you and strip you clean, right down to your teeth."

"I'd like to see 'em try," said Derek, matching the gleam in the old lady's eyes with his own.

She cackled again. "You are a firebrand, ain't you?"

Derek said nothing. He'd survived a childhood at the edge of a blasted desert— he was not easy to intimidate.

The old woman looked at them closely. "I know just the path," she said. "A few days march from here, through barren country. No homesteaders out that way, at least, not many." She nodded. "Yes, I believe it will do nicely."

She described to them a rough trail that had its start a few miles to the north. Three or four days' travel would take them up through a long series of switchbacks and high ridges. If they followed the path true they would find themselves at the edge of a seemingly impassable cliff. They were to look for a notch in the cliff's edge, where they would find a slope, a steep slope, but one that such fine adventurers as themselves should have no trouble braving.

"Follow that slope down into a stony valley," said the old woman. "From there, your Wasteland is due east, straight into the rising sun."

Derek, Teddy, and Leggy, walking on his hands and stumps, came upon John and Magdalena sitting in the grass several hundred yards from the cabin. They sat cross-legged, facing each other, lost in a rapture of quiet conversation. Goats grazed nearby, the tiny bells fixed round their necks tinkling. Minna and Ahfa strode over to Teddy and nuzzled his hands.

"Let's go," ordered Derek, nudging John with his boot.

Teddy, who'd carried all their gear from the cabin, busied himself cinching Ahfa's saddle around the donkey's scrawny belly and heaving Leggy onto the back of the beast.

John looked up at Derek as if he didn't recognize him. A shadow crossed his face. "I don't...." started John. "Fellas, I'm thinkin' maybe...."

Derek let him stammer. He knew exactly what John was wrestling with, and exactly to how put a quick end to the nonsense.

"I want to stay," said John finally, unable to look at his companions.

Derek let the moment linger, let John's words hang uncomfortably in the air. Though he said nothing, the menace radiated from him like heat from a fire. Leggy nudged the donkey toward Derek, ready to shove the beast between him and John if need be. Magdalena rose from the grass, the long rifle cradled in her arms.

Derek stepped forward and pressed his face into John's. "I always knew you'd quit." Derek pushed John back with his body. "We all did. But don't cry to me. Explain it to God. Explain it to the angels."

He bored into John's head with his gaze, dug in with hooks crueler than iron. Derek looked as if he meant to drive over John, to stomp him to dust into the ground. Instead Derek spun and walked away.

"Let's go," he said to Leggy and Teddy. He moved off down the path and didn't look back.

They hadn't even gone a mile when John caught up to them, his head bowed in shame and embarrassment. Derek saw his friend's cheeks, wet with tears, but he didn't say a thing.

CHAPTER FIFTEEN

The path the old woman set them on avoided the cool forests of pine and oak that marched up the mountain in favor of a steep, rocky ascent into the Sierra Nevada range. As they cleared the foothills, the landscape became hard and craggy, cracked and broken.

All that day they marched in silence. Leggy regarded his troop with concern. Derek had prevailed over John, but at what price? Leggy had assured the lad with a hearty clap on the shoulder that whatever didn't kill him could only make him stronger. But Leggy wasn't so sure. The venom was gone from John's leg, but another poison was seeping into his heart.

And there was something else, something about the landscape they moved through. These rocky wastes had cast a pall over the travelers, and they stumbled forward reluctantly, like prisoners to the gallows.

Teddy was the most visibly uneasy. He walked tentatively ahead and was prone to stopping without cause and refusing to budge until Derek consoled him with secret whispers and urged him forward again. Teddy clutched his Bedouin flute tightly in his fist and held it out protectively in front of him, perhaps hoping to ward off any evils that might be marking their passage. And when the world grew the most quiet, when the shrill wind for reasons unknown decided to cease its busy passage around weathered rocks, he would play. He would lift his flute to his lips and blow. With no rhythm or tune discernible to the others, Teddy would fill the dangerous silence with the discordant, untuned sound of their passage.

The "music" annoyed the bejeezus out of Leggy. But he would admit that he preferred it to the stretches of eerie quiet that dogged their path. Let Teddy have his flute. If it kept him moving forward, then Leggy wouldn't complain.

For two days they climbed in silence, save the wind and the flute, and neither saw nor heard any signs of life—no birds of prey circled above, no insects crawled below. The enormous moths had not reappeared at night, and they were free to light a tentative campfire without intrusion. Leggy had fully expected to hear the clamor and scream of mountain cats by night. But only silence had accompanied the harvest moon's lazy sojourn across the ruined sky.

On the morning of the fourth day out from the homestead, they stood at the top of a sheer cliff, just as Mother Morgan had described. Above them, still thousands of feet overhead, the hard, high spine of the Sierras ran to the north and south. The peaks were tipped with white snow. Mist draped the hills and valleys beneath them, obscuring their view of what lay ahead.

Maybe it was better that way, thought Leggy.

"Now what?" asked John.

Derek related the old woman's instructions to search for the notch that the she had said would lead them down into a stony valley.

"There," Derek said.

The notch lay between two huge knuckles of rock. They peered through it to see a steep slope that led to a series of switchbacks.

"I'll be damned," said Leggy.

"Why?" asked Derek. "You thought maybe she was lyin'?"

"I don't know," said Leggy. "Somethin' about this path makes me uneasy. Like maybe she'd put us on a wild goose chase, sent us wandering in circles until we died out here, just because she'd think it was funny. But her directions were right as rain. At least, so far."

He re-arranged himself in the saddle and patted Ahfa on his flanks. "Hope you're as sure-footed as Tariq thought you were, donkey," he said. "Goin' up is hard work, but goin' down is careful work. One slip and…." he made a falling gesture with his hand.

"Anyway," he said, "that crone was right about this being a short cut. If we had followed my route, we'd still be on the way up."

During the first afternoon of their descent they heard *Tap! Tap! Tap!*

The sharp sound assailed their ears, which had become accustomed to the soft breath of wind and flute.

Tap! Tap! Tap!

They stopped and listened for a time. The tapping was intermittent. It echoed throughout the hills, making it hard to locate its origin. But after a few moments Leggy smiled.

Derek had noticed the old man's lips moving, a quiet counting between echoes.

Tap! Tap! Tap!

"There's a trick to it," Leggy confided. "Counting the echoes to locate the source. I'll teach you sometime. C'mon, this way."

The noise grew louder and sharper as they eased down into the valley, the dull *tap* resolving into the sharp *clink* of metal on hard stone.

Perplexed, they continued their steady pace, descending the rocky slopes and switchbacks, making their way doggedly toward its source. After days of silence, the source of the tapping was a welcome mystery.

The switchbacks ended at a gravel-strewn and slippery slope between two steep cliff walls. Teddy took the lead. Placing a huge hamfist firmly against each wall to either side, he braced himself and formed an immovable human barricade should any of the others, mules included, lose their footing and begin to slide. Their descent was slow and arduous. Pebbles and gravel broke loose and rolled down the hill ahead of them, mini avalanches which announced their coming to any who might reside in the canyon below.

The tapping stopped.

Eventually, having given up any hopes they might have had about remaining inconspicuous, they reached the bottom of the slope and turned a corner into the canyon. Not knowing what to expect, Derek pushed his way forward, fingering the barrel of his shotgun. He squeezed past his brother and stepped into the wide opening. A movement at the opposite end of the valley, about a hundred yards away, caught his eye. Someone was sitting on a pile of rocks and waving to him.

The strange figure that reposed on the mound of gravel was thin and pale. Dressed in faded rags, he was nearly indiscernible from the slate and granite all around. As they neared, they could see that it was a man, a very old man, much older than Leggy.

The old man stood up from the rock pile and waved both arms. "Heloooooo-eeeee, there," he called, squinting his eyes and peering in their direction. "I wuz waiting fer you slowpokes ta git here!" He laughed gruffly and then sat back down on the rocks, waiting for the group to come to him.

The old man's ash-gray hair was long and flowed down past the tops of his shoulders. Despite the loose rags and his advanced age, it was obvious he was strong. Hard knots of muscle wrapped their way across his shoulders and down his disproportionately large forearms and wrists. A ragged white beard covered most of his shrunken face. What wasn't hidden by his whiskers was blanched by wind and sun and pulled taut over his skull. His eyes peered out from behind bushy gray eyebrows. Though it was hard to make out his expression beneath his rampant beard, he exuded an air of merriment.

"Sorry, but you boys missed lunch," he remarked when they were close enough to speak without yelling. "But that's okay. Dinner's coming up on us real quick." He glanced up at the sky. The sun was out of sight behind the lip of the canyon and the shadows were beginning to grow long. "'Nother hour or two, I should guess. Drop your bags wherever ya like, you'll be camping here. For tonight at least."

The old man extended a hand. Derek reached out and the man grabbed it and pumped his arm enthusiastically and with unexpected strength. He shook everyone else's hand in turn, as they introduced themselves.

"I'm Teddy!" said the giant, caught up by the man's enthusiasm

"Oh my," the old man looked up at Teddy, who stood a full head and shoulder taller than Leggy, mounted on the donkey.

"We're goin' to New York," Teddy announced proudly.

"Oh my!" repeated the old man. "Ya don't say?"

"And what's your name," Derek asked, looking him over with distrust.

"Me?" said old man. He appeared surprised, as if he'd never before considered that he might one day be posed such a question. "Well, I don't rightly have one, I guess you could say. Never needed one. No one around to call me by it even if I did have one."

It took a moment for Teddy to comprehend, but when he did grasp the old man's predicament, he exclaimed in surprise, "You don't got no name?"

The old man shook his head. He was smiling widely now, a long thin horizontal U-shaped split formed in the hair of his beard, revealing a collection of brown and twisted teeth.

"I'll give you a name," Teddy offered.

"Will you, now?" The stranger chuckled.

"Stu…. Stu…. Stubert!" said Teddy. When there was no reaction from the man he tried again. "Horace!" The giant wrung his hands and chewed on his tongue. "Bartlefish! Monkos! Humpety-Dumpety," he offered.

"Those are all good names there, Teddy," said Leggy. "But why don't you think about it for a while, and tell us what you come up with later?"

Teddy nodded in solemn agreement and sat down on his huge haunches. He began silently mouthing syllables, compiling a list of potential appellations for the mysterious stranger, a man who, at least in Teddy's mind, would remain a stranger until he could be fixed with a name.

"So, you live right here in the canyon?" Leggy asked, in an attempt to provoke conversation.

"Yep," said the man. "Always have."

"All by yourself?" asked Derek.

"The winters must be Hell," said Leggy.

"Purtle-pus…." muttered Teddy.

The nameless old hermit nodded. "Yep and yep."

"Why?" asked John.

The old man looked surprised again, as if the answer was obvious. He swept his hand around to indicate the pile of gravel. "Why? Because there's work to be done."

The old hermit's "work" turned out to be as much a mystery as everything else about him. He led them around to the other side of the hill of gravel he'd been sitting on and showed them a deep hole in the ground, a pit so wide Derek doubted even Teddy could leap from one edge to the other at its widest part.

At the pit's north edge was an even stranger site. A concrete abutment, nearly twelve feet across, and as tall as the old man's shoulders, was set into the ground, half-buried. On the top of the structure, fixed into a small, second level of concrete, at a roughly a forty-five degree angle was a large round rusted steel door, nearly four feet in diameter.

The door was quite obviously sealed tight. It was marked with numerous scrapes in the rust and dents in the metal where the old man had taken a pickaxe or shovel to it. Likewise, the concrete all around the door was chipped away and broken, several feet deep in places. In some of the deeper burrows, John could see the brown rust of metal framing set within the concrete.

Suddenly, John realized that the pit next to the abutment was an excavation. The hole had been dug into the ground next to the concrete structure. In fact, the old man had managed to bore himself a tunnel of sorts that ran several yards downward and into the very heart of the concrete. The mountain of gravel that the old man had been resting upon was, in fact, countless decades of concrete chipped away from the strange artifact.

"What is it?" asked Leggy.

"Damned if I know," exclaimed the hermit. "If I knew what it was, do you think I would have spent my whole life diggin' away at it? And my daddy before me?"

Leggy shook his head. "Your whole life?"

Derek leaned over and whispered to the old hauler. "Is it one of your stockpiles? One of those army bases you was talking about?"

Leggy shrugged. "Don't know. To tell you the truth, I've never seen anything quite like it."

Something occurred to John. He turned to the old hermit. "You said your daddy used to work on digging this thing up before you. He must've named you, then. He must've called you *something*."

The old man smiled broadly, revealing cracked lips and more rotting teeth.

"'Course he did. He called me 'Boy.' But considering my age, and your youth, I don't think it'd be appropriate fer you to be calling me that."

They all laughed at this. "Bingo!" Teddy offered. "Barney?"

John peered into the pit. From here he could see the nearest wall of the pit sloped downward at a steep sixty degrees, a slippery access to the point of primary excavation.

"You dug this all by yourself?" he asked.

"Yep," grinned the hermit proudly. "Well, my daddy started it, but I been chippin' away at it long as I can remember. It's my life's work."

"No doubt," said Leggy. "You try blasting?"

"Yep. But it's reinforced like a motherfucker." The old-timer looked Teddy up and down then walked in a circle around him, sizing up Teddy's enormous form, his strong arms and solid back. "There's as much steel down there as concrete. I'm beginning to think I may not see my way into it in my lifetime. And I've no progeny to hand over the shovel to."

Leggy turned to the old man. "I take it not too many lady-folk pass through here. 'Specially not the motherin' sort." He laughed.

"Not a whole lotta anybody passing through here," the old man agreed. "Occasionally a coyote. Every couple'a years or so a mutie or two'll wander up from the Wastes. But that's about it. Used to be, when I was a lad, there was some trouble with raiders, but not no more. And the traders, they never come through here. Hell, I haven't seen a trader or Bedouin in well over fifteen years. I ain't seen no one worth talking to in…shucks, in quite a long time."

John poked Derek and pointed. A few yards past the strange excavation, where the valley floor met the base of the canyon wall, something gently stirred on the ground. Indeterminate shapes seemed to blend in with the white granite and gray slate. He squinted, and then gasped and jumped back with a start.

There, nestled together, emitting soft purring and chittering sounds, huddled three of the moth-creatures, fast asleep.

Their wings were folded like paper fans and held tightly against their backs. In the light of day, John could see that their bodies were translucent. He could just make out the grayish coils of internal organs and the motion of ichor through veins and arteries. The translucent skin was covered with a sparse down of white fuzz. Long feathered antennae drooped lazily over closed eyes. The delicate bodies of the creatures were dusted with a fine white powder that also covered the ground and wall where they lay.

In their sleep, John thought, *they looked all the more angelic.*

Each of the creatures was pierced. A fist-sized, rusted eye-hook broke the skin at the rear of each of the three bulbous bodies. The skin appeared to have healed and grown around the hooks, as if they'd worn the metal adornments for a long time, perhaps all their lives. Each hook was affixed to a thin silken length of cord, which was coiled neatly on the ground and staked securely into the cliff face with an iron spike.

"What's with the bugs?" asked Derek.

The old hermit smiled. "Them's my pets. Caught 'em myself. They make a pretty sight at night, fluttering toward the moon and stars."

When no one spoke, the hermit bent forward and picked up an armful of shovels and a pickaxe. He handed one to each of the group, including Leggy, "Well, let's say we get in a few good hours of digging before dinner, eh?"

CHAPTER SIXTEEN

"Fuck that," said Derek, tossing aside the pickaxe. "We're not digging. We can still get in a few miles before dark."

The old man raised his eyebrows in surprise. "Not dig? But with your help I might be able to crack this nut." He turned and patted Teddy's shoulder. "Especially this one."

"Flabia!" said the giant. "How about Flabia?"

The old man shook his head no.

Teddy bit his lip and returned to his word hoard.

"Just think how quick we could get this done," said the old man. "We could work two shifts, day and night. At that rate, I figure we'd open this old whore in three, maybe four years!"

"Four years?" scoffed Derek. "We don't even know who the hell you are. Why should we spend four years diggin' your hole?"

Now the old man's eyebrows threatened to leap straight off his face. "Why help? To find out what's in there! Saints and angels! Don't you got any curiosity?"

"Who cares what's in there?" said Derek. "Probably a lot of useless junk from the Before Times."

"Useless?" hooted the old man. "Useless?" He scrambled toward what appeared to be the mouth of a small cave set into the canyon wall. He was amazingly spry, considering his age.

"Let's go," said Derek. "This old man is cracked."

But before they could make their exit, the hermit re-emerged bearing a large crate. He staggered over to them and dropped it at their feet.

"Useless?" he said, reaching into the crate. He emerged with a brick-shaped tin. Pulling a ring tab at one end of the tin, he popped it open. "You call that useless?" he said, shoving it under Derek's nose.

Inside the tin was shredded beef, mashed potato, and carrots and green beans, all divided into neat portions. The food looked fresh and smelled good.

"Go on and try it," insisted the old man. "I got stacks more just like it. You just try it, and tell me if it's useless."

Derek turned his nose away, but Teddy stuck a big finger into the beef, which was covered in gravy. He licked his finger thoughtfully then lifted the tin out of the old man's hands and proceeded to devour its contents.

The old man reached into the crate again, this time emerging with an armful of rattling bottles. He lined up several on the ground.

"Pills," he said. "I take these ones when I get sick," he said, pointing to a bottle labeled Amoxicillin. "I take these if I can't sleep," he said, indicating a second bottle. "And I take this one if I ain't feelin' so energetic—pep me right up, it does. And these ones." He indicated yet another plastic bottle. "They just make me feel sorta funny. You know, in the head. So I only take those ev'ry now and then."

Next, the old man pulled out a fat, short wand with a black grill at one end and several buttons on the other. Leggy, Derek, and John leaned in. The old man also took out a pair of small stoppers and inserted one into each ear. Then he grinned slyly at his guests and hit one of the buttons.

Instantly they were blasted by a shriek of noise, a two-tone siren that seemed to detonate in their ears. They fell back as if struck by a blow. Ahfa reared, threatening to throw Leggy from the saddle. Teddy put his hands over his head and howled, his own roar of pain drowned out by the siren. The moths awoke with a start and leapt into the sky. They were halted painfully by the lengths of rope affixed to their piercings. The sound rocked back and forth between the canyon walls.

The old man pushed the button again. The horrible siren cut out, but it took several long seconds for the echoes to exhaust themselves in the canyon.

"Pretty good, huh?" he said, removing the stoppers from his ears as the group recovered themselves. "I ain't had no trouble with muties, raiders, bears, coyotes, or bugs since I found this little beauty."

Derek, who was torn between anger and awe, said "Where'd you get all this?"

"From the first bunker," said the old man. "The first bunker my daddy dug up."

"You mean this isn't the first?" asked John.

"Heck no. That's number two," said the old man. "Number one is a couple hundred yards south of here. We cracked it about thirty years back. Daddy figured since we found so much good stuff in *that* bunker, we might as well try this one. Problem is, this one turns out to be a Helluva lot tougher than the first. A *Helluva* lot tougher. Which indicates to me that the things inside must be that much better." He turned and winked at Derek. "You still think what I'm doing here is useless?"

106

"Youslus," shouted Teddy. "That's it that's it that's it. Your name is Youslus!" He grasped the old man and shook hands properly.

Youslus eventually extracted himself from Teddy's grip and looked them all in the eye. "Well then, now that we're on a first-name basis, what do you say we get started diggin'?"

"I must admit," said Leggy, scratching his head, "I'm mighty curious about what might be in there."

"Who wouldn't be?" agreed Youslus.

"But four years?" John said. "That's an awful long detour."

"Way too long," said Derek. "Not gonna happen."

"Well, maybe three years," said Youslus. "I got a few things I ain't showed you yet that might help speed up the dig."

"I think," said Leggy carefully, "that we'll just be on our way. But good luck to you."

Youslus frowned. "You sure? Really?"

Leggy nodded his head.

"Well, I suppose I can't expect everyone to be as curious as me."

He looked them over once more, and then turned his eyes up to the darkening sky. The sun had dropped completely behind the Sierras, and daylight was fading rapidly to dusk.

"I don't suppose you'd consider stayin' here for the night? I got plenty of food and water. And I ain't had no one to talk with since Daddy died. I'd appreciate your company."

"I believe we could stay the night," said John, stepping forward before anyone else could decline.

Derek opened his mouth to protest, but John was already moving toward the small cave, his eyes fixed on the captive angels. Teddy followed quickly, asking Youslus if there were any more of the delicious tins.

Youslus chuckled. "Round here you got two choices for vittles—whatever's in the tin or whatever's on the ground." He reached down and picked up a rock. "And this is all that's on the ground."

Teddy took the rock and sniffed it. Licked it. Frowned. And chucked it far into the distance.

"Tin," said Teddy.

"Yep," agreed Youslus.

For an insane man, Youslus made a good host, thought John.

Youslus invited them into his cave. It was dry, high-ceilinged, and crammed with food tins, digging implements, and other strange items—presumably salvaged from bunker number one—including some kind of lantern that didn't run on oil or batteries. Youslus simply turned a switch and two white tubes inside the thing began to glow. When Leggy asked about its power source, Youslus just shrugged. It was another excavated treasure, but he had no idea how it worked. He placed the lantern on a niche in the rock wall, and led them to a small, spring-fed pool near the back of the cave.

As they washed trail dust off their hands and faces with clear, cold water from the pool, Derek turned on John. "What the Hell is wrong with you, volunteering us to stay the night?"

John looked at the ground. "The old coot's lonely. He wanted some company. I just felt sorry for him."

In fact, that wasn't the reason at all. John had a plan, one that he didn't want to share with his companions. He was going to set those moths free. He still felt guilty for the moths that had been killed at their campsite. If he freed these creatures, it might ease his mind.

"Well, let's just hope we don't end up feelin' sorry for ourselves if he decides to pickaxe us in our sleep," said Derek.

When they returned, they found Youslus had peeled the lids off a number of food tins. He pressed them into his guests' hands. John asked how old they were.

Youslus shrugged. "Don't know. My daddy and I found 'em maybe thirty years ago. But I'm sure they're a lot older than that. Don't make no difference. The food's still good. Look at me—I been eatin' 'em for decades, and I'm fit as a fiddle."

John thought he might contest that point, but the rich scent of beef and gravy trumped his arguments. As they ate, Youslus inquired about their journey. He regarded their attempt to cross the Wasteland as sheer madness, but that didn't stop his questions. He was thirsty for talk, and he soaked up everything he could about them.

"Any of you fellas have experience with motors and such?" he asked at one point.

John looked at Leggy. "He used to fix our generator back home."

"I see," said Youslus, "and how did you come across that skill?"

Leggy pursed his lips. "You could say I have an affinity for mechanical parts. I used to work on engines when I was a hauler—motorcyles, automobiles, mostly. Even a couple military vehicles way back."

"Is that so?" asked Youslus. A delirious grin split his beard like Moses parting the seas.

As the stack of empty tins grew, John felt himself growing sleepy, almost irresistibly so. He fought hard against the feeling. He wanted to stay awake so that he could sneak out in the middle of the night and free the moths. He looked around at his companions and saw that they too were droopy-eyed and yawning—everyone except for Youslus. The old man was wide awake and as sharp as a tack, watching his guests with eager, hungry eyes.

John didn't like that look. He considered standing up and rousing his companions, but a great weariness had entered his limbs. The urge to sleep was growing stronger now. He thought it must be left over poison from the snakebite, but then he remembered the bottles that Youslus had shown them earlier—the one with the pills to help him sleep.

"I think…I think something's wrong," murmured John. He turned to Derek, who was now fast asleep on the floor. John nudged him but got no response. Leggy's head had drooped forward onto his chest, and Teddy, who had eaten almost a dozen tins, began to snore.

John looked at Youslus, who was watching him fight the sleep.

"What'd you do?" asked John. He was flickering in and out of consciousness now, so that the old man's face seemed to double and jump in and out of focus.

"Nightie night. Sleep tight. Don't let the bed bugs bite," said Youslus with a wide grin.

John sank into a long and dreamless slumber.

John awoke with the sun in his eyes and curses in his ear. He squinted and held up a hand against the light. As his vision came into focus, he realized he was outside, at the base of the canyon wall. His ankle hurt, and he bent to examine it. He was surprised to find himself in irons. A steel cuff was strapped around his left ankle. The cuff was attached to a short length of thick, rusty chain that ran to a bolt driven into the rock wall of the canyon.

He looked to his right and saw the source of the curses. It was Leggy, cuffed at the wrist, his chain also ending in a bolt in the rock face. Derek was to his left, still asleep, with a cuff on his left ankle. Beyond Derek were the moths that John had hoped to set free.

In front of them lay Teddy, unbound. His chest rose and fell with the deep, easy rhythm of drug-induced sleep.

"That goddamn son of a bitch," cursed Leggy, heaving himself into a sitting position. "He must've pilled us. My head is killing me." He turned and looked at John. "You all right?"

John nodded. He was as all right as he could be, considering the situation.

"Can you reach Teddy?" Leggy asked. "He ain't tied for some reason."

John stretched forward to the full length of his chain, but Teddy remained out of reach.

"He's not bound because he's going to help me," said Youslus, emerging from his cave. He stopped and looked them over. He had Derek's shotgun in one hand.

At that moment Derek began to stir. They all watched him as sat up, rubbed his eyes several times and then looked around. It didn't take long for him to comprehend their predicament. When he did, he cast a withering look at John.

"Just a harmless old coot, huh? Just lonely for some talk, huh? Swear to God John, you sure got us in a fix."

"Oh, don't be so hard on him," said Youslus with a grin. "You'll see it differently when we crack that bunker open."

"Why hasn't Teddy woken up yet?" asked Derek.

"He got a larger dose than the rest of you," said Youslus. "I might've overdid it a bit, just to be sure he went down. Not to mention, he ate quite a lot of the tins. But he'll wake up, by and by."

"What do you mean to do with us?" asked Leggy.

"Why, get your help," said Youslus innocently.

"You mean digging?" asked Derek.

"Yep."

Leggy rattled his chains. "But how are we supposed to dig when you got us staked to the side of the canyon?"

"Oh, I got plenty of chains and anchors about. I can fix you up just about anywhere I'd like. I just put you all here to begin with, so there won't be any trouble."

"But you said it would take us three or four years to open that bunker," said John. "You plan on keeping us locked up that long?"

Youslus's eyes gleamed. "I hope it won't come to that. No, no, no. Not if this man here…" he gestured to Leggy, "…is truly good with motors. And if that ox over there…" he pointed at the sleeping giant, "…is half as strong as he looks. And if we get a little luck. Just a little."

He reached down and patted Teddy on his back. "Your friend here is just what I need for the Stone Biter. He'll be perfect—assuming Old Legless can get it working."

"What's this Stone Biter?" demanded Leggy, but Youslus declined to answer.

After a few minutes, Teddy's breathing sped up and his eyes fluttered open. He sat up unsteadily, mashing his huge fists into his eyes and yawning like a hippopotamus.

He squinted in the daylight, and then recognized the old man. "Hi, Youslus. How come you got Der-Der's gun? You oughtn't to have that. Der-Der gets mad."

"Now listen to me very carefully, Teddy," said Youslus calmly and slowly. "I want you to do exactly as I say. Don't make any sudden moves. Just sit and listen to my instructions. If you leap up or try and attack me, I'll put both barrels into you." With a double click, Youslus pulled back the twin hammers of Derek's gun.

Teddy thought for a moment, then turned and saw his brother and his companions. He looked at them curiously.

"Why you chained up, Der-Der? You been bad?"

"We're in trouble, Teddy. All of us," said Derek. "You just sit tight and do like Youslus tells you. Otherwise, he might hurt us."

Teddy turned back to Youslus, confusion in his eyes, but he didn't move.

Youslus smiled. "Good, that's good. Things will be so much pleasanter if we cooperate. Now Teddy, you go on into the cave. Toward the back you'll find a big old cart. I want you to drag it out here."

Teddy emerged from the cave wheeling a flatbed dolly loaded with heavy equipment. When he returned to the group, Leggy saw what looked to be a generator among the gear, though bigger than any he'd ever seen before. There was also a large metal cylinder, about three-quarters as high as a man, and thick as a telephone pole. At one end it had hand grips that stuck out from it like the stubby arms of a crucifix. At the other end gleamed a metal shaft that tapered to a thick point. The cylinder was connected to the generator by a length of thick, black cable.

Youslus was quivering with excitement. "This is Stone Biter," he said, gesturing at the strange device. "That's what my daddy called it, anyway. It's a mechanical hammer. They used them in the Before Times to pulverize rock and stone, to drill holes in the ground, to break up concrete, to build cities and break mountains. We found it in the first bunker.

"My father knew what it was, and he told me how quickly it could speed our work. But something's wrong with the motor. In here." He tapped the generator casing. "Daddy and I never could get it to work. We tampered with it off and on for years, but we just don't know machines very well. Do we Daddy?" Youslus looked off into the sky.

"For twenty years it's sat in the cave, untouched. Just think about that—twenty years of possessing a magnificent tool that you could never use? Imagine havin' an itch you couldn't scratch…for twenty years! A body might just go crazy."

Might? thought Leggy.

"My poor daddy died and never once saw his prize in action," continued Youslus, "and here I was beginning to think the same might happen to me. Yet now, you fellas drop in outta the sky."

He pointed to Leggy.

"You can fix the motor. And Teddy here can operate the hammer. It will be fantastic! Absolutely fantastic. We'll crack that bunker wide open. Do you hear? Open!" The word echoed off the canyon walls.

Then Leggy asked, "And what if I can't get this motor to work? Then what?"

Youslus shrugged. "Well, we'll just have to dig without it. The old fashioned way, or maybe it's the *new* fashioned way, with pickaxe and shovel until we get inside. Or until we die tryin'."

CHAPTER SEVENTEEN

Leggy tinkered with the motor all throughout the morning. Youslus had brought a tool kit and a crate of spare parts that may or may not have belonged to the motor. Then he crouched down on his haunches, just out of reach of his prisoners, the shotgun straddled across his knees, and watched Leggy work.

Teddy worked with a pickaxe down in the pit. Steady, ringing blows echoed throughout the canyon. Derek and John sat against the cliff wall, husbanding their strength. The cliff faced east, and the bright sun stared them in the face as it rose through the morning sky. By noon the sun stood directly over their heads, baking their skulls. They were parched with thirst, tongues thick and swollen in their dry mouths, heads pounding.

Finally, Derek spoke. "Water," he said. "You got to get us some water. Especially Teddy. He's been workin' all morning."

Youslus looked up and blinked, as if he'd forgotten about everything but the motor. Now he shook his head as if waking from a daydream, noting the position of the sun in the sky.

"Lordy, lunch time already?" He stood up, stretched his legs, and strode into his cave. He returned a few moments later with an armful of food tins, which he tossed to his prisoners.

"What about Teddy?" asked Derek.

"Don't worry—I'll take care of him next," said Youslus.

As the prisoners were tearing into their meals, Youslus returned again with a bucket and a dipper. He put them down near Leggy, and stood back again.

"Go ahead and drink up. This one gets first dibs," he said, pointing to Leggy. "He's the one doin' all the work. He and the big fella. For the rest of us, it's a little holiday, right fellas?" He smiled at John and Derek. "Lazy day off! Ooh, Daddy would be maaa-aaad!"

"Sure," said Derek. "A fuckin' holiday. You're crazier than a two-headed baby."

Youslus said nothing. He merely squatted down to watch Leggy get back to work.

Throughout that day, and the next, and the one after that, Leggy had come across a slew of problems with the Stone Biter—loose wires, misaligned rotors, corroded gears, and the like. He'd done his best to remedy or work around problems, but still the motor refused to start. Youlus urged him to persevere.

It wasn't until late afternoon of the fourth day that Leggy shouted, "Aha!" and removed a frayed belt from deep within the guts of the motor. He showed it to Youslus, who practically beamed.

"Very good," said the old man, his forearm muscles pulsing as he opened and closed his hands with excitement.

"Maybe, and maybe not," said Leggy. "If you don't have another one of these somewhere, it ain't gonna run."

Youslus motioned to the crate. "Look in there. It's gotta be in there. It must!"

Leggy heaved himself over to the box, convinced there wouldn't be a spare belt. As he pawed through an assortment of parts, he wondered if Youslus would blow them all to Hell if the motor couldn't be fixed.

Impatiently, Youslus snatched up the box and dumped it out. Nuts, screws, washers, bits of wire, and other detritus clanked to the ground. Several bolts rolled away. Youslus searched through the pile, then shrieked.

"This is it, this is it!" He held up a small gray belt, no larger than a rubber band, and thrust it under Leggy's nose. "This is it, yes?"

Leggy compared the damaged belt with the replacement. They looked similar, so he nodded. "Yup, that's it. Or close enough that I can maybe make it work."

Youslus kicked away the other bits and scraps of metal to give Leggy a clear space to work. "Well, put it back together then," he shouted. "Plenty of daylight left. Oh yes, plenty."

By dusk the motor was reassembled. As Leggy reattached the last screw on the metal housing, Youslus dashed away. He returned with a large red can with a handle and long spout.

"Gasoline?" croaked John, his throat parched with thirst.

"That's right, boys. It's go-juice for Stone Biter."

Youslus poured gas into the tank then hunted around the generator until he found the start button. "You know how many years I've dreamed of this?" he asked them. "How many times I've pushed this here button, just wishin' to hear something—anything?"

"Now here we go!" He stabbed the start button with an eager finger. The motor shook. Inside the housing, moving parts began to stir. The motor backfired several times, and then suddenly barked into furious, roaring life.

They covered their ears against the noise—everyone but Youslus, who grinned so wide it seemed the top of his head might come off.

Teddy came up from the pit, face coated in blood, sweat and dust. Through a series of wild hand gestures, Youslus ordered Teddy to carry the Stone Biter to the pit. The mad hermit then followed along behind, pushing the generator. Soon they were lost to view behind the mountain of gravel that Youslus and his father had built up over the decades.

Although they couldn't see, the prisoners didn't need to. Sounds told them everything that was going on. The motor continued to roar, but then a loud clattering erupted from the hole that made them all jump. It sounded like God Himself pounding on a mile-high door. It was the hammer. The noise rang out intermittently at first, and then grew more regular and sustained, presumably as Teddy grew more accustomed to the hammer's operation.

By now darkness was falling rapidly. Several stars peppered the night sky, and the moths were beginning to stir. Leggy expected the hammering to stop as the light faded, but Youslus had other plans. He went to his cave-house and returned with the lantern that had lit their dinner what seemed like years before. He placed it on the lip of the excavation pit nearest to where Teddy was working.

"I believe he means to have Teddy hammer all night," said Leggy, noting the appearance of the lantern.

"Is he lookin' over here?" asked Derek.

"No," said Leggy. "Least I don't think so."

"Good," said Derek. "You tell me if he comes over this way."

John turned to see what Derek was up to. He had taken a ring tab from a food can and inserted it into the locking mechanism of the cuff around his ankle. He twisted and jiggled without result.

John watched carefully for Youslus to reappear, but after what seemed like hours of staring into the dark, his concentration faded. His head ached from the relentless noise of the hammer, and hunger and thirst began to plague him again. They'd had no food nor water since breakfast.

As night fell, his eyes were drawn back to the moth creatures that Youslus kept as pets. They were fully awake now and fluttering up toward the moon, which had risen full and round above them, their progress hindered by the cruel hooks and lengths of rope that bound them to the insane man's canyon. John felt foolish. He'd wanted to set them free, but now he needed saving just as badly as they did.

As he watched the moths' stunted arabesques, his mind wandered back to the cool green of the plateau from which the travelers had descended nearly a week ago and to Magdalena. A deep regret sat on his heart, and he felt his soul fluttering out toward her, yearning and straining against its own bonds. Perhaps, if and when they got out of this, he might just turn and head back into the mountains, forsake the Wasteland and his friends to find her.

Hours later the banshee howl of the generator finally cut out, along with the awful pounding of the hammer. Silence descended like a thunder clap, causing Derek to look up from his failed attempts to jimmy open his ankle clamp. Immediately he slipped his crude lockpick into his sleeve.

A few minutes later Youslus appeared, lantern in one hand, shotgun in the other. Behind him came Teddy, staggering with exhaustion. Derek's brother was covered in a thick layer of dust and grime. He sat down heavily and looked at the ground, too tired to even raise his head.

"Is it open?" asked Leggy.

"No, no, not yet," said Youslus. "But Teddy here did a good day's work. A damn good day's work. He's earned himself a bit of rest. I'll be back in a minute with some food and water." He patted the giant on the head.

Teddy had fallen asleep by the time Youslus returned. The old man nudged him with his foot, but Teddy didn't stir. Youslus shrugged and left several tins on the ground, then disappeared back to his house.

The prisoners did their best to get themselves comfortable. The canyon wall, which baked like an oven in the sun, had gradually given up its heat as night fell, and was hard and cold now. The companions had to huddle together for warmth. Teddy, who had collapsed out of their reach, was so deeply asleep that even the chill of the night didn't rouse him.

In the dark silence, Leggy, Derek, and John discussed their predicament, and how they might get out of it. It was clear that Youslus meant to keep them here until he got inside the bunker, which by every indication wouldn't be any time soon. How long could Teddy stand being driven like this?

"How you comin' on that lock?" Leggy whispered to Derek.

"I'm not," said Derek. "I been at it for a long time with nothin' to show for it."

"So what are we gonna do?" asked John.

"Keep at it, I guess," Leggy said. "Maybe we should all take a crack at it. That son of bitch has been pretty careless about leaving those tins around. We got enough lids for each of us. Maybe my lock or John's is more pickable...."

"Not likely," said Derek.

"Well, what else are we gonna do?"

"Pray," said John.

"Shit. Maybe I will," Leggy sighed.

Before they drifted into sleep, they noticed that spasms occasionally wracked Teddy's body, his large frame jerking as the muscles in his arms, chest, and back quivered arhythmically.

"Why's he doin' that?" asked Derek.

"Not sure," said Leggy, "but I'll bet it's from that goddamned hammer. Vibrations and such, messin' with his nerves."

Derek turned his face to the canyon wall. "I promise you right now," he said darkly, "if we get outta this, I'm gonna make that bunker into the old man's tomb."

The next day was much like the previous. Youslus appeared just after dawn, eager to tackle the pit. This time, however, Teddy was harder to rouse. He didn't respond to prodding, shouts, or even kicks. Finally Youslus threw a bucket of cold water over the boy. Teddy sat up suddenly, violently sputtering and shaking his head.

"You okay?" asked Derek.

Teddy shook his head, tears mixed with the icy mountain water dripping from his hair. "Hurts." He frowned. "Really sore, Der-Der. Don't want da noisy hammer today."

"Buck up there, Ted," said Youslus cheerfully, clapping him on the back. "You're doing great. Really great. Now saddle up and let's get crackin'! Your muscles'll get used to it. It'll get easier." He cackled.

"And look what I brung you." He tossed a pair of earplugs onto the ground. "That way you won't go deef while ya work."

"No," said Teddy petulantly. "Don't wanna go in the pit today."

"Now, Ted," cajoled Youslus. "What say we make a deal—you get to work, and you can have all the food tins you want."

"No," said Teddy.

The old man frowned. "How's about you get to work and I don't let you friends starve to death?"

Teddy said nothing.

Youslus scratched his beard for a moment, then hefted the shotgun. "Well, if that's the way you're gonna play." He strode over to his prisoners.

"Whadda ya say, Ted? How about I blow off your brother's arm, just above the elbow? Or would you rather I take off his leg at the knee?"

Teddy grimaced.

"It's your choice, Ted. What's it gonna be? Arm or leg?"

Teddy said nothing.

"I'm gonna count five," said Youslus, "and then I'm gonna cap your brother at the knee. If he doesn't bleed to death, he and that other cripple there can start a club."

"Fuck you," said Derek.

"One," said Youslus.

Teddy bit his lip.

"Two...Three...Four...."

"Okay." Teddy lumbered to his feet and trudged toward the pit.

Youslus followed at a safe distance behind, once again bubbling with excitement. Soon the generator began to howl, and the jagged pounding rocked through the canyon.

The hammer stopped twice that day—once to refill the motor with gas and once for Teddy to wolf down some food.

The others worked feverishly at their manacles but without success. The locking mechanisms were too sturdy for their flimsy, makeshift tools.

Youslus let Teddy stop at nightfall. This time he ate and drank several portions before collapsing in a heap.

The next day, Youslus set Teddy to work again. It was the hottest day yet. As the sun beat down on the prisoners, John found himself slipping in and out of consciousness. His head pounded from noise and sun. Was it heatstroke or something more sinister? His leg throbbed where the snake had bitten him. He had difficulty concentrating on the only task he had—namely, attempting to pry his lock open with the ring from a food can.

As he worked at the lock, his mind wandered back to Magdalena. He missed how she would lay a cool palm against his cheek, and the way her fingers had scanned his face, as if reading him. John wished she were here now—to bring him cool water to drink or to wipe his brow with a damp cloth.

He had read to her from his Bible while they sat together in the green pasture. No one had ever read to her before, she said. She said she liked the sound of his voice. She had listened intently to the Psalm of the shepherd, for she herself tended a flock. And she gasped in disbelief at the story of Jonah—how could there be a fish so big it could swallow a person? She had made John read that story over and over.

He regretted leaving her. And yet, he knew he had made the right choice. God had called him. How could he refuse that call and refuse his companions? It had been hard to leave her, but wasn't God's way always hard? Moses had wandered in the desert for forty years, the Elders said. How long would John and his companions wander in the Wasteland?

But first they would have to escape from here. Maybe they had failed already. Maybe this was their punishment, to be chained to a canyon wall until they died because John had been weak—because he had almost abandoned their quest for a woman.

These dark thoughts followed him down into a restless sleep.

He awoke to the quiet. After the near constant hammering of the Stone Biter, the silence was almost deafening. Youslus was rushing from his cave to the pit. John's mind swam.

"What's going on?" Derek called.

"Your brother passed out," said Youslus, sounding annoyed. "Gonna throw some water on 'im. Git some food in his belly. He'll be all right."

But the old man sounded less than convinced. He descended into the pit, and after a quarter of an hour, Stone Biter started hammering again.

CHAPTER EIGHTEEN

The prisoners lost count of the days. Youslus proved an efficient jailer. Empty food tins turned into receptacles for the prisoners' waste. Once a day he'd toss the keys to Derek, who was instructed to unlock John and toss the keys back to Youslus. Then, covered by the shotgun, John would gather up the fouled tins and dump them into a nearby hole. Then the process with the keys and the lock would reverse.

Once, when Derek refused to toss the keys back to Youslus, the old man shrugged and pulled one of the triggers. The rock wall above Derek's head splintered, showering the captives with bits of stone and smoke.

"Next time it's your face," said Youslus with a smile.

Derek tossed him the keys.

Meanwhile, Teddy had grown distressingly haggard. His arms and legs convulsed uncontrollably whenever he was not down in the pit.

Sleep did not refresh Teddy. He shook, and his hamfists clenched and unclenched, as if trying to control the powerful Stone Biter. Even in his dreams he struggled to keep the metal demon from escaping his grip and turning its hungry bite away from the unforgiving stone and back toward more delectable flesh—a booted foot or sweaty calf.

Stone Biter was a greedy, violent beast, weakening and deadening its captor's muscles with endless pounding vibration. Teddy knew it was only a matter of time before it would taste flesh. The impossible metal contraption seemed to grin assuredly up at Teddy, metal teeth throwing sparks and chomping the granite and cement to bits as easily as it would bone.

Oh, it seemed to say, *I'll have you. Maybe not today, maybe not tomorrow, but I'll have you.*

When awake, Teddy's eyes were dull and glassy. Derek had to yell in his brother's ear to be heard, and Teddy complained of the endless ringing. It was beginning to affect his equilibrium, and when he walked he would often stagger and veer to the left or right of his intended destination, sometimes crashing tiredly into the valley walls or piled debris. The cruel hermit was working him to death.

The rest of the group fared little better. They roasted in the day and shivered through the night. Their bones ached from the hard stone. The cuffs had rubbed their skin raw, making even the smallest movements painful. They existed in a near constant state of hunger and thirst.

Afha and Minna had been relieved of their burdens and turned loose to fend for themselves. Each morning they wandered away to forage. At first Derek thought he'd never see them again, and he added the two mules to his tally of injuries. But each day the animals returned. Their fidelity was a comfort, but it did nothing to help their predicament.

As the first week turned into the second, Youslus grew increasingly agitated. While Teddy was making steady progress, no end to his toil was in sight. The concrete of the strange bunker proved thicker and deeper and more fortified than even Youslus would have predicted. The steel with which it was reinforced proved nearly impenetrable to even the godlike fury of the Stone Biter. The old man took to swearing anxiously under his breath, and shortening Teddy's rest breaks. Once, Teddy heard him mutter, "Not sure what's gonna give out first—Ted or my gas supply."

The companions were growing frantic. The iron locks had proved impenetrable to their meager attempts at picking them, and the companions had no other ideas. In the absence of anything else, Leggy stressed patience, that they could only bide their time.

"That crazy fucker will make a mistake," insisted Leggy. "Maybe leave the gun in our reach or turn his back on Teddy. We have to be ready to jump on Youslus when he does."

Two weeks turned into three. The days now filled with a new sound—the guttural, animal wails and moans of Teddy rose above the beat of the Stone Biter. All day long he cried. He was dying.

Derek shut his dried and sunburned eyelids and thought only of escape.

Escape…and murder.

CHAPTER NINETEEN

A broken bridge, larger than imaginable—spanning a deep valley as far across as the eye could see. Mist obscures the floor of the valley, thin white clouds drift lazily by far below.

He walks out as far as the failed bridge will take him, a quarter mile, a half mile.... His throat is parched and dry.

To the end of the ruined bridge he comes. It has been sheared off at its highest point, now just an iron and steel cliff hanging over the center of the enormous valley. Metal spires rise up on the bridge's sides, rusted cables dangling and creaking in the wind.

The valley stretches on endlessly to either side, unfathomable in its depth. Clicking, chittering, snapping sounds—dulled by the wall of cloud—hint at unknown dangers below. Deep, rumbling moans roll through the mist like thunder lumbering across the valley.

A rusty, corroded girder balances precariously on the bridge's edge. He grips the girder with his tired fingers (noting how withered they are, and dry—the skin is cracked and raw) and begins to shove. After a moment's exertion, the tired metal moves. He uses this momentum to begin rocking the thing—forward and backward, over the lip of the cliff, in wider and wider arcs until finally it goes over.

Falling... Falling...

The girder breaks through the clouds below and disappears into the mist. There is no sound of impact. Only silence...

He sits down on the edge, his feet dangling over the abyss and waits. Waiting for what, he does not know. His legs hang over the broken abutment, he feels the rough concrete and steel on the backs of his thighs, warmed by decades under the hot, ultraviolet sun. Looking down at the mist that rises up from the valley to obscure the distant horizon, he feels as if he is sitting on the edge of the world.

Suddenly the clouds and mist begin to swirl. He can hear the distant gale of a rapidly approaching wind, rushing down the valley. He feels the temperature drop as the gust draws closer. Then it hits him, knocking him backward onto the bridge. He scrambles away from the edge and lies flat on his stomach, gripping the corrugated ground with all his might to keep from being swept away. He can feel the gigantic structure swaying beneath him, and he prays that it will hold....

Then, as quickly as it had come, the wind is gone. He stands and rubs the dust from his eyes.

The mist has lifted; the clouds have all blown away. Before him is a sight that is nearly incomprehensible—he's seen pictures in books, but this was like nothing he'd ever imagined.

New York City.

Countless buildings, taller than mountains, loom on the horizon. Black and gray, brown and crumbled, many of them have long since fallen over, only to be propped at awkward angles, leaning heavily against their sturdier brothers. Had people actually lived in this place? From smashed windows and broken walls he imagines that he can see eyes: glowing, unblinking, ever watching.

Strange trees (some few nearly as tall as the skyscrapers themselves) have sprung up everywhere, blending with the buildings, taking root in the tarmac and cement, and gripping the shattered city in the clenched, wooden fists of their branches. Thick, evil vines have overrun the place, strangling the buildings, sprouting poisonous crimson leaves the size of caravans, twisting and tangling the edifices in their snakelike embrace.

But most terrifying of all are the heads. Carved onto each of the buildings are dozens of glaring, staring demonic faces. Piercing stone eyes, snarling grins, fanged teeth. Stark eyes, despondent faces, mouths frozen in painful agony. They silently smile, frown, laugh, scream and accuse. The shrill wind cuts through the city like the clamor of a thousand voices.

What is this?

He begins to tremble and shake with fear under the powerful gaze of the skyscraper totems. He closes his eyes and presses tightly to the ground, wishing that he could bury himself in the stone, make himself disappear. In the distance, a grinding sound suddenly pervades the air, the harsh scrape of stone moving against heavy stone. The sound is joined by another, then another. He opens his eyes, and his heart leaps into his throat. The gargoyle heads are slowly turning, grinding on concrete necks to gaze directly at him, to scrutinize him with their evil, apocalyptic stare. Those with mouths that were closed begin to open them. Chunks of stone fall from the buildings where the heads move, falling to the ground with a cacophony of sharp smashing, breaking, and crunching reports.

Hundreds of the heads, thousands of them, begin to turn in his direction. The sound of the grinding, breaking stone fills his ears, threatening to split his eardrums.

Then, just as suddenly as it had begun, all is silent.

He screams.

Derek awoke screaming, a desperate, burning thirst in his throat and a strange silence in the air. He shook his head, confused, wisps of nightmare still clouding his brain. Someone was yelling in the distance.

"Whoooooouuueeeee! It's open," shouted Youslus. "Open at last! Open at last!" Youslus appeared on the lip of the pit, leaping up and down and waving. "It's open boys. Open. Teddy cracked a hole. Hallelujah!" He lifted his hand in the universal sign of okey-dokey. "Won't be long now before we're in. Yeee-haw! Where's my lantern?"

Derek frowned. He was about to ask about his brother when Leggy interrupted.

"Well, aaall right." Leggy smiled a wide, shit-eating grin. "That's dandy," he exclaimed. "Now, I know you're not gonna keep this moment all to yourself—you're gonna want some help bustin' in there!" Leggy wrung his hands in anticipation.

Youslus stopped.

Leggy continued, "Bustin' a hole with old Stone Biter is one thing. But widening that hole, getting inside...well, that's a bird of a different feather." He was speaking fast, not giving Youslus a chance to respond. "Widening the hole is careful work. You want to get inside, but you don't want to cave the place in. Take it from an ex-hauler, I busted into more'n a few bunkers an' vaults in my day, let me tell you."

He paused. "You don't want to damage the merchandise." Youslus opened his mouth to speak, but Leggy cut him off. "'Sides, we got nothing to lose, now. We're in! Won't be long. Few hours most likely. A day at the most, maybe two. With five of us hammerin' away, we'll be in there in no time."

"Enough," Youlous said. "Wait here." He grinned crazily, then turned and marched back into the pit.

Leggy's smile instantly dropped. He looked grimly at the boys and spoke with deadly seriousness. "He's gonna let us help him. He can't wait. He wants to get in there now. He'll let us help. Doesn't think we'll run, not when we're this close."

Derek squeezed his hands together and smiled coldly.

"No!" Leggy hissed at Derek. "Now you listen to me, and you listen carefully. He's gonna let us go but most likely he'll do it one at a time, so's he can chain us up down in the pit. Don't you jump him the second he undoes those chains, you hear me? You wait until we're either all free or all down in the pit. I'll choose the moment, Derek. You jump too soon, you'll fuck us all—"

Youslus's head popped up over the edge of the pit. "All right. You boys wanna help?" He grinned maniacally.

All was silent from down in the pit. Youslus climbed out and walked over to the three, a ring of oversized iron keys dangling from one hand, the shotgun held firmly in the other. "All-righty then." He fit a key into Leggy's wrist-cuff. "Ya get yerself down into the pit, Hauler."

Leggy shot Derek a warning look then scrambled on his hands over to the edge of the pit and began to tentatively work his way down into it.

Youslus tossed Derek the keys and pointed the shotgun at him. "You unlock your friend. When he's down in the pit, you can unlock yourself."

Derek took the keys and unlocked John's cuffs. John rose unsteadily and groaned.

"Little sore, are ya?" asked Youslus with a grin. "Don't worry, that old Stone Biter and a little hard work will smooth you out. I figure the two of you can handle it if you work together."

Derek's heart sank into his stomach. "What do you mean, handle it? What about Teddy? What's wrong with my brother?"

"Nothin' a little rest won't cure. In the meantime, you and your friend should get to work."

John walked down into the pit.

"Go ahead then," said Youslus, jiggling the shotgun at Derek.

Derek turned the key in his own lock and then stood as the chains fell from his wrists to the ground. He was free. He thought about Leggy's warning, and then thought Leggy could go fuck himself. He measured the distance between him and Youslus. He readied himself to lunge. Just then there was a scream from down in the pit.

"Aw, no, Teddy, no," Leggy bellowed. "Quick! Bring water. Aw, Teddy, don't you die on me, now, Don't die!" Leggy's voice echoed back and forth between the steep valley walls.

Don't die…don't die…don't die…

Derek broke into a run. Without looking he swept past Youslus and leapt into the pit. It was deeper than he had thought, certainly deeper than it had been the last time he had gazed into its depths three weeks ago. He landed hard, twisting his ankle and rolling awkwardly down the steep incline into a pile of debris and concrete dust. He could see Youslus's hole, a dark opening into the interior of the bunker. It was no larger than a fist. And beneath the hole lay Teddy. The giant looked gaunt and pale. He was sheened with sweat, and blood ran from his ears and nose and from beneath his broken fingernails.

Derek hobbled to his brother. Teddy breathed intermittently in awkward, straining heaves. He was struggling to stay alive, fighting for each breath, each moment of life. He lay on his back, eyes staring into the eternal blue above. Stone Biter lay next to him, seeming to grin.

"He needs water or he's gonna die," said Leggy.

Just then the giant's body was racked with convulsion. His arms flailed uncontrollably at his sides. Leggy heaved himself on top of the boy, as if the frail weight of the half-man could possibly restrain the enormous child's spasms.

"Get water," Leggy yelled. And then, "Aw, easy there, Teddy, easy." He brushed the boy's ragged hair from his sweaty temple in a soothing, motherly gesture. "You rest easy there, big guy, just relax."

Derek turned and found a rope ladder leading up the side of the pit. But before he could mount it, he saw Youslus and John peering down from the edge. John was holding a large canteen.

"Throw it down," shouted Derek.

John dropped it over the edge. Derek caught it and ran back to his brother.

"I'm gonna kill him," Derek hissed, handing the water to Leggy. "He's dead. You just watch."

"Not yet," Leggy said, carefully placing the canteen at Teddy's lips.

At first Teddy gagged and refused the water, but Leggy was persistent.

"There'll be time for him later. Plenty of time. Don't you worry 'bout that. But first, we gotta help your brother. It might not be too late." Leggy shook his head. "It probably is, but it might not be...."

Unexpected tears welled up in Derek's eyes, and he dropped to his knees before his brother.

"Oh, Teddy," Derek urged, "Come on. You can do it, I know you can. You're strong. Stronger than any of us. Take the water. Drink."

Teddy gagged again. The convulsions had momentarily subsided and now the giant lifted his tremendous hand to push away the canteen.

"No," Derek commanded, "You drink! Teddy, you listen to me. You drink that water or I'm gonna be very mad at you. You drink that water or I'm gonna leave you here. Alone. All by yourself."

Tears streamed down Derek's cheeks and he turned away from his brother. "I'll leave you. I swear I will. Now drink! Please, drink...."

After a moment he heard the sound of Teddy gulping and swallowing.

"Good boy," he whispered, putting his arms around his brother. "Good boy." Then he heard footsteps behind him.

Youslus stood at the floor of the pit, pointing Derek's own shotgun at him. John stood nearby. Derek saw that Youslus had shackled John to a length of chain that was spiked into the wall of the pit.

"I don't recall sayin' it was break time." Youslus giggled. "In fact, I distinctly remember saying that it was work time. Help that big feller over to Johnny—he can play nurse to your brother."

Teddy rose unsteadily and would've toppled back to the ground, but Derek steadied him. Groaning under the weight of his brother, Derek helped Teddy shuffle over to John, where the giant sprawled onto the ground.

Derek turned in time to see Youslus reach into a leather satchel at his side and remove six long, thin objects. "TNT," the old man declared. "Die-No-Might!"

"Holy shit," said Leggy.

Youslus winked at him. "That's right, Hauler. You know what this is." He pointed to the small hole that Teddy had bored into the bunker. "We'll just tamp these fuckers in there and crack that nut. Oh yeah, we'll crack 'er!" He giggled again, his lips flecked with spittle.

Leggy hauled himself over to Youslus and looked at the sticks. They were coated with a sticky white substance.

"You crazy bastard, these things are sweating nitro," cried Leggy. "They could blow any time."

"Guess we better treat 'em real gentle, then." Youslus winked and turned to Derek. "Take these and stuff 'em in that hole."

"How about I stuff 'em—" started Derek.

Leggy cut him off. "Just take 'em. Gently, Derek. Very gently." He followed Derek to the hole and guided him in positioning the TNT. With great care Derek placed the sticks into the hole.

"This is too much," Leggy whispered to Derek. "This is way too much TNT for this hole. I know cause I used this kinda stuff a couple times way back. If he sets this off, he's gonna blow the whole pit to Hell."

"Should we tell him?" asked Derek.

"We're just humoring him," Leggy whispered back. "This game's up. We gotta get out of here now, or we ain't never gonna get out."

Derek nodded. For once he agreed with the old hauler.

"Fuck it, then." Derek gripped one of the seeping sticks and hurled it with all of his might to the ground at Youslus's feet. There was no time to duck, or even to blink. But the stick bounced impotently off the stone floor and rolled past the stunned Youslus.

"Son of a bitch," muttered Derek.

"Boy, you're a bigger fool than I thought," said Youslus. "You try a stunt like that again, I'll give ya both barrels."

Behind them, Teddy regurgitated a good portion of the water he'd drunk. Mixed with blood and bile, it formed a dark puddle on the ground before it quickly evaporated. Leggy crab-walked himself over and helped Teddy with the canteen.

"Move Stone Biter and its generator away," ordered Youslus, toeing the unexploded TNT stick with a frown. "It'll come in handy if there's other bunkers around here."

Derek dragged the devilish machine away from the hole and over to where his friends were nursing Teddy. He had to pull with all his might. He couldn't believe his brother had single-handedly worked the massive thing. Teddy caught sight of the machine and cringed, squeezing his eyes shut to the thought that he might again be forced to wield it.

"Whee!" Youslus squeeled. "Okay boys, you stand back now. I'll do the honors."

He removed coils of fuses from his satchel and strode over to the jam-packed TNT. He put the shotgun on the ground and carefully twisted his fuses into the caps at the end of the sweaty sticks.

Derek looked up at Leggy. "Now?"

"Now or never," said Leggy.

Derek sprinted across the pit. With surprising speed Youslus whirled round, scooped up the gun, and clubbed Derek across the side of the head just as he closed the distance. Derek fell hard, clutching his bloodied jaw.

"Dumb, dumb, dumb," said Youslus. "Now you're gonna miss what's inside." He cocked a hammer and pointed the gun.

As he did, a dog barked above them. Its echo bounced back and forth between the walls of Youslus's excavation. Everyone looked up.

Magdalena stood at the edge of the pit, flanked by her two dogs. She held her rifle in her arms.

"Why Hello, Maggie," said Youslus. "Nice to see you again. Have you brought me some eggs? I do love Mother Morgan's eggs. I'm just about to take care of some business here, and then I'll greet you properly."

The woman pivoted toward the sound of the old hermit's voice and raised the rifle.

"Don't shoot," cried Leggy. "There's dynamite—"

The blast of the rifle echoed through the pit. The bullet exploded into the rock just behind Youslus's right shoulder. Everyone in the pit, Youslus included, flung themselves to the ground, hands over their heads, waiting for the blast that would blow them skyward.

It never came.

Youslus peeked out from behind his hands. "Hee! That was a close one."

As he pushed himself off the ground, a long dark shadow fell over him. A terrible mechanical shriek split the air.

"Bad man! Bad man!" shouted Teddy, towering over his cruel taskmaster and holding Stone Biter high above his head. The evil machine thrummed with life, vibrating and screaming bloody Hell on earth. Teddy brought it down—he brought it down hard.

Stone Biter writhed and convulsed and almost seemed to laugh as it burrowed into Youslus's belly and legs. Blood and gore spattered the walls of the pit. Youslus screamed.

Then Teddy turned the machine on its own motor. The hammer punched into its own heart as eagerly as it had Youslus's. The pounding turned into a scream, high and shrill. Shards of hot metal slashed the air as the thing devoured itself. In seconds its cacophonic shriek died to a whine. The hammer-blade slowly came to a stop. The generator was obliterated. Stone Biter was dead.

Teddy heaved its twisted remains across the pit, and then turned to his brother.

Derek recoiled, fearful of what he saw in Teddy's eyes—unbridled fury, incomprehensible anger. It was his brother's face, but the eyes that looked down on him were his father's, the man's only legacy, bequeathed to both brothers. Derek knew that anger well, he'd felt it himself, even basked in it. But he'd seen it on Teddy's face only once before—the night that Teddy had murdered the man who'd passed on that birthright of all-consuming anger.

He's going to kill me next, thought Derek.

"He's gone, Teddy," cried Derek. "He's gone and can't hurt you anymore. It's just us now, Teddy. Just us."

Teddy flinched, as though he'd been slapped. The terrible anger drained from his face. He peered down at his brother quizzically, and then looked all around him.

"He can't hurt you anymore," said Derek.

All was silent but for the ringing in their ears.

Derek staggered to his feet and retrieved his shotgun.

Leggy stared up, open-mouthed in awe, at Magdalena, who still had her hands pressed over her ears.

John pulled frantically at the chain around his ankle. "Undo me, dammit," he shouted. "Undo me!"

Leggy blinked. This was first time he'd ever heard John swear.

"John," shouted Magdalena from the top of the pit. "Are you okay?"

"The keys." John strained to pull the length of chain from its anchor in the stone. "Where're the keys?"

"Shit," said Leggy. "Youslus had 'em." He turned to look at the remains of the old man. "It's gonna be a bitch tryin' to fish 'em out."

Miraculously, the old digger was still alive. Everything below his waist was decimated. Both legs were missing, blood and flesh and bone painted the ground all around him. His face was a mask of madness. Propped against the wall of his cherished bunker number two, one hand was absently trying to shove entrails back into his torn bowels. The other hand reached into a pocket sewn into his robe and retrieved a thin wooden match. The mad hermit struck it against the rocky floor of the pit.

"No, oh no," whispered Leggy.

The others turned to see.

Youslus stared at the flame for a moment, and then touched the match to the fuse. The line hissed to life, and a maniacal spark raced down the wire.

"Crack…that…fucker," Youslus said with a grin, his mouth full of blood.

"Run," screamed Derek. He raced for the rope ladder, but his brother grabbed him by the shirt.

"Teddy what—?" shouted Derek, and then he was in the air, the world twirling underneath him. Teddy had flung Derek out of the pit. He crashed on hard stone and looked up to see Leggy in the air, the man's arms and stumps flailing. Before the old man landed, Derek was on his feet. He raced to the edge of pit. The fuse was more than halfway gone.

Down below, Teddy was straining to pull John's chain from its anchor.

"John," shouted Magdalena, her rifle at the ready, "tap the chain."

"What?" screamed John, his eyes wide with panic and confusion.

"Tap the chain!"

John grabbed a rock and hit the chain as if he were trying to strike sparks. "Again," shouted Magdalena.

The ringing echoed around the pit until it was silenced by a sharp crack from Magdalena's rifle—and he was free! John and Teddy tumbled backward, the chain broken about halfway down its length by the blind woman's bullet.

The spark had nearly run its course. The flame was inches from the sweating sticks of dynamite. Teddy braced himself and flung John out of the pit.

John landed on his belly, the length of his chain dangling over the edge. Derek grabbed John's arms and pulled him up over the lip of the pit. Teddy's oversized hands appeared next, his weak and trembling fingers grasping for purchase. Derek let go of John and seized one of his brother's hands. He pulled as hard as he could until Teddy came up out of the pit and tumbled down on top of him.

"The cave," screamed Leggy.

With superhuman effort, Teddy untangled himself from his brother, snatched up the legless hauler under one arm and Derek under the other. John grabbed Magdalena's hand. They raced for Youslus's shelter.

They were nearly to the cave when the TNT went off.

A massive fist of hot air punched them from behind. Teddy was thrown forward, spilling his human bundles. Derek sprawled onto his face inside the cave, head ringing. He felt the stone floor tremble and wondered if the whole side of the mountain would come down on them. A fiery wind roared inside the cave, scorching their ears and coating them with dust.

The roar of wind was replaced with a pattering sound like rain as bits of stone, concrete and steel fell to earth. The patter was punctuated by crashes as larger chunks tumbled from the sky.

When the inferno had begun to subside, Derek and Leggy left the cave to see what damage Youslus's dynamite had wrought. The ground everywhere was coated with grit, which crunched beneath Derek's boots and dimpled Leggy's palms as he pushed himself along on his hands. They had to detour around several car-sized hunks of smoldering concrete skeined with rebar.

As they approached the edge of the pit, Derek felt a rising excitement. They were alive, Youslus was dead, and the old man's treasure trove was blown wide open. Whatever might be inside—food, weapons, strange artifacts of power—was theirs.

They stopped at the lip of the pit. Smoke and dust still swirled around the blast site, but they could see that Youslus's dynamite had done more than its intended job. A huge hole had been blown out of the face of the bunker, big enough for three to walk abreast straight through.

Derek began to smile, but then faltered. He scrambled down the rope ladder into the pit. He pulled his shirt up over his mouth to block the dust and smoke, and shimmied through the jagged mouth of the blast hole. He stepped inside and walked five or six feet, reaching out a hand.

Three yards in, a large steel door blocked any further passage. It was smoothly fitted into a steel frame. The frame itself was set into the granite of the mountain. The door had no handles, and Derek could find no hinges, nor any gaps of any sort that might show how the door opened. The way was barred to them.

Its metal face was scarred and pocked from the blast, but otherwise unaffected.

He put his palm to it. The steel was cool. Derek thought he felt a slight vibration, a tiny ripple of force from powerful engines churning somewhere deep within the bunker. He rapped it with his knuckles, but the steel was so thick he could tell nothing about what might lay on the other side.

He stepped outside and climbed back up the ladder. Derek sat down at the edge of the pit, his legs dangling over the side. Suddenly he felt more tired than he ever had in his life. So tired, that he thought he might never move from this spot.

"Well?" asked Leggy.

Derek sighed, summoning the energy to speak. "There's another door," he said. "Made of steel."

"Closed?" asked Leggy.

Derek nodded and spat into the pit.

"Fuck me," said Leggy.

"Yup," said Derek. He cupped his hands behind his head and lay back on the ground. The stone was warm against his back, and the sky above was cloudless. For a long time he stared into blue oblivion.

CHAPTER TWENTY

John sat up in the cave and found himself eye to eye with a sleek German Shepherd, Sheba. She licked his face. The dog wore a harness, and holding that harness was Magdalena. Her blind eyes were aimed straight at John.

"You came," he said.

"Yes."

"How did you find us?" he asked. "And why did you come?"

Magdalena's cheeks reddened. "My dogs knew the way. We've been here before."

"Huh?" said John, rising to his feet and brushing dust from himself. "What do you mean?"

"Mother Morgan sent you this way on purpose," said Magdalena. "She sent you into his hands."

"She knew about this guy?" exclaimed John. "She knew he'd put us to work?"

"We both did."

"But Magdalena, why would you do such a terrible thing?"

"Mother Morgan and the old man, they've known each other for years," she said. "They had an arrangement. If she sent him travelers, he would bring her things he'd uncovered from his dig. Tins of food and such."

"Is that why you came then?" John asked. "To collect your reward?"

"No," she said, tears welling in her blind eyes. "I…I wanted to help you. I came to free you, if I could."

"Free us?" shouted John. "We were trapped here for weeks!"

Sheba growled and bristled her teeth at John. Magdalena pushed the dog's snout aside. "Please," she said, reaching a hand out to John.

He batted it aside.

"Please. I was a prisoner myself."

"What do you mean?" asked John.

"Mother Morgan. She knew I wanted to go after you. She could see it in me. She trapped me in the house."

"Then why did you come now? Did she think we'd be dead?"

"No. I escaped," she whispered. "I ran away."

"How?"

Magdalena put her hands over her face. "I killed her."

John felt his knees buckle. He steadied himself against the cool wall of the cave and crossed himself. For a moment he thought about running, running without stopping and never looking back.

"You don't understand," said Magdalena. "You don't understand what she did to me. I was scared, John. Terrified. There were four of you, and you were armed. I was scared that maybe you hadn't been captured."

"What?" cried John. "You *wanted* him to catch us? He worked Teddy nearly to death. He would've done the same to us if—"

"Listen," said Magdalena. "I was scared that I'd come here and find you already long gone. But I came anyway. Because I had to know."

"I don't understand," said John.

"If you were his captives, I would've tried to help you escape," she said. "And if you were gone, I would've killed the old man and followed you."

John's head reeled. Who was this girl that he'd thought he'd fallen in love with? She was as cold and vengeful and as full of killing as Derek.

"Why?" he asked.

She wouldn't answer.

"Please," said John. "I have to understand. I can see that he was a bad man, a crazy man, but why kill him? Especially if he weren't keeping us captive?"

Hot tears of shame flowed from her eyes.

"Magdalena," said John.

"She sold my body to him," said Magdalena. "The old woman sold my body to him. The first time was when I got my bleeding. That was six years ago. But that wasn't the only time. She used me, used me as trade."

John sat down on the dusty stone floor of the cave. Ever since leaving San Muyamo, he'd felt as if he'd been descending into Hell. Every turn on this journey uncovered some new horror, some new human cruelty. Back home the Judges said God had abandoned the world, and now John understood why. Because all its people were wicked.

"I came for you," said Magdalena. "But maybe I shouldn't have. Now that you know what I am."

John could hear the pain in her voice. Part of him wanted to hurt her more, to drive his shock and disgust into her like a stake. A voice spoke to him, the voice of Elder Hale. The voice was full of righteous condemnation.

This woman was a fornicator, a liar, a killer. Perhaps even possessed by demons.

134

If John valued his soul, if he loved Jesus Manchrist, he would turn his face away from her. Avert his eyes.

But he didn't turn away.

He looked. John saw her misery and sorrow and felt the anger wash out of him. He went to her and put his arms around her. She put her face in the hollow of his neck, and he felt her tears against his dry skin.

"It's okay," he whispered to her, stroking her hair. "It's okay. We're safe now. You found me. And I'm glad."

CHAPTER TWENTY-ONE

The group, their number now increased by one woman and two dogs, spent three days recuperating in Youslus's cave. They slept sixteen to eighteen hours at a stretch. They ate their fill from Youslus's tins and drank from the spring-fed pool.

On the morning of the fourth day, Leggy drew John and Derek away from the cave. They hunkered down near a large boulder.

"We should be moving on," said Leggy.

Derek and John nodded.

"That means it's time to send the young lady home," said Leggy.

"What? No, she's going to to come with us," said John.

Leggy glanced at Derek, but Derek was toying with his boot. No one spoke.

Finally, Leggy cleared his throat. "I don't think so, Johnny Boy. She's just gonna slow us down."

"She won't," said John. "In fact, I expect she can get along quite a bit better than you, Leggy. No offense, but she's a lot more able-bodied. With those guide dogs of hers, she'll be all right. She tracked us this far, didn't she? She saved us from the pit."

"Well, that may be true," said Leggy, "but I still don't think it's right. We're on the verge of some hard travelin'. Very hard. You fellas are gonna think our whole trek up to now was just a picnic compared to what's waiting for us. I think that girl'd be better off goin' home. The Wasteland's no place for a girl, a blind one, at that."

Leggy also had another concern—Derek had bedded this girl. That fact hadn't been shared with all parties yet, but Leggy would bet a hundred food tins against a lump of shit that it wouldn't stay secret. And when it came out, Leggy could only see two outcomes: the end of their fellowship or blood. Likely both.

"She's got no home," said John. He explained her predicament to them. "If she doesn't come with us, we'll just be leaving her alone."

"Shit," said Leggy. "I still don't like it. What do you say, Derek?" Leggy knew Derek was a master at bending John to his will.

136

But Derek simply shrugged his shoulders. "Why not? We already got a cripple and a mutie donkey. Might as well have a blind girl too. Maybe we can pick up a deaf-mute along the way and we'll have a complete set."

Leggy raised his eyebrows in surprise but didn't press the debate.

"So if we're all settled up, I suggest we get the fuck out of here," said Derek.

"Just one more thing I have to do," said John.

While the others gathered together as many food tins as could be carried, John and Teddy walked over to the moths chained to the base of the wall. They'd found a hammer and chisel among Youslus's tools, and they walked purposefully toward the creatures.

At their approach the insects stirred from their sleep and rose as far as the cords would allow, chittering and clucking down at the men. John gripped an arm's length of rope and held it on the ground with his foot. The moth attached to it shrieked in alarm and strained to pull away. The others began to swoop upon the two men, battering them with powdery canvas-like wings.

"Quick now," shouted John, but Teddy needed no urging. He pinned a moth to the ground and with three quick blows split the link at the base of the creature's abdomen. The creature shot skyward, free of its bond.

John wasn't sure how smart these things were, but their cries suddenly sounded excited rather than fearful, and the remaining two stopped swooping. They slowly settled to the ground at Teddy's feet. A half dozen more blows were enough to set them free.

John and Teddy watched as the creatures spiraled upward on a draft of air and over the canyon wall. Soon they were gone from sight.

"Fly up to Heaven now," whispered John. "Fly up to Heaven and pray for us."

Finally, the group was assembled. Leggy, saddled up on Afha, looked at his companions. "We must be the most unlikely band of travelers to ever dare the Wasteland," he said. "We're going to need all our strength and all our resources. We've already been in some pretty tough scrapes, and come out the other side. But the Wasteland's a whole other ballgame. Now let's shake the dust of this place from our shoes and get our asses goin'."

"Amen to that," said John.

And they were on their way.

CHAPTER TWENTY-TWO

Several hours after the travelers had left Youslus's valley, a humming noise came from deep within the bunker that had so obsessed the old hermit. Beneath the humming came another noise, a two-note alarm that repeated itself for perhaps thirty seconds. Then the alarm cut out and the great steel door inside the bunker split down the middle and began to swing open. Air—cool, climate-controlled and scrubbed of particulates—hissed through the widening seam. The wings of the door swung out flush against the bunker walls, revealing a shadowy tunnel. The humming noise died away.

A boy appeared in the opening. He was slender and delicate, as if his bones were made of straw. He was dressed in a sky-blue singlet with long pants and sleeves and wore sandals on his six-toed feet. He was bald. His skull was slightly ovoid and perhaps a touch too large to be in proportion to his narrow body.

The boy blinked in the bright sun and climbed carefully out of the pit. When he reached the top, he noted Youslus's cave and the stony lane that led down into the desert.

The boy stood for a moment then reached out with his mind, searching. He found the cave empty and the surrounding valley desolate. Then, extending his search, he ran his mind along the lane and caught up with the travelers. Curious, the boy probed gently, and discovered four men, one woman, and four beasts. One of the animals stirred in its mind, aware of the mental probe, and snorted inquisitively. The boy withdrew and let his consciousness hover above the travelers.

The boy monitored their progress for several minutes, gauging the roiling flow of their thoughts and emotions.

Then the boy turned his mind upward, focusing on a narrow band high above the common channels of perception. His consciousness rose like a hawk on a thermal column, sensing, testing, seeking a signal. Background noise had overwhelmed the meta-psychic band after the missiles had fallen so many years ago. Now, finally, the noise had subsided somewhat—but enough to let communications pass? It had been so long since he had reached out to the others. Had any of them survived?

The boy strained for a contact, temples throbbing, breath coming in short gasps. He had been asleep for so long his ability was rusty. With redoubled effort he concentrated, ignoring a sharp spike of pain that stabbed across his forehead. Suddenly he felt a blip, the touch of a mind, like fingertips brushing against another hand in a dense fog. And then it was gone. His mind tumbled from its high place, and a whirling vertigo dropped him to his knees.

The boy cried out, a small, despairing sound. He was alone. He had awoken to find Karen, his "mother," dead—her stasis chamber had failed some time ago. None of the scientists, techs or solider men in the bunker had made it through the long sleep. And the others like him, secreted in bunkers and compounds around the world, were out of reach and likely dead, too. He was alone. He put his strange head to the stony ground and cried.

After a few minutes of tears, the boy stood and wiped his face. Crying wouldn't help him. He'd have to help himself. He shaded his eyes and looked up at the blue sky and the unfamiliar, unyielding sun above. He ran a hand over the smooth, pale skin of his skull and felt the heat gathering there. He knew that if he stood in front of his dressing mirror he would see a red bloom beginning on his head and his cheeks.

He went back inside, emerging a few minutes later with a makeshift turban fashioned from a section of white sheet. He also had a knapsack stuffed with supplies and a gurgling canteen. The strange boy took a last long look at the bunker then started down the lane and into the desert.

The valley where Youslus had imprisoned them sloped gently down toward the desert. The Sierra Nevadas were behind them now, and Leggy pointed them toward the rising sun, due east.

They traveled for two days, and each day brought more changes. The air grew hotter, the landscape drier and more desolate. Foothills gave way to a brown plain that stretched out before them, flat and unvarying for miles and miles.

"Is this it?" asked John. "Is this the Wasteland?"

"This is the hem of it," said Leggy. "We've still got a few hundred miles before we reach the Wasteland proper."

"Do you know where you're going?" asked Magdalena.

"I'm trying to get my bearings," said Leggy. "If we're where I think we are, we should be runnin' into a small lake soon. From there we can strike for an old roadway that I've traveled before."

"Who made it? Bedouins?" asked Derek.

"It was from the Before Times," said Leggy. *"Afore-the-War.* Bedouins travel it occasionally, but there ain't many settlements out this way, so there's no reason for Bedouin traders to come through here."

"What *is* out here?" asked John.

Leggy grinned. "Bugs. Loners. Muties. And Lord knows what else."

That comment ended the question-and-answer session, and the travelers moved on in silence.

By mid-morning of their third day out from Youslus's pit, they struck the shallow, polluted lake Leggy was seeking. Thin, gray wisps of chemical haze floated languidly above the still, stagnant water.

"From here we follow the lake north and then east again. That should get us to the road, and the road will take us right through the heart of a place called Death Valley." He smiled at John. "And that's where the Wasteland proper begins. Sounds good, huh?"

John said nothing. As they followed the banks of the dead lake north, Magdalena asked if the water had a name.

"I don't know what it used to be called in the Before Times," said Leggy. "When I was working as a hauler for Rasham, we just called it Blue Lake. But maybe we should give it a proper title, like Lake Nicodemus."

"How about Lake Crippled Old Drunk?" suggested Derek.

Leggy threw back his head and laughed. "Tell you what, son. You ever run into a map maker, you have my blessing to call it that."

Eventually they struck Leggy's road, an old two-lane highway. A sign stuck into the side of the road told them it was once called Route 190, but that meant nothing to them. Ghosts of heat shimmered up from the aging blacktop, which was cracked and broken in many places. But the way was clearly marked, and ran on ahead of them to the horizon.

The highway bent southward, but Leggy assured them that soon it would turn east again.

As they traveled, Magdalena began to show signs of strain. The heat seemed nearly suffocating to her, and she felt the sun as a merciless presence, beating on her with fiery fists. Flakes of sand and bits of dust, kicked up by hot winds, scratched at her face. John showed her how to fasten a kerchief across her nose and mouth, and wrap her head against the sun, but while this helped with the dust and grit it only increased her feeling of being smothered.

The dogs, Cole and Sheba, were also suffering. Their smooth coats, so suited to a cool mountain climate, were a liability down on the arid plain. The rough, old roadbed was hot under foot and abraded the pads on their paws. At night when they camped, the dogs would lick sorrowfully at their sore feet.

John tried his best to encourage Magdalena. "You'll get used to it," he said. "Really, it's not so bad once your body adjusts."

Magdalena nodded. Despite her suffering she did not complain.

Their fourth day on the blasted highway they spotted a structure. It was near dusk, and daylight was fading when Derek glimpsed the low building. They approached carefully, but the place seemed deserted. A sign had been set into the side of the road next to the building.

WILLY'S GAS 'N GO

"'Water. Pop. Snacks. Maps. Film. Clean restrooms,'" read Derek. "Must be some old way station, right?"

"Yup," said Leggy. "There's the gas pumps. No more gas, though. I know because we used to hole up here on runs."

Three pumps stood on a concrete island—the nozzles of their hoses tucked neatly into their sides, like a trio of saluting dwarves. Next to the pumps stood a one-story clapboard store designed in a faux Old West style, complete with a porch that ran the length of the store, a hitching post, and a wagon wheel nailed to the façade.

"Looks like it's in pretty good shape," said Derek, tilting his head toward the store. "Might be suitable for the night."

"Yup," said Leggy.

"Maybe there's snacks, Der-Der," said Teddy excitedly.

"Sorry, Teddy," said Leggy. "The place has been cleaned out of food and drink for ages."

"Can we lookie-see?" asked Teddy.

"Might as well," said Leggy. "But let's do it real cautious. Me and Ted and Derek'll scout it out. You two keep an eye on things out here," he said to John. Then he turned to Magdalena. "Ma'am, can we take one of your dogs inside?"

"Of course," said Magdalena. "Take Cole."

Derek whistled. "C'mere Cole. Let's check this place out."

The shepherd trotted to Derek's side, tail wagging. Despite having threatened to blow the dogs' heads off on their first encounter, Derek found he liked the animals, and their relationship had improved tremendously on the journey. In the evenings, Derek would tend to their sore paws and stroke and scratch them with affection. For their part, the dogs had quickly learned that Derek was a soft touch when it came to sharing food, which raised his standing with them considerably.

Leggy scrambled off Ahfa's back and onto Ted's, and the three men and the dog stepped cautiously inside the building. Derek took point, his shotgun at the ready.

John tied Ahfa and Minna to the hitching post and stood next to Magdalena. She took his hand and smiled. He squeezed her hand in return. Then he cast his eyes up and down the road but saw nothing. Magdalena's head was cocked to one side, which meant she was listening intently.

They waited in silence.

Five minutes later Derek appeared at the door. "All clear. C'mon in," he said.

John led Magdalena inside. The store was one large room with a wooden floor and ceiling. Bits of paper and trash were scattered everywhere, and dusty old cobwebs had gathered in corners of the sagging ceiling. Empty shelves had long been knocked over and broken. Along the far wall stood a row of tall glass cases, also long empty.

A counter stood at the other end of the room. A large banner, dusty and fading, hung on the wall behind it. The words CALIFORNIA LOTTO were barely visible.

Leggy appeared from behind the counter, scooting along on his hands. "Pretty good mess, huh? But it'll do for a night's shelter."

"You shoulda seen all the scag-rats that went running when we came in," said Derek. "Ol' Cole there almost caught himself a couple." The dog was rooting in a corner, scratching at a baseboard and sniffing. Sheba strained in her harness, eager to join her fellow in the search. Magdalena released her and she raced over to Cole, yipping with excitement.

"Where's Teddy?" asked John. "I'd like some help unloading Minna."

"We found a cellar," said Derek. "He's still hopin' to dig up some snacks."

"Where is it?" asked John.

Derek jerked a thumb behind the counter. John went around and found a small corridor. There was a pair of bathrooms, a utility closet full of old cleaning supplies, and a small door with a staircase leading down. John stuck his head in the door.

The basement was full of shadow—the only light coming from a couple of small, dust-covered windows. John went carefully down the stairs. He could hear Teddy rooting around below him. At the bottom of the staircase he stopped to fill his lungs to call for Teddy when he heard a scream.

"Aaahhhhhhhhh!"

It was Teddy. He wrestled with something man-sized. Suddenly Teddy was hurtling through the air. He crashed heavily against the wall.

"Muties," shouted John.

The creature spun around. John had time to see its face—sallow skin wrapped around a misshapen skull, one eye gone, the other yellowed and alive with menace. Then it raced at John with unbelievable speed. John fled but only made it up a few stairs before a hand locked around his ankle and pulled him back down.

Derek raced down the stairs. The creature looked up as Derek shoved the shotgun barrel in its face.

"Eat this, you fucker," screamed Derek. He pulled the trigger, but instead of a vengeful blast there was merely an impotent click. The firing mechanism had failed.

"Huh huh huh! Huh huh huh!" It was the mutant, guffawing.

Then Derek felt knobby fists on his chest and upper thigh, and suddenly he was flying through the dank air. He hit the wall hard and slumped down next to his brother. The mutant scuttled toward them then stopped in the middle of the room, unsure which of its victims to dispatch first—Derek and Teddy at the wall, or John by the staircase.

Derek, dazed and in pain, looked up to see dark bodies leaping onto the creature—Cole and Sheba. The dogs knocked the mutant to the ground and began seeking its throat. The mutant gurgled with pain as the dogs tore open its right cheek and bit off an ear. It lashed out, cuffing the dogs aside with brutal blows. Then it leapt to its feet.

"Hey freak," came Leggy's voice from the stairs.

The mutant caught a thrown knife in its one good eye. It screamed with rage and hurt.

Leggy watched in horror as the mutant raised one hand and pulled the blade from its skull. Now blind, it walked jerkily toward the staircase, holding the knife and slashing at the air.

Then the basement exploded with thunder and light, and the creature was halted by a rifle bullet punching through its abdomen. It howled and then continued its advance.

Magdalena chambered another round and lifted the rifle again. The second round obliterated a lung and flung the mutant backward against the ground, but, in an instant, it sprang up again, raced for them, and howled with demonic ferocity. The mutant was just three steps from the staircase when Magdalena's final shot exploded its head. The creature flopped backward, convulsing on the floor. Its arms and legs furiously pounded the ground until finally it was still.

Leggy looked up at Magdalena in surprise.

"How did…? How can you…? You hit that thing three times."

Magdalena smiled grimly. "What I lack in sight, I make up for in hearing."

She scrunched her nose. "And smell." She moved the rifle toward Leggy and touched the barrel to his chest, exactly over his heart.

"If I concentrate, I can hear it beating," she said. "I can hear John at the bottom of the stairs, and the two brothers at the far wall. And my dogs…." Here she faltered and looked confused.

"Excuse me," she said, moving carefully past Leggy.

Leggy turned to follow her, then saw John, who was getting groggily to he feet at the bottom of the stairs.

"Okay?" asked Leggy.

John nodded.

Leggy snaked his way over to Derek and Teddy, both of whom were sitting up. "You fellas all right?" asked Leggy.

"Shit," said Derek. "I hope that fucker didn't crack m' ribs."

Leggy probed with experienced fingers. Derek gasped.

"I think you're okay," said Leggy. "But you're gonna feel it for a few days. How 'bout you, Ted?"

The giant rubbed his neck. "I'm okay. The bad thing tried to bite me."

At that moment John came over, wobbling slightly on his left ankle. "I thought you said this place was clear. Did you even bother to check down here?"

"Sure I checked," said Derek defensively. "It must'a been hiding."

"Hiding? You must be pretty goddamn stupid to let a mutie hide from you," shouted John. "Didn't you *smell* it?"

Derek's face flushed red with anger. He tried to rise to his feet but fell back again, clutching his ribs.

"Hey now," said Leggy sharply. "It was a mistake, that's all. We took our licks for it, and that means it won't happen again. Let's be thankful we can all walk away from it."

"Not all of us," said John, jerking a thumb toward Magdalena. She had felt her way over to the far corner of the basement, where her dogs were.

"Cole's dead," said John.

"What?" asked Derek.

"The mutie broke his neck," said John, hobbling away from them, going to comfort Magdalena.

They buried Cole that night. John and Teddy took turns digging a grave with a shovel they found in the utility closet. Then they wrapped the German shepherd in an old blanket and lowered him gently down into the desert.

"Goodbye Cole," said Magdalena, her ruined eyes wet with tears. "You were a good dog, faithful and true. You guided me well and protected me. I'll miss you." She sprinkled a handful of dirt over the grave, and then wept openly.

John stood, taciturn, one arm around Magdalena's waist. Leggy and Teddy waited in respectful silence. Then John led Magdalena away. Teddy bent to the shovel and began to fill the grave. Sheba howled mournfully as Teddy worked.

Derek watched it all from the shadow of the store, leaning up against the wall. He held his sore ribs and said nothing.

They spent the night inside the store, after barricading the entrance with old shelves and other junk. Without a fire to gather around, they set up their blankets and bedrolls apart from each other. Leggy didn't like it, but he didn't say anything. Besides, they'd had a hard day and needed rest, not chit-chat. Still, the death of the dog had driven a wedge into the group. Something should be said, but Leggy was too tired to deal with it. Not tonight. Let them sleep.

But Leggy himself found it difficult to get comfortable. He'd grown accustomed to sleeping outdoors, and he found it strange to be staring up at a cobwebbed ceiling rather than a magnificent sweep of stars. The old store felt stuffy, and the warped floor creaked and popped as the others turned in their sleep.

He thought about taking his own bedroll outside, but that would mean waking one of the boys to undo the barricade. So he settled himself in as best he could. A nip or two would help settle him, but that was moot—his flask was empty, and the last drink he'd had was some moonshine swill that Mother Morgan had dished out. Oh well.

Eventually he must've dozed off because he sat up with a start, his mind fuzzy and confused. He felt a sense of alarm, some instinct that had triggered him awake. He looked around the store. The others were asleep, breathing slow and easy. A patch of moonlight had crept inside the room from a high window above the counter. Leggy looked. There was a flash of movement. Had there been a pair of eyes at the window?

Fully alert now, Leggy swept the store with his gaze, listening closely. He thought for a moment it might be another mutie, but that was unlikely. Muties were solitary creatures, with a cannibalistic bent. They had no qualms about turning on one another when there was no other prey to be found. Besides, muties didn't sneak up on you. If one were outside, they would've heard it trying to smash through the barrier.

That left only outlaws. He looked to where John and Magdalena and Sheba lay in a far corner. The Shepherd was asleep. Surely she would've scented something. Wouldn't she?

Leggy watched the window, and then the barricaded door, but saw nothing. He watched and waited a full thirty minutes, but all seemed quiet. He thought about waking Teddy, getting him to clear the barricade so he could check the perimeter, but decided against it. It was probably nothing. He lay down again.

The next morning Leggy was first out the door once Teddy had heaved aside the shelves and junk that blocked them in. The old man's bladder was full and he was heading for the side of the building to take a piss when a sight brought him up short—sitting in front of the rusting gas pumps was a boy.

He was dressed in a faded blue singlet with a makeshift turban tied incorrectly over his head. The folds of linen threatened to fall down over his bulbous head. Leggy swallowed and made no expression as he noticed the boy had six toes on each foot.

The boy was sunburned, and his narrow face gaunt. He leaned against the gas pumps like he might fall asleep. As Leggy approached, the child stirred.

"Hello," said the boy. "My name is Samuel. Why did you bury the dog?"

"Bury the dog?" asked Leggy.

The boy studied Leggy carefully. As he did so, Leggy felt a strange warmth on his forehead, like sunlight concentrated through the lens of a magnifying glass into a hot point.

"Oh," said Samuel. "He was killed by a mutant. That's very sad. He seemed like a nice dog. I've always wanted to meet a dog. Do you think Sheba will play with me?"

The heat continued to penetrate Leggy's skull, and suddenly he felt as if his mind were being rummaged through. It was a nauseating feeling, and his stomach quivered. In his thoughts he shouted, *"Stop that. Leave me be. Get out!"*

The heat dissipated immediately.

Samuel said "I'm sorry, Mr. Nicodemus. Karen said I should never read people without their permission, but sometimes it's the easiest way to find things out."

Leggy rubbed his forehead with one hand. His stomach settled itself. He stared at the strange boy. "Samuel," was all he could think to say.

The boy made no reply.

"Do you...do you live out here?" Leggy asked.

"No. I lived back in the valley, down in the bunker." He smiled. "You called it bunker number two. Karen called it Bag End. Did you ever read *The Hobbit*?"

"Valley? Bunker? Jesus H. Christ, are you tellin' me you lived down in the ground? Inside that place old Youslus was tryin' to dig up?" asked Leggy.

"I don't know who Youslus is, but somebody sure was trying to get in. I could hear them knocking, at first. And then later, I could hear the drill. It wouldn't have worked though. They built the compound to survive a direct hit, even from bunker busters and nukes."

"Right," said Leggy, unsure how to respond.

"Did you know I was in stasis for eighty years? That's what the computer said. When I was little, I used to think they said they were going to put me in Stacy. Isn't that funny? You don't put someone in Stacy. You put them in stasis. That means they can go to sleep for a long time."

At that moment the door opened, and the rest of the travelers emerged onto the porch.

"Holy shit," said Derek. "Who's the kid?"

"Kid?" asked Magdalena in surprise.

Sheba barked.

Samuel's eyes went wide and a huge grin erupted on his face. "Hi dog," he said. "C'mere Sheba. C'mere!"

Sheba, tail wagging, leapt from the porch. Samuel dropped to one knee as the dog approached. She sniffed him eagerly and began to lick his face. Samuel shrieked with delight and buried his hands in the dog's fur.

After a long minute of licking, Samuel stood up again. "Sit," he said.

Sheba sat.

"Shake."

Sheba raised a paw, which Samuel took in his hand and shook.

"Good girl," he said, releasing the paw and patting Sheba on her head. Then he looked up at the people on the stairs.

"She's a great dog. Really great. Can I come with you to New York?"

CHAPTER TWENTY-THREE

They walked all morning but spoke very little. Derek led the way, while behind him Teddy led Minna and Afha, who carried Leggy. John and Magdalena brought up the rear, lagging behind and frequently turning to scan the highway behind them while Sheba panted and trotted alongside.

Because there had been no supplies worth looting at the GAS 'N GO, Derek had offered to skin and filet the mutie, just in case things got really bad. Leggy laughed at him.

"You gonna eat that shit?" The old man choked. "You just see how friggin' sick *that* don't make you! Haw haw, you sure are a newbie, ain't ya, Derek? First day in the Wasteland, eh son? Haw ha ha." Leggy held himself until his giggling abated, then he remarked, "You know what they say, 'Ya'eat one, ya'are one!'" Then he burst into a renewed fit of laughter.

"What's so goddamned funny?" demanded Derek.

Leggy snorted again. "Well, it's not exactly funny. It's just that we got our asses handed to us by a single low-grade, border-waste, run-of-the-mill, half-starved, half-assed mutie. That mute didn't got a *tenth* o' the muster of a full-blown Wasteland mutie. 'Bout time you boys got a taste of what we're heading into. And I'm talkin' to you too, John."

"That 'run-of-the-mill' mutie," said Magdalena, "killed my dog."

Leggy's smile froze and slumped into a frown. It was late afternoon and the heat seemed to be pouring down in sheets from the hot, radioactive sky.

"Well, gee Missy, I didn't mean it like that. He was a good dog and all, and I'm genuinely sorry for your loss. But, and I mean no disrespect, we got away lucky. I'm just saying that we're on a dangerous road. We've got to be prepared is what I'm saying. All of us."

The company walked on in silence—the cracked tarmac warm beneath their feet, unfolding seemingly without end before them. The mountains shrank behind them, and the flat desert stretched on endlessly ahead and to the sides. Puddles of heat shimmered in the distance.

At one point the highway came to a stop before a dry creek bed. It had once been bridged, but the bridge had tumbled to ruin. They were forced to climb down a ten foot embankment, hike through a tangle of gorse and sage, and scale the steep cement abutment back up onto the highway again. It was grueling work, especially for Minna and Afha, who would not have been able to make the climb without Teddy's help.

The travelers were thankful that, for the most part, the interstate seemed to have survived weather, wear, and the passage of time—not to mention nuclear weapons.

At the end of the day the sun dipped low onto the horizon, looking to Leggy like a fiery egg breaking on the radioactive frying pan of the world. He smiled grimly at the thought. He reckoned it would be a long time before he tasted eggs again.

He turned himself on Afha and looked back at the highway in the direction from which they'd come.

Derek noticed and called, "He still followin' us?"

"Yep."

"Aw Hell, I was hoping he would've turned back by now."

"'Nope," Leggy said.

John cleared his throat. "Seems a pity to leave him straggling like that."

"Pity?" said Derek. "If you really felt pity, you'd send him back to his bunker. Or put a bullet in his head. The Wasteland is no place for a kid."

John rebuked Derek with a look. Leggy sighed.

"He must be so thirsty," said Magdalena. "Such small legs for such hard walking."

"Fine. Fuck it, then," said Derek. "We'll stop here. He can catch up and we'll camp for the night."

Leggy sighed again and then cupped his hands to his mouth and hollered down the highway, "All right kid. You win. You can come with us. Now hurry up, cause we got some chores for you to do. If you wanna ride with the big boys, you're gonna earn your keep!"

Samuel staggered into their camp thirty minutes later. His singlet was sweat-stained and torn at one arm. "Hello," he said. "Does this mean you'll let me come with you?"

Derek said nothing. Leggy just rolled his eyes.

Samuel sat down next to Sheba and shrugged out of his pack. He drank deeply from a large water bottle and looked at the campfire. He thought for a moment and then said brightly "Does anyone have marshmallows?"

"What the Hell are you talking about?" Derek was already irritated by the strange child's presence.

"Or not," said Samuel. "I've never had a marshmallow before. I never ate outside before, either. The doctors didn't like me going outdoors."

"Hungry?" asked John, handing a tin to Samuel.

"What's a marsh mellow?" grunted Derek.

"Thank you," said Samuel. He gave the tin a disappointed look. "This is the same stuff we ate at Bag End." He frowned.

They sat around the fire in uncomfortable silence, watching the boy eat. Though they all had questions for Samuel—about the bunker and what he had been doing in there, about why he wanted to go with them—they also found him disconcerting.

No one knew quite what to say to the strange boy, and no one seemed willing to ask the first question. And so, they ate in silence until, after a while, the small newcomer began to hum softly to himself, and then to sing,

The Road goes ever on and on,
Down from the door where it began...
Now far ahead the Road has gone,
And I must follow, if I can...

Derek rolled his eyes. This couldn't possibly get more annoying.

Samuel had finished his meal. His lips and chin were stained with gravy, but he seemed not to notice. Nor did he notice the uncomfortable mixture of rapt curiosity and embarrassed tension with which the others regarded him. Only Teddy seemed truly comfortable around the boy and soon took out his flute to accompany the strange song.

The next morning they cleared camp and hit the road again. The day was overcast, with skeins of dark cloud obscuring the sun. Samuel walked happily alongside Teddy, his head bobbing from side to side, trying to take every detail of the blasted landscape into his wide eyes.

As the morning wore on, the air grew still and was charged with electricity. When they stopped for lunch, Leggy appraised the sky.

"Storm comin'," said Derek.

"Yup. And it looks like it's gonna be a rager. Too bad there ain't shit for shelter."

"What do we do?" asked John, looking worriedly around at the flat, featureless landscape.

"Get wet," said Leggy.

"Don't think I'd mind," said Magdalena. "It'd be the nearest thing I've had to a bath in too many days."

By two o'clock the sky had turned dark, and a harsh wind kicked up across the dirty, dry valley floor, throwing sand into the faces of the travelers. Sheba whined.

Samuel looked around nervously. "What's going to happen?" he asked, his voice tight and high.

"Just a storm," said John. "A little rain, maybe some thunder an' lightning. Ain't you ever been in a storm before?"

"No," said Samuel. "They only ever took me outside twice and never in the rain." He reached up and took Teddy's hand.

"Well, here's your chance," said Leggy. He pointed to a bank of thunderheads rapidly approaching from the west, dark and swollen. The wind grew stronger, tugging at his hair and beard. "Help me off this donkey, Ted. He's getting skittish, and I don't want to get thrown."

Teddy, who looked as frightened as Samuel, helped Leggy off the donkey. Derek scanned the desert and highway all around them. Not even an old car to hunker in.

A thunderclap suddenly exploded behind them. Teddy shrieked.

"Easy there, Ted," said Leggy. "You just hold onto these reins. Don't let our mules go runnin' off."

Teddy nodded. He tightened his grip on the leather straps, his lower lip trembling.

There was another clap of thunder, closer than the first, and a fork of lighting stabbed down out of the sky. White light popped in their eyeballs and illuminated the grim landscape. The dark clouds raced toward them. Now they could hear the hiss of rain. A shrill wind whipped over them.

"Here it comes," shouted Leggy, and then it was on them.

Sheets of rain hammered the travelers, soaking them instantly. Thunder exploded over their heads. Samuel cringed against Magdalena's leg. His cries of fear drowned in the drumline of falling water.

Another thunderclap and another stab of lighting, so near that they could smell ozone. The mules' eyes were wide with fear. They strained against their reins, ready to bolt. Teddy held them fast, his own fear adding to his strength.

The rain fell as a solid curtain now, obscuring their vision. John groped blindly for Magdalena's hand and clung to her as if she might get swept away by the torrent of water.

Then, as suddenly as it had begun, it was over. The clouds raced ahead, sweeping aside the veil of rain. The sun emerged, making them squint. The blacktop beneath their feet steamed, and they sputtered and gasped in the aftermath of torrential downpour.

"Shit," said Derek, "I thought I was gonna drown standing up."

Leggy laughed. "You look like you *did* drown. Hell, we all do."

Indeed, they were bedraggled with water, dripping where they stood. John pulled off his shirt and twisted it up, and everyone cackled at the amount of water he wrung from it. Sheba shook herself vigorously, dousing the group in a fine spray of dog water and making Samuel giggle. Only the mules didn't look amused. Their ears were back and they stamped impatiently at the road.

Leggy screwed the lids onto several plastic jugs that he had fitted with funnels. "While the rest a' you's were gawkin' and trembling, old Leggy took the opportunity to replenish our water supply. In the desert, you never waste a chance to collect rainwater. That's lesson...well, let's start fresh and call it lesson one." The old man winked good-naturedly.

"Well, now what?" asked Derek. "Should we make camp and dry off or keep goin'?"

"I say we keep goin'," said Leggy. "Take a look around. Ain't a dry place to sit, and there won't be for awhile. Me, I'd rather dry off walkin' than sit in a puddle."

The valley floor was a muddy mess, and water had collected in shallow pools all along the blasted highway. So they pressed on, wringing out their clothes and hair as they walked.

They soon came to another gully. The bridge across was still intact. Lucky for them because the gully was alive with floodwater, dirty rapids that raced through the bed, too high and swift to be forded.

As they reached the other side of the bridge, Afha suddenly pulled to a halt. Teddy yanked at the reins, but the animal wouldn't budge.

"Now what?" asked Derek.

"He don't wanna go, Der-Der," said Teddy.

"Give him a nudge there, Leggy," said Derek.

Leggy prodded the beast with his stumps, but without effect.

"Aw, what the Hell," said Derek. He grabbed the reins from Teddy and gave them a shake. "Listen, you stupid fleabag, if you don't get a move on you're gonna end up dog food."

Afha brayed once, the milky cataract in his third eye swirling, but he would not be moved.

"He's scared," said Samuel, who was holding Teddy's hand.

"Scared? Of what?"

"Bugs," said Samuel.

"Course he's scared of bugs," Derek said. "Everybody's scared a bugs. What's that got to do with anything?"

"He says there's a nest up ahead," said Samuel. "It sounds awful."

"He says?" asked Derek. He reached down and grabbed Samuel's chin, forcing the boy to look into his eyes. "I'm in no mood for kiddy games."

Samuel winced, his face pale with fear. "I'm not playing a game. I can see his thoughts."

"You what?" asked Derek, squeezing harder.

"I can see his thoughts. Please stop, that hurts."

"Let him go, Derek," said John.

Derek released Samuel's chin, but continued to hold his gaze. "Mules don't think."

"Yes, they do. Not like you and me. But they do have thoughts. Especially Afha."

"And you can hear them? Boy, you're a dirty little liar. I ought to chuck you off this bridge."

"Wait," said Leggy. "Maybe there's something to this. Remember back up in the Sierras, just before we came across Magdalena? Afha pulled up short just like he is now. Wouldn't budge. And then John got bit by a snake."

"Holy Christ," said Derek. "You really think this donkey and this kid are some kinda...mind readers? Tell ya what, everybody stand back. Samuel and Afha are gonna lead the way. Onward to New York, fellas."

Leggy shrugged. He hadn't told them everything about his first encounter with Samuel because he still wasn't sure he believed it himself, but certainly there was something going on with this boy.

"Afha *is* a mutie," said John. "Maybe that's got somethin' to do with it."

"Yes," said Magdalena. "All animals have heightened senses. Like hawks that can spy a mouse in the grass from a great height. Or my sheep, who will smell a bear a mile away. Maybe this donkey has a sense for danger."

"There's one way to find out," said Leggy.

John turned pale. "You mean walk into the nest, if it's there?"

"Hell no, John. Don't be stupid. Derek, you still got that spyglass from the Bedouins?"

Derek rummaged through his sack and produced the telescope. He extended it to its full length and put it to his eye. He slowly swept the horizon.

"Ain't nothing...ain't nothin' for miles and m...wait a minute. Ah, shit."

He gave the spyglass to Leggy. Leggy peered through the eyepiece, aiming the glass in the direction Derek pointed. At first he saw nothing, but then detected movement in the distance. Black shapes scurried on the ground.

"There's somethin' there, all right. And right in our path," Leggy said.

"But if it's bugs, why would they be stirrin', unless they caught somethin'?" asked John.

Leggy returned the spyglass. "I bet the rain drove 'em out. Maybe the nest got flooded."

"Fuck," said Derek, taking another look. "They're right in our road." He closed the spyglass and put it back into his pack. "So now what?"

Leggy shrugged. "I guess we go around."

They stepped off the road and began trudging southward through the mud. It sucked at their boots and splashed up onto their legs.

Magdalena shook her head ruefully. "So much for being clean."

"I'd rather be dirty than eaten," said Derek.

They tramped south, using Afha as a sort of rough compass to define the perimeter of the nest. Every so often they tried to steer him back east, but each time he resisted. Finally, after several miles Afha allowed himself to be turned.

Though they could still see shallow pools glinting in the afternoon light, the desert valley was greedily absorbing the rainfall. The mud transformed into a dirty yellow paste and the ground grew firmer beneath their feet.

As they walked, Derek turned his attention to Samuel. "Now what's all this bullshit about mind reading?"

"It's true," said Samuel. "It's just something I've always been able to do. Karen says I was born that way."

"So you can look inside my head?" asked Derek.

"Yes, if I wanted to." Samuel turned his eyes down to the ground.

"Okay, what number am I—"

"Seven," said Samuel.

"Lucky guess. Now what number?"

Two thousand four hundred and eleven."

"Fuck me," said Derek. "He's right."

"Can you do that with everybody? All of us here?" asked Leggy.

"Yes," said Samuel.

"Now do me," shouted Teddy. "What's Teddy thinking?" He squeezed his eyes shut and furrowed his brow.

Samuel smiled. "You're thinking about peanut butter. Your dad bought some off a trader from the coast, a long time ago. That was the first and last time you ever tasted it."

"Mmmm," said Teddy with a smile, his eyes still closed. "Peanut buttteeeeeerrr."

"I don't like it," said Derek. "What's in my head is mine. Private. Travelin' with you is like travelin' with a thief. I'll never know when you're rifflin' through my gear."

"That's not true," said Samuel. "It's easy to read thoughts if you project them to me, like you did with the numbers. The doctors said it was like someone throwing me a ball—I can just catch the thought. Then there's the other way. I can go into your mind, like going into a house. And you'd feel that."

"What…what's it feel like?" asked Leggy.

Samuel peered up at him. Leggy felt a hot point on the inside of his skull, and a strange dizzying sensation, as if he'd been swept up by a wind high into the air and then dropped. He wobbled a bit, and then the heat and the vertigo vanished. Suddenly his stomach took a flip—he turned and vomited on the side of the road.

"He's right," said Leggy, gasping and wiping his mouth. "It's awful."

They trudged for a time in silence, before Derek finally spoke. "I still don't like it. This is mutie behavior. It makes me nervous."

"I don't see that we've got much choice," said Leggy.

"Sure we do," said Derek. "We can send him packing."

"What, out here?" asked John.

"That'd be murder," said Magdalena.

"Maybe not," said Derek. "He's a resourceful little shit. He can read minds." To Samuel, he said, "You could make it back to your bunker, I'll wager."

Samuel looked scared. "Please," he said, his voice tight with fear. "Don't leave me. I promise I'll be good. I promise I'll never go into your minds. Please."

Derek looked around at the others. He sucked his teeth and then spit into the dirt. "You just stay away from me, kid. Stay out of my way. Stay out of my head. And if I catch you playin' any mutie tricks…." He fingered his knife.

Samuel, clearly terrified, nodded his agreement and tried his best to disappear behind Teddy's enormous calf.

They moved on, continuing to use Afha to gauge the perimeter of the bugs' domain. The group was back on the blacktop by nightfall. They walked until the moon was riding high in the clear night and then made camp. There was little talk, and, after eating, they rolled into their blankets and closed their eyes.

Samuel, who had curled up with Sheba, gazed at the stars. He hadn't told them about the *third* way of reading thoughts—how easy it was to probe deeply into a mind when the person slept, how they would be completely unaware of it happening. He had probed all of them over the past couple of nights, peering deeply into their psyches. He knew it was a bad thing. Karen had warned him against it, but he had to. They were strangers, and he had to protect himself. And he was curious.

All of them had scars and wounds in their psyches, and bad things in their minds, bad things they'd done that they didn't want anyone to know. So Samuel would keep their secrets. He was good at keeping secrets.

But Derek—he was different. His psyche wasn't just scarred, it was twisted. He was the dangerous one. His threat with the knife had been real. Samuel vowed to go quietly around him, like a mouse around a cat. But if Derek ever threatened him again, Samuel would protect himself. He'd burst Derek's brain like a rotten grapefruit.

CHAPTER TWENTY-FOUR

In the morning they woke to a desert bloom. Sage and gorse brush, invigorated by the rains of the previous day, opened shoots of green and gold. Cactus flowers perched among the spines in full blossom, pink and bold in the morning sun. Wildflowers, hidden beneath the hard ground, emerged and unfolded in a dazzling carpet of yellows and reds and oranges. It was as if a magician had passed in the night, transforming the dry wastes into a desert garden.

"Beautiful, ain't it?" said Leggy. "Worth a little wettin', I'd say. It's a shame you can't see it, Missy."

John plucked a cactus flower and stroked Magdalena's cheek with it. She took the bloom in her hand and inhaled its fragrance.

"It's amazing to think that anything could live here," she said.

"We're livin' here," said Derek. "And I expect if we want to keep livin' we should hit the road."

After a quick meal they broke camp and continued east, following the highway. They had gone less than a mile when Teddy poked his brother.

"Look, Der-Der. Somethin' shiny up ahead."

Derek, who'd been watching his feet, his mind lost in thought, looked toward the horizon. Teddy was right. The sun glinted off something, sending up shards of light like a beacon. They were too far away to make out what it could be, or how big. Derek took out his spyglass and peered through it, but the land ahead dipped into a slight valley, hiding whatever was catching the sun.

"You see what it is?" asked Leggy.

"Nope," said Derek. "I expect we'll run into it soon enough, though."

Derek glanced at Afha. The donkey was calm. Derek didn't believe that the beast could sense bugs, or trouble, or anything besides a patch of sage grass—the creature hadn't sensed the mutie in the basement, and had given no warning of the menace of Youslus; but nevertheless, he felt reassured by the beast's calm.

So they plodded on, and waited to see what the road would bring them.

It was a house made almost entirely of glass—magnificent silver beams held the panes together. The sun reflected off the crystal, throwing rays in all directions, obscuring the house and preventing anyone from looking directly at it.

"Why dat house made of glass, Der?" Teddy chewed nervously on his lower lip. For someone who'd spent his life fighting a desperate, daily war against weather and radiation, mutants and marauders, a glass house seemed an idea of utter madness.

"It's a greenhouse, I'd guess," Leggy said.

Teddy looked more confused than ever.

The house wasn't green, not by a long shot—the reflected beams of light were blinding hues of yellow and orange.

"I'll bet they…." but Leggy didn't finish his thought. He didn't want to set the group up for disappointment if his daydreams of homegrown vegetables and hydroponic herbs proved wrong. He just shook his head. "Let's go."

For a moment all stood in silence, contemplating the strange sight. But when no one could offer a reason not to trek down off the broken highway and over to the glass house, they began the rugged hike in silence. Even Samuel, who was prone to humming, was unusually quiet.

They eased their way down a shattered exit ramp onto the desert floor. Just before they reached the end of the ramp Derek removed his spyglass and lifted it to his eye.

"I wouldn't if I were you," Leggy said. "You gonna blind yourself looking at through that thing."

"I'm not stupid," Derek chided, "I'm not gonna look *at* it. I'm looking *around* it. Make sure no one's out there waiting to ambush us."

Leggy sighed. The kid was right. If the greenhouse was functional, there would no doubt be measures to protect it. *Damn*, Leggy thought, *a greenhouse in the desert. Would miracles never cease?*

"Well, I don't see no one," Derek said after a moment. "Maybe it's abandoned."

The band of travelers continued in silence, picking their way through the desert scrap and scrub. The bloom that had followed the morning's rain had been brief, and had long since retreated back into the hard-baked earth and shriveled stalks and stems.

They cautiously approached what they assumed to be the front of the house—the side facing the highway.

As they drew closer, the sun's reflected rays lost their power and the glass construct came into better focus. If it was a greenhouse, there was nothing inside it. They could see clear through the building. From its base to its peaked roof it stood perhaps one hundred feet tall, but its length was difficult to judge. All four sides and the angled roof were transparent crystal, nearly invisible and untouched by dust or blowing sand.

"You've been this way before," said John to Leggy. "When you were running freight. You never saw this?"

Leggy shook his head. "There's no way I would've forgotten something like this."

"When's the last time you made a run out this way?" asked Derek.

"Shit, must be…twenty, thirty years," said Leggy.

"So it's less than twenty years old?" asked Derek.

"Maybe," said Leggy. "Though I suppose if we passed it at night, we would've missed it." The old man scratched his chin.

"You mean if you weren't passed out drunk," said Derek.

"I never drank on the job," said Leggy stiffly. "Least, not enough to impair my scoutin'."

Teddy, still amazed by the structure, walked around it, leaving smudgy handprints, which quickly disappeared, all around its exterior. The glass appeared quite solid.

The others watched Teddy knock on the panes as he walked the perimeter of the house. His gait grew more assured, his knocks louder and harder against the transparent walls. He looked back at his audience, grinning, and smiled through the glass at them as he turned the second corner, which Leggy guessed to be about twenty-five yards away.

Teddy leaned forward to rap heavily, and stumbled as his hand met no resistance. He fell into the house. The others startled and raced around the corner to his aid.

Teddy lay on the floor of the building, just inside.

John carefully felt the wall and found that an ovular, door-sized entrance was cut from the glass. It was nearly imperceptible to the naked eye, such was the pure crystalline quality of the structure.

Derek stepped inside to help his brother. The floor was a polished mirror, and looking down into it, Derek could see himself looking back up. He was shocked by the wild face that stared back at him—the dirt and grime etched into his brow, a tangled beard, and the grim expression of a haunted man.

Teddy clambered to his feet. He and Derek began to cautiously explore the seemingly empty interior. Walking was careful, tedious work. The floor reflected the empty blue of the sky above, and their brains refused to believe they were on solid ground.

After a careful inspection of the interior, Derek and Teddy discovered, almost by bumping into it, the building's one interesting structure. A crystal staircase, nearly invisible, was set in the exact center of the room. It spiraled up to the roof, and it spiraled down through a shaft that opened in the mirrored floor. The edges of the shaft were glass-smooth, and its diameter was an exact fit for the circular staircase. The shaft was too deep to see its bottom.

Derek put a foot onto the first step.

Teddy grabbed his arm. "Don't go down, Der. It's scary. And I won't fit to go with you."

It was true. The diameter of the shaft wouldn't admit Teddy's bulk.

"I ain't goin' down, Teddy. Not yet anyway," said Derek. He glanced at the ceiling. "I'm goin' up."

Derek ascended several dozen steps, but was forced to stop when he reached the peaked ceiling. He felt around for a hatch or opening of some sort, but could find nothing. Eventually he gave up and returned to the floor.

"Nothing up there," called Derek to the others, who hesitated in the doorway. "So I guess we see what's down there." He began to descend the stairs.

"Now hold on just a damned minute," Leggy called, but Derek ignored him.

Teddy whimpered.

"Well, he can't go down there alone," said Magdalena. She stepped inside and walked smoothly to the center of the house. She felt for a stair, and put her hand on the center column for a guide.

John glanced back and forth between the group outside and those inside. Magdalena was already on her way down, her body disappearing beneath the mirrored floor. Teddy was beginning to cry. And to John's dismay, he could see activity on the horizon—skeins of sand spiraling up from the ground in miniature funnels, propelled forward by currents of air. He tapped Leggy on the shoulder and pointed.

"Oh, shit," Leggy snarled, "That's a sandstorm brewin'. Wait!" he called to Magdalena, but she had already sunk out of sight. "Mother of fuck," Leggy cursed. "Come on fellas, we gotta try and squeeze these animals inside before we all get shredded by that storm."

The sky darkened. Lightning flashed . The sand on the ground outside the glass house was already being disturbed by the increasing wind.

John looked over at the strange hole that Magdalena had just descended—the hole where she was all alone facing God knew what. Alone with Derek.

He moved to enter the structure when Leggy put an arm on his shoulder.

"Hold up there, John. We got to get everyone inside first. Teddy seems to be out of commission, and I can't wrangle these mules inside by myself."

John looked toward the staircase again, then turned back to help Leggy off his donkey. The old man scampered inside, then turned to Samuel.

"Come on, youngster, you and that dog get in here."

Samuel obeyed, guiding Sheba through the opening. The dog whined, disoriented by the mirrored floor. Her paws slid on the smooth surface. Samuel led her several steps into the house, and rewarded the dog with a strip of jerky. Sheba huddled against the boy, gnawing at the meat, her sides trembling slightly.

"Now the mules," said Leggy.

John grabbed Afha's bridle and tugged. The beast walked up to the house but wouldn't step inside. John strained at the reins, but Afha set his hooves into the sand and would not be moved.

"Teddy," shouted Leggy. "Quit your cryin'. We need you over here."

Teddy lumbered over, wiping his eyes and nose with a dirty sleeve.

"See if you can give him a push while I pull," said John.

Teddy stepped outside. The sky was purple and gray, and the air was alive with a hissing wind. Teddy squinted against the gritty sand that swirled through the air. He wrapped his arms around Afha's midsection and heaved. The donkey brayed, its ears flat against its head, and the beast stayed put.

"Goddamit," said Leggy, as the two men struggled to budge the beast, "if those mules don't get in here the storm's gonna strip the flesh right off their bones!"

"Wait," said Samuel. "I think I know what to do." The boy ran back outside. He staggered in the surging wind, and unstrapped a bedroll from Minna. He ran back inside, and unrolled the blanket.

"It's the floor," said Samuel, shouting to be heard over the gale. "The reflection makes them skittish."

"Good thinkin'," said Leggy. "Hey Ted, get them bedrolls off and toss 'em in here."

They quickly spread several blankets across the entrance. John tugged at the reins. Afha stuck his head through the door and put one hoof gingerly on a blanket. Once the creature was satisfied of its footing, it came inside without a fuss. Minna followed easily. Teddy came last, his cheeks raw, abraded by the gritty winds.

161

Sand was coming in through the opening, falling in drifts against the inner wall. Outside the wind roared. They moved away from the door, sliding blankets ahead of them to keep the mules moving. They made their way to opposite end of the structure, where they cowered in the corner as the sandstorm unleashed its full power.

Leggy watched, pop-eyed, as the storm squatted directly over them, lashing at their shelter like a screaming child intent on smashing a toy castle. Dark clouds of desert particles shrieked against the glass ceiling, the glass walls. Gusts of wind blasted through the opening, carrying stinging grit to their eyes, ears, and mouths. Cannon shots of thunder battered the crystal frame. Leggy was certain the whole structure would shatter, and they would be shredded to bloody bits by infinite shards of glass and sand.

Teddy howled in absolute terror. Samuel buried his face in Sheba's fur, and both boy and dog whined and trembled. Only John had eyes for the crystal staircase, and the black pit where Magdalena had descended.

Magdalena counted fifty steps before she met up with Derek. Her fingers and her ears told her they were in a narrow shaft, the circumference of which exactly fit the staircase. In the closeness of the shaft, the rank smell of Derek's dried sweat and unwashed clothes struck her like a blow.

"Can you see how far this goes down?" she asked.

"No," said Derek. "It's getting darker as we go. I can see maybe a dozen more steps, and then it's black as night."

Magdalena opened her mouth slightly. She caught the gentle motion of cool air wafting up from beneath them, and, perhaps, a distant hum. But otherwise she could hear nothing.

"Why'd you follow me down?" asked Derek.

"Because I wanted to speak with you, in private."

"Go ahead, then."

"Does John know?"

"Know what?" Derek asked.

"Know that you laid with me?"

"No," said Derek. "And I'm not gonna tell him."

"What about the others? Your brother? Nicodemus?"

"Teddy was asleep. Leggy'll keep his trap shut."

"And the boy—do you think he can truly read minds?" she asked

"Hell if I know," said Derek. "Nothin' we can do about it if he can."

Magdalena was quiet for a long moment. "You understand then that I—that

I'm going to be with him? That I'm going to be with John?"

"Sure," said Derek, gritting his teeth and continuing his descent. "I had my jollies."

"And those nights in my home?"

"The old lady sold you for a poke," said Derek. "I had my fun. Now we're done."

Magdalena frowned. From the direction of Derek's voice, she could tell he was not looking at her.

"And now…?" she asked.

There was a soft rasp, the sound of steel slipping from leather. Derek had drawn a knife.

"We keep goin' down," he said.

"I'd rather go back up," said Magdalena

"Suit yourself," said Derek.

Magdalena listened to the sound of his steps as he descended. Then she turned and began to make her way slowly back up the stairs.

Above, the storm raged on. A jagged pitchfork of lighting licked out from the black clouds. Then another and another. The flashes had a strobe effect, freezing the storm for a moment of time. In those instances Leggy saw each individual grain of sand, pausing in their mad swirl around the edges of the crystal house. The sand gave shape to the wind, tracing the coiling vortices of its movement, becoming skin to its invisible sinews. Beneath the cold fear Leggy felt awe, as if the designs of nature had been revealed to him for an instant.

"Look," he said, prodding John. "It's beautiful."

John had no eyes for the spectacle. He fixed his attention on the crystal stairs and the dark hole. His belly was tight with fear—of the storm, yes, and for Magdalena's safety, yes, but another note hummed on, striking an anxious chord in his guts. If she had gone down by herself, or with Teddy, or Leggy, this third note would not be ringing. But she was alone in the dark with Derek.

Ever since their boyhood, John had deferred to Derek—after all, Derek was stronger and more clever, and there were advantages to letting him lead. It was Derek who schemed new ways to fill their bellies. It was Derek who fought off the camp bullies who would've preyed on John. But in the pattern of their lives, John had come to understand two things: Derek resented what others had and Derek always took what he wanted.

John had been content to live with these conditions until Magdalena had joined the group. For reasons not quite clear to John, Magdalena had chosen him over the others. Though he was pleased with her choice, the geometry of the group had been altered, and John was keenly aware of the change. Before Magdalena they had been a band of brothers, uneasy ones sometimes, but brothers. But now, with the addition of a woman, suddenly they were men.

John had mulled over the new equation. Teddy did not worry him. The man-boy blushed furiously if Magdalena even addressed him, and he had welcomed her into the encircling arms of his simple loyalty. Leggy had a chivalrous streak in him, a quality that John had been surprised to see shining through the rude hide of the old goat. His talk was still inappropriate with a woman present, but John knew the old man would never try anything without Magdalena's consent.

But Derek.

Derek never even spoke to Magdalena, barely acknowledged her presence. At first John thought it was because Derek was upset to have a woman join them. But then another idea took root—perhaps the effort that Derek put in to ignoring her meant she was ever present in his mind. And now Derek had her to himself, alone in a dark, strange place.

The anxiety in John's guts became too much. "Damn the storm," he shouted. "I'm goin' down!"

"Wait!" called Leggy.

At that moment a fork of lighting struck the peaked roof. Lighting ran along the crystal frame, and the walls thrummed with electricity. Tingling energies ran from the soles of their feet up to their heads, making their hair stand on end. A blast of noise rocked the structure, and the house itself suddenly went opaque. The transparent glass turned to sheets of cold white. Even the mirrored floor had been transformed, like a frozen pond under a dusting of snow.

The noise of the storm cut out, leaving the travelers in a ringing silence.

"What the Hell?" said Leggy.

"Look," said Teddy. "The door is gone!" He pointed to the place where they had found their way inside. Now the wall stood unbroken, the opening vanished. They were trapped. The air inside was still, no wind could penetrate.

John ran to the stairs. The spiral staircase still stood, but the stairs ended at the floor. The shaft had vanished.

"No," shouted John. He fell to his knees and banged on the floor with his fists.

"Magdalena! Magdalena, can you hear me? Magdalena?"

CHAPTER TWENTY-FIVE

"The stairs end here," said Derek, speaking over his shoulder. "I'm standing on a floor, and there's some kind of archway."

"Can you see anything?" asked Magdalena. She had tried to go back up the staircase and found the way blocked, and so had returned to Derek.

"No. It's still too dark."

Derek waited as Magdalena made her way down the last few stairs to stand next to him. He felt her put a hand on his shoulder.

"I'd guess we're in a large room or open space," she said quietly. "The air is cool and fresh. Can you feel the way it moves?"

"It does feel cooler down here," he said. "Hey! Hello?" Derek called loudly. A faint echo returned to them, filled with distant reverb. "A *very* large room," he agreed.

"What do we do now?" she asked.

"I've got matches," he said. "I'm going to risk a light." He took a match from his pocket and lit it. The head sputtered to life. Derek winced against the pinpoint of flame for a moment, then held the match out in front of him. He was relieved to find that his eyes still worked. The match cast a tiny halo of light, enough that he could see his hand, and Magdalena's face. But by itself the match was too weak to penetrate the deep darkness, and they had no better idea of where they were.

The orange flame ate its way quickly down the matchstick, singing his fingertips before he dropped it to the floor, where it sputtered and died. Darkness covered them like a black hood. The sulfur smell of the match was sharp in the air, and suddenly he realized what a target he'd made of them.

There came a sharp crack of noise. Derek's fingers trembled on the railing of the spiral stairs.

"What the Hell?" he said.

At that moment the room filled with white light and a burst of discordant music. Derek flung his arms up over his eyes. White patterns and shapes danced behind his eyelids.

165

As suddenly as it had begun, the music stopped. Derek dropped his arm and blinked owlishly against the bright light.

"What happened?" asked Magdalena. "What was that?"

"Somebody turned on the lights," said Derek.

"What do you see?"

"Not much. Everything's kinda hazy and white. But we're in a big…bunker, or warehouse or something. *Really* big. I—"

Derek stopped. He heard footsteps—hard, heavy feet clocking against the smooth floor, coming toward them out of the bright haze. Magdalena swiveled toward the sound, unslinging her rifle from her back.

"Who's there?" shouted Derek, knife ready in his hand. He peered into the cavernous room, his eyes still adjusting to the bright glare of a million overhead lights.

"Greetings," a voice answered. "Welcome to your new home."

It had been nearly an hour since the lighting strike. Leggy and Samuel sat in silence on the white floor, watching the animals sleep, huddled together on the makeshift carpet.

Teddy paced around the staircase, clenching and unclenching his fists. John walked the inner perimeter of the crystal house, its walls and floors still an opaque white. He tapped and pressed and pushed, hoping to trip a hidden button or switch.

Suddenly Afha's ears perked and his eyes opened. He tilted his head toward the stairs and brayed. John and Teddy stood still. A distant, mechanical *Whiiir-klomp, whiiir-klomp* sound came from beneath their feet. It was growing closer. Beneath the floor, something was slowly ascending the stairs.

Leggy grabbed Derek's shotgun and ordered Samuel to take cover behind the mules. "Teddy! Johhny! Stand tall. Something's comin' up."

"Der?" cried Teddy, running toward the stairs. "That you, Der?"

"It ain't them," Leggy said, "Get away from there, both of you." Teddy and John backed away from the staircase.

"I don't like this," Samuel squeaked from his spot behind Minna. "I have a bad feeling about this."

"Really?" Leggy asked.

"In general," Samuel clarified. "I'm not sensing anything, if that's what you mean. Strange, but I'm not sensing…*anything.*"

At that moment the crystal dome went transparent again. The night sky was brilliant with stars, the desert landscape lit with silver.

The sandstorm was over.

And the shaft beneath the stairs was open again.

John leaped for it and then pulled up short. A small head popped over the edge of the stairs. It was made of metal with antenna jutting from either side. The antennae quivered, and then it pulled itself up onto the mirrored floor with heavy, treaded wheels.

"What the Hell?" Leggy asked.

The thing was boxy, about the size of a dog. It was made of a dull metal, and rolled steadily across the floor on its treaded wheels. Except for the antennae and the short, elephantine hose-like trunk that protruded from its front, the contraption reminded Leggy of a miniature version of the hulking burned out husks of the tanks that littered the no-man's land of Old Tijuana.

"Should I step on it?" Teddy asked. "Should I squash it?"

"Wait," Leggy ordered. "Give it a minute. Let's see what it wants."

John took a step toward the staircase.

"Hold on," called Leggy. "Don't go down by yourself."

John looked over his shoulder at the old man. "Sorry," he said. "I can't leave her down there." He descended into darkness.

"Fuck," shouted Leggy.

"What do we do?" asked Samuel.

Leggy didn't like John going down by himself, but he also wasn't keen on following him, because it would mean leaving Samuel and Teddy behind—and frankly he was more worried about Teddy than the boy because the man-child was already on edge with his brother gone.

The wheeled visitor didn't seem to want anything from the intruders. In fact, it seemed not to even notice them.

Leggy, Teddy, Samuel, and the animals watched as it rolled casually across the mirrored floor, headed in a straight line toward where the door had been. It stopped a few feet shy of the wall, just in front of a drift of dust and sand, and its trunk-hose began to tremble and sway as if it were sniffing the floor. Suddenly the sound of a loud motor erupted from its belly, causing the others to jump, and it began to suck up the sand through its snout. It continued to roll around the floor, snorting up the errant drifts of sand and dust.

Within a few minutes it had sucked up all the sand in the drift. Then it headed toward the place where the door had been. With a *zapping* sound, it emitted a stream of electricity from its antennae to the glass, and the door reappeared.

The robot casually rolled through the door, turned in a few circles as if choosing a spot, then raised its trunk and expelled all of its gathered sand in a pile on the ground outside. Then it turned, came back in, and headed for the stairs.

Just then, three more machines emerged from the hole. They were flat and disk-shaped, and moved silently on soft, furry undersides, polishing the floor as they went.

"Well, I'll be," said Leggy.

Eventually the disk-bots made their way over to the blankets where the humans and animals sat. The bots began to emit a series of frantic, annoyed beeps.

"Sam, get up," Leggy ordered. "Teddy, see if you can't move those blankets out of their way. Sam, get those mules up. Quick!"

With a confused bustle of activity, Teddy attempted to yank the blankets out from beneath Samuel and the animals, who in turn lost their balance and began to dance frantically for footing on the mirrored floor. To add to the panic of the mules, the disk-bots immediately saw their opening and *wooshed* in, gliding deftly between and around panicked, shuffling hooves, cleaning all the while.

Once the inside was finished, the three robots went out the open door. In less time than Leggy would've imagined possible, the machines climbed the walls and polished the outside of the house, returned to the ground, formed a neat line, and came back in.

And with no further ado, the four robots descended the stairs and were soon lost to the darkness below. The house was as clean as it had been when the group had first discovered it.

An hour had passed since the departure of the robots. And then another. Teddy was frantic with worry about his brother.

Leggy bit his lip. Surely something was wrong. He wouldn't put it past Derek to let them worry, but he was certain that Maggie and John would've checked back by now. Their absence could only mean that they were in danger. And if they were in danger, someone had to go down and get them out of it.

But who? Teddy couldn't fit down the shaft, which left only himself and Samuel—the legless wonder and the child freak. Not much of a rescue crew.

Leggy sighed, a sinking feeling in his gut accompanied the knowledge of what he knew he must do. He put two fingers to his lips and whistled, "C'mon Sheba. C'mere doggy." Then he frowned, "Samuel, I'm gonna need you to help me down those stairs."

Sam nodded.

Leggy took a deep breath. "Teddy, you have to stay up here and guard the mules. I'm going down there and I'm going to come back up with your brother. That's a promise. But you're going to have to promise me that you will stay with the animals and protect them if you have to. Can you do that, big guy?"

Teddy thought for a long moment, and then nodded.

"And you're going to have to promise me something else, Teddy. Okay? You're going to have to promise me that if something dangerous comes up those stairs...or if we don't come back up by tomorrow night, that you'll leave the next morning. You'll have to head back to Moses Springs, find Silas, and tell him what happened. Can you do that, Teddy? Can you make that promise to old Leggy?"

For a while Teddy said nothing. He mulled over what the old man had said, considering it as carefully and as quickly as his cloudy mind would allow. Eventually, wordlessly, he nodded, his eyes brimming with tears.

"Good then," Leggy said, and left it at that.

Leggy, Samuel, and Sheba moved quickly but cautiously down the stairwell. Samuel tried to assist him, but it proved easier to simply let the old man climb down of his own accord.

At the bottom of the shaft was a doorway through which light poured. Leggy stopped. His arms were sore from the descent, and his heart was thumping heatedly in his chest. Samuel stood behind him, nervous and silent. Sheba whined softly. Leggy took several deep, long breaths to calm himself, and then peered through the doorway.

It opened onto a vast, brightly lit room. High, stone walls arched upward toward a ceiling, from which hung thousands of lights. Leggy eased himself through the doorway and out onto the floor. The floor was cool against his palms and slightly damp. The size and shape of the place reminded him of the arena in Los Angeles, where the locals went to take in public executions and mutie fights. This place was in much better shape though and didn't stink of blood and urine like the other.

The shaft they had come down opened into a far end of the grand room, so that the wide expanse of the place spread before them, inviting them inward.

Samuel eased his way past the old man, followed by Sheba. The boy looked up at the great domed ceiling. Leggy watched his face for signs of awe or distress, but the boy seemed calm. If it was true that he'd come out of that bunker that Youslus had blasted open, then maybe he was used to being underground.

As the trio made their way forward, they saw a pair of signs standing on the floor, one larger than the other. The nearer sign was made of tarnished brass and though clean and free of rust and dust, was scuffed with age. It read:

WELCOME!
FOLLY OF MAN:
Museum of the Past, Present (and Future?)
Open to Visitors

The second sign was smaller and made of yellow plastic. This sign read:

CAUTION!
Wet Floor

Beneath the letters was the black silhouette of a figure slipping on a wet surface.

"Well, this is just plain weird," said Leggy, who had been expecting to be set upon by some dark horror, not given a polite warning to watch his step. He wondered if maybe the others hadn't been waylaid. Perhaps they were just exploring the vast wonderland. He cupped his hands to his mouth and was about to holler for John, when he stopped. He looked at Samuel.

"Can you...can you sense anyone?"

Samuel shrugged. "Not really. There's a smattering of brain activity, but it's faint and distorted. If anyone's down here, they must be catatonic."

"Cata-what?" asked Leggy.

"Out cold," said Samuel.

"Hmmm," said Leggy. He stroked his grizzled chin as he looked about him.

He saw that all around the circumference of the room large, square panes of glass had been set into the walls, like old-fashioned shop windows that storekeepers used to have—before the nukes had shattered them all. Roughly half of the windows were lit from within, but there seemed to be no discernible pattern to their illumination.

Not knowing what else to do, Leggy and Samuel strode over to the glass window to their left. This window was dark, but by cupping his hands to the sides of his head and peering inside Leggy could see that it was empty. Gray walls and no obvious features.

They worked their way slowly around the perimeter, checking each darkened window as they went. More of the same. And then they came to the first of the lighted windows and peered inside.

Samuel gasped. In the room were three large dogs with glowing red eyes. Each was clad in powered armor with mounted weapons. Their teeth were barred. Foam and spittle clung to their lips. Behind them stood two soldiers, also heavily clad in battle armor and rebreathers. All were silent and still. A sign bolted next to the window read *Dogs of War, circa 2085*. The back wall of the room was a photo diorama of a burning city, a generic battleground of the last World War.

"They're dummies." Leggy breathed a sigh of relief. "They ain't real. Just statues."

He and Samuel passed to the next display of a shanty town like the kind that had sprung up outside of major urban centers after the bombs had fallen. The diorama focused on a tin shack with a tarp roof, the family inside suffering various advanced stages of radiation sickness. At the center of this Hellish tableau a young woman offered her infant a breast to suckle. The artist had carefully detailed the sores and scabs on the mother's skin, and the wasting body of her son, his eyes wide with pain as cancer devoured him from the inside. The sign read *Madonna and Child, circa 2087*.

Each window they passed took them through the dark history of the Last War and its aftermath. *The Toxic Upheaval - The Arrival of the Bugs - The Extermination Volunteers - The Cleansing of the Cities - The Rendering of The Word*. In this way they made a nearly complete circuit of the arena, their steps describing an oval that took them back toward the door to the shaft.

Eventually Leggy and Samuel came to a lit window almost directly across from the door through which they had entered. A sign inside read *Desert Dwellers, Commonly Referred to as "Muties" – Present Day*.

Inside the room was full of sand. The background was an image of endless desert and rolling dunes. A bright, hidden light poured heat and glare from above. Lying in the middle of the room, huddled together, were three vaguely human skeletons. The remains of a fourth skeleton were scattered all about.

"That's weird," said Leggy. "Where's the mannequins? Those ain't muties, just dried bones."

Samuel gulped. "Maybe…maybe this used to be a live display."

"You mean with real muties?" asked Leggy.

Samuel nodded.

"But eventually they would've just…if they couldn't get no humans to eat, they woulda…."

"They would've what?" asked Samuel.

Leggy shook his head. "Never mind. C'mon."

The next lit window stopped them dead in their tracks. Inside, the room was made to appear as a comfortable bedroom, of the sort that neither Leggy nor Samuel had ever known. A painting of a pastoral red barn hung on the wall. A King James Bible lay bookmarked on the end table. Two half-empty glasses of water stood between the Bible and a shaded reading lamp. A large bed with a fluffed down comforter was positioned catty-cornered for maximum viewability.

And laying side-by-side on the bed were Derek and Magdalena. Their scruffy traveling clothes had been removed and replaced with....

"Pajamas!" Samuel sputtered.

Derek and Magdalena seemed lifeless and pale. Their complexions were waxy, their eyes were closed. They looked dead. A sign inside read *Recent Additions—Classification and Nomenclature Pending.*

Leggy pounded against the glass, wondering if he could break it when Samuel called excitedly from the next window. "Nicodemus! Hurry. Over here."

Leggy scrambled over and was surprised to see an identical room to the one which Derek and Magdalena reposed. John sat on the bed, his face buried in his hands, weeping. Samuel jumped up and down in front of the window, but John apparently could not see him.

"Holy crow," said Leggy. "Stand back there, Samuel. Let's see if I can break the glass." He drew his knife, determined to shatter the glass with the haft.

But before he could swing, a mechanical voice from behind them declared, "Now, now, sir, please don't do that. Visitors aren't permitted to tamper with the displays."

Leggy and Samuel spun around. A tall, mechanical creature peered down at them. It was man-sized and man-shaped and stood with its hands clasped in front of its waist, long fingers worrying with muted clicks and taps. Its body was composed of burnished steel. The lines of its torso and legs were shaped to give the appearance of clothing tinted a deep burgundy, giving the robot the appearance of a carnival barker.

Its polished face had a host of fine qualities, such as one would assemble if building an ideal actor or politician—high cheekbones, patrician nose, strong jaw line, and a pleasant, polite, permanently affixed smile. Whatever craftsman had created this artificial man had even hammered in a pair of dimples. Its eyes were a soothing blue, and they glowed calmly, almost cheerfully, as the robot spoke, growing brighter as it grew more animated.

"Now then, let me introduce myself," it said softly. Its voice, though mechanical, had a warm, melodious quality. "My name is Mr. Tines, and I'll be your guide during your visit. Feel free to ask me any questions you like. We don't get visitors often, and I've got *sooo* much information to share."

"Whu...." said Leggy, his mind struggling to make sense of things.

Sheba growled, her hackles raised.

"Oh!" said Mr. Tines, rearing back a bit. "I'm afraid pets aren't allowed in the museum."

Samuel put a hand on Sheba's back, quieting her.

"Oh well," clucked Mr. Tines. "I suppose we can make an exception." His blue eyes sparkled. "I don't think the other patrons will mind…because there aren't any!" His mechanical voice tittered.

"Now then, I can see that you're interested in our most recent acquisitions." The robot gestured toward the windows with their friends inside. "I haven't had time to conduct a full curatorial analysis because they just arrived today, but I can tell you a thing or two if you don't mind my engaging in a little bit of speculation?"

He paused, waiting for a response.

All that Leggy could muster was a grunt.

"Excellent," said the robot.

Mr. Tines folded his fingers and turned his eyes up to the brightly lit ceiling. "Based on their relatively unblighted physiognomies, it's very doubtful that they are dwellers of the deep wastes. More probably they come from the pockets of humanity that were outside the most lethal effect areas of the fallout or the genetic toxin bombardments. That is, well away from the toxic coastal clouds, or any military targets or bug-infested Heartland. While nothing remains unaffected by the fallout or toxin clouds, these specimens do not appear to exhibit any external abnormalities. While I can't say with certainty from where they originate, I would guess that they're representative of the population in the central farmlands of what was once known as the Great State of California."

The robot sighed, and though the smile didn't change, the blue light in his eyes dimmed slightly. "I do so hate to speculate, though. My master abhorred speculation. 'Always the facts, Tines!' he would say to me as he worked. 'If there's one thing this museum will preserve, it's the facts!'"

The robot tsked. "What ever would he say now? I haven't even had time to mount them correctly because I'm not sure what kind of background to construct. And here you are, the first visitors we've had in years. Surely you're thinking it *unforgivably* inappropriate to have them in a pre-War motel setting. I couldn't agree more. The anachronism just grinds my gears. But it was all that I had handy, and it *is* better than just laying them on a bare floor."

Leggy, who'd been listening in utter astonishment, straightened himself up. He didn't like the way the robot loomed over him, and the machine man's dignified bearing made him feel awkward and shabby. He cleared his throat.

"Listen, ah, sir—"

"Mr. Tines," insisted the robot politely.

"Are they dead?" asked Leggy, glancing at the prone figures of Derek and Magdalena.

"Dead? No, not yet. Unfortunately I have not yet had time to fully prep the taxidermy lab. For the moment they are unconscious. They'll revive in several hours, unless I administer another dose of soporific."

"You got to let these people out," said Leggy. "They ain't exhibits. They're our friends."

Mr. Tines, who had bent obsequiously at the waist as if to better hear Leggy, straightened up in surprise.

"You know them? You know where they came from?"

"Well, sure," said Leggy. "We all came from a little shit-heel place called San Muyamo." He didn't feel inclined to explain Samuel's provenance.

"I see," said Tines, sounding disappointed. "I haven't heard of this...San Muyamo. Perhaps it's in the master's atlas?"

"Doubt it," said Leggy. "But it is about fifty miles from a place they used to call Fresno."

"Ahh," said the robot excitedly. "Then I was right about their origins. Oh, this is good! Can you tell me what their environment was like?"

"Mr. Tines," said Leggy, not liking the direction this was heading. But before he could continue, the robot cut him off again.

"For example, did they live in neo-adobe structures? Or a sandstone domicile like those dreadful Bedouins?"

"RVs," said Leggy. "And shanties. Whatever you could dig out of the ground or salvage from a scrap heap, is what we turned into shelter."

"Oh, very good," said Mr. Tines. "How quaint! Simple, yet sublime. This will really add some color to the exhibits. It's a shame the master's not here to construct the display. He had such an amazing eye for detail. I'll do my best, but I'm sure to leave out that poignant quality he imbued in his work. Master had a real empathy for the plight of humanity."

Mr. Tines leaned in conspiratorially. "Not being human, it's hard for me to get that bit." He nudged Samuel with a burnished elbow.

"Now then, can you describe this shanty-town?" he asked, turning back to Leggy. He held his hands in front of his face, long metal fingers extended in an open gesture. "I'm picturing worn-out old shacks with corrugated iron roofs, the hulks of long-abandoned cars half-buried in hardpacked mud. Sand drifts, tufts of shrub grass, maybe a tuber root or two protruding from the dry ground. Have I got it?"

"No," said Leggy. "I mean, yeah, you got the picture all right, but you're missin' the point. You can't have those people in there."

Mr. Tines turned his head to the side, his blue eyes pulsing. "I can't? Why not? They're perfect. They'll bring the museum right up to date, and it will be such a fascinating project."

"Because they're with us," said Leggy. "And we're moving on."

"You're welcome to leave whenever you like," said Mr. Tines, "but these exhibits must stay. If you're concerned about their preservation, I can assure you that after I've embalmed them, they will remain unchanged for the next millennia." Mr.

Tines pushed out his chest proudly. "The master taught me to seek only the highest standards in the curatorial arts."

"I don't know what you said, but it don't matter because you're crazy," said Leggy. "C'mon Samuel, let's bust 'em out." He raised the haft of his knife and struck at the pane. The glass was thick and strong, and Leggy's blow had no effect other than to galvanize Mr. Tines.

The mechanical man reached out and snatched Leggy's wrist. The robot squeezed, and Leggy cried out in pain. The knife slipped from his hand.

"Now, now," said Mr. Tines, the cheerful tone in his voice never once slipping. "I warned you not to touch the exhibit." He slapped Leggy with a powerful backhand, knocking the crippled man onto his back.

"Stop it," cried Samuel, running to Leggy's aid.

Sheba snarled and leapt at the robot, but Tines batted her aside without effort.

"Did your master program you to attack visitors?" demanded Samuel as he helped Leggy sit up.

The old man was dazed and blood trickled from the side of his mouth.

Mr. Tines twitched once, as if jolted by a momentary surge of electricity. "My first duty is to the museum and its contents. I'll allow you to stay only so long as you behave yourselves. But I will not tolerate tampering with the exhibits. Now, if you will excuse me, I've got a display to assemble."

The robot walked over to the steel divider between the case that held John and the one that held Magdalena and Derek. There was a small numeric keypad set into the wall, and Mr. Tines tapped out a quick code on the pad.

Samuel tried to count, and thought there might be six or seven digits.

A door slid open in the space between the cells, and Mr. Tines glided through it. Before they could react, the door slid closed again with a hiss. A few moments later, Mr. Tines appeared behind Derek and Magdalena's window. The robot easily lifted the humans and placed them gently on the floor. And then like a stagehand striking a set, he began carefully dismantling the motel setting.

Leggy stirred himself.

"Are you all right, Mr. Nicodemus?" Samuel leaned over him, offering his tiny, six-fingered hand.

"M'allright," said Leggy, "but we're in a fix, no doubt about it." He wiped at his bloody mouth with a dirty handkerchief.

Sheba came to them and sat on her haunches. Samuel ran his hands along her body, probing for injury, but she was sound.

The trio watched as the robot moved smoothly through the display case, emptying it of its contents, even peeling off a layer of wallpaper to reveal smooth, white walls beneath.

"Samuel, I'm out of ideas," said Leggy. "That tin man in there has all the cards."

Samuel frowned. He had an idea, but was afraid that Mr. Tines could hear them even from the display case. He had no choice—he projected his thoughts into Leggy's consciousness.

The old man startled as Samuel's voice rang out inside his skull.

DON'T BE ALARMED MR. NICODEMUS—IT'S ME—THIS WAY THE ROBOT CAN'T HEAR

Jesus that's weird, thought Leggy. And then, *Are you...are you hearin' me?*

YES—I THINK IF WE HUMOR MR. TINES WE CAN GET OUT OF THIS

Humor the robot? What are you talkin' about?

I'M GOING TO TRY AND CONTACT JOHN NOW

Samuel went and stood in front of the last display case. John paced the room, searching for some way out. Samuel took a deep breath and pushed his thoughts toward John. He stopped and looked up in shock. His hands flew to his head.

"Who's that?" he shouted. "Where are you?"

IT'S SAMUEL—MR. NICODEMUS AND I ARE ON THE OTHER SIDE OF THE GLASS WALL—CAN YOU SEE US

John stepped forward and pressed his face against the glass. *No. It's a mirror. Is Magdalena with you? Is she all right?*

THE ROBOT HAS MAGDALENA—SHE'S DRUGGED

At that moment, Mr. Tines entered John's room. John whirled around, and Samuel recoiled from the surge of fear and anger that overflowed into him. Mr. Tines picked up the water glass on the bedside table and approached John.

He wants me to drink it, but I think it's poison.

DONT DRINK IT—TELL HIM YOU CAN HELP WITH THE DISPLAY

"What?" said John. "I don't understand." He backed away from Mr. Tines, who advanced cheerfully on the human with the water glass extended in one burnished steel hand.

SAY YOU CAN HELP WITH THE DISPLAY—SAY YOU WERE BORN IN SAN MUYAMO—SAY YOU KNOW EVERY DETAIL OF THE PLACE projected Samuel, his brow knit in concentration.

The robot backed John up against the glass and used its own body to hold him in place. One hand reached up and took John by the chin. Steel fingers forced his mouth open. The other brought the glass to bear.

"Samuel, help me," shrieked John.

TELL HIM urged Samuel, pounding the glass with his fists. YOU HAVE A LIFETIME OF KNOWLEDGE OF CUSTOMS, RITUALS, FOODSTUFFS, LIVING CONDITIONS, CLOTHING, CRAFTS—TELL HIM—TELL HIM—TELL HIM

Samuel heard an echo of John's frantic babbling, but couldn't make out his words.

Whatever John said worked. Mr. Tines backed off and escorted John out to where his companions waited.

"Leggy! Sheba!" shouted John, running to the old man and the dog. "What is this place?"

"It's a goddam nuthou—"

"It's a museum," said Samuel brightly, cutting off Leggy. "This is Mr. Tines. He's the curator. We're going to help him with his newest display."

"His what?" asked John.

"Display," said Mr. Tines, coming around from behind him. "And your assistance is going to be so very valuable. The master would be quite pleased."

John turned and saw Magdalena and Derek on the floor of the now-bare display room. He ran to the glass. "What've you done to her?"

CALM DOWN Samuel focused the full strength of his mind on John.

John recoiled as if slapped. The words were like a knife in his head. A thin trickle of blood appeared at the corner of his left nostril, which he quickly wiped away with his sleeve. Turning back to his friends, John noticed a similar trickle of blood from Leggy's nose.

TRUST ME—OKAY—JUST TRUST ME

John wiped his eyes and tried to breathe more steadily. "Okay," he said aloud, the hysteria gone from his voice.

"I assume," said Leggy, turning to Mr. Tines, "that you've got some idea for a particular scene in mind?"

"Oh yes," said Mr. Tines. "We must think it through very carefully, and it's essential that we get the details right. Now then, what should our subjects be doing?" The robot looked around at the humans. For the first time he seemed to take notice of Samuel. "And *what*, exactly, pray tell, are *you*?

"Cooking?" offered Leggy with a sidelong glance at Samuel. "Skinning hides?"

"Excellent," said Mr. Tines, his attention back on the subject at hand. "A splendid idea. The action of cooking and tanning will give exquisite movement to the scene, while also providing an intimate look at the daily routine," The robot put a hand to its cheek, a disconcertingly human gesture. "But when should they be cooking? At dawn? Perhaps the mid-day meal?"

"I'm thinking dusk," said Leggy, his mind racing. "Just before the sun sets and darkness falls, and all the dangerous stuff comes out."

"Ah now," said Tines, one finger following the outline of his metalworked cheekbone, "I like it. Perhaps we can manage to get a look of anxiety into their eyes as they hurry to finish their chores before the coming of the dark night and its deadly denizens. Yes, that should work well. I see a gloaming dusk, the sun a fiery orb sinking behind the rim of the continent, the cloak of night looming. Dangerous eyes peeping from the shadows of the wild. Very poetic."

"Now then," said the robot. "What else do we need?"

"Well, we'll need a campfire, of course," Leggy began, cautiously studying the automaton for any sign of adversity.

"Yes," said Tines, nodding. "I believe I can simulate that."

"You'll need some gear—you know, cook pots, a couple of tin plates, a knife. Probably a rifle. I think Magdalena had one of those."

"Who?" asked Tines, distractedly. "You mean the female? Yes, she did. It's in the workshop."

"And you'll have to have a donkey, of course," added Samuel. "No one in San Muyamo does anything without a donkey, right John?"

"Uh..." murmured John, nodding dumbly. "That's right. Donkeys all over the place."

"Oh dear," said Mr. Tines, his blue eyes dimming. "I think a donkey might be outside my capabilities."

"No problem," said Samuel. "Teddy's got two donkeys. You could embalm one of them."

"Teddy?" asked Mr. Tines.

"Another companion of ours," said the boy. "He's still upstairs."

"Upstairs?" asked Mr. Tines. "In the reception hall?"

"Is that what you call the glass house?" asked John.

The robot nodded.

"Then yeah, they're in the reception hall."

"Well, this is just wonderful," said Mr. Tines, his eyes brightening again.

"There's a problem, though," said Leggy. "The opening in the shaft isn't big enough for them."

"Ah, that is most definitely *not* a problem," said Mr. Tines. "They can come down the freight elevator. Shall I send it up?"

"May I go up too, to tell Teddy what's happening?" asked Samuel. "He'll be so excited!"

"Of course," said Tines. He swiveled quickly around and bounded excitedly across the open plaza.

Samuel followed. As he walked, he put his mind in connection with Leggy.

I WILL BE BACK WITH TEDDY

And, just for good measure, Samuel projected an image of Mr. Tine's head being smashed into a cloud of sparks and wire between Teddy's enormous hamfists.

Mr. Tines approached another divider between two blackened display windows. He pressed a button recessed into the wall and the divider slid up, revealing an access passage. Samuel followed him inside. They passed through a narrow corridor about six feet long that opened onto a workshop the size of a gymnasium. It reminded Samuel of the labs that had been housed in the bunkers where he'd been raised, although the equipment here included woodworking and machinist tools along with silicon fabricators, nano-assemblers, computer terminals, and a gene sequencer. The room was tidy and dust-free, but it still gave the impression of long disuse.

"The master's workshop," said Tines, his voice low and reverent. "It was here that he created the displays you see in the cases in the plaza. He built me here, too," Mr. Tines said with pride. "His greatest achievement, he often said, though were he alive to see how things are now, he would know it wasn't true."

"Did he build those cleaning robots too?" asked Samuel.

"Ah, yes. My dumber cousins. But essential. I couldn't manage the place without them."

"How long ago did your master die?" asked Samuel.

"Die?" said Tines. "I don't know that he's actually dead. Fifty-three years ago he went to the surface with the sand crawler. He said he was going out to collect artifacts. But he never came back. He was quite old by then, of course, so I must assume he's perished. But still, I've tried to maintain the museum, waiting for his return."

"How sad," said Samuel, feeling a momentary pang of sympathy for the robot. Samuel knew what it was like to live at the bottom of a hole, alone for ages. But he put his feelings aside, knowing that he had to focus on himself and his companions.

As they passed through the workshop, Tines pointed to a small corner that showed signs of recent activity. A mannequin stood in various stages of assembly, but even up close, Samuel couldn't tell what it was supposed to be.

"What is it?" he asked.

Mr. Tines sighed, his blue eyes nearly fading to black. "A mutant. At least that's what it's *supposed* to be. I tried to fabricate it myself, but I just couldn't get it to come out right."

Tines brightened. "But now you're here. I haven't felt this hopeful in so long!"

They came to a pair of doors set back into the wall. Mr. Tines pushed a button and the doors slid open, revealing an enormous elevator.

"This is how the master brought equipment and materials into the museum," said Tines, stepping in.

Samuel followed. Like the workshop, the elevator was neat, but stale with disuse. Mr. Tines pushed a button on a small white control panel. With a gentle lift, the elevator began to move.

"The lift arrives just inside the eastern face of the reception hall," said Tines.

"We looked all over the reception hall," said Samuel. "We didn't see any entrance for an elevator. It's just a big glass room."

"Not glass. Nano-crystal," said Tines. "Strong as steel but infinitely malleable. To your friend inside the reception hall, it will look as if the floor is suddenly sprouting an elevator. In fact, it's just the nano-crystal re-arranging itself to accommodate the elevator."

"Neat," said Samuel. "Did your master invent that, too?"

"Oh no," said Tines. "Though he was one of the first to stabilize it enough for industrial applications. But the war engulfed the world long before his processes could be put into widespread use."

"Is the whole museum made from nano-crystal?" asked Samuel.

"Heavens no. Just the reception hall and the windows for the display cases."

"How did your master build this place?"

"He didn't build it. The museum itself is an aquifer that ran dry decades and decades ago. My master stumbled across it before the war during a vision quest in the desert. Under the divine influence of the peyote cactus, he fell in love with the place and realized its potential. He purchased seven hundred acres of land above the aquifer and began making the underground chamber habitable.

"You see, initially, this wasn't supposed to be a museum," admitted Tines.

"No?" asked Samuel.

"My master originally built this place as a refuge. In his vision, he saw that a catastrophe was looming on the horizon. A worldwide calamity, he called it. A paradigm shift. A redefining of human consciousness. He planned to populate this refuge with like-minded friends and family, as well as other scientists and artists and craftsmen. They would preserve the best technologies available to humans and then emerge after the catastrophe and help remake the world.

"But the end came much sooner than he'd anticipated. The bombs fell while he was here alone, making final touches. How lonely he was, then! How often he contemplated killing himself—just another corpse among the millions, this one courteous enough to have had himself pre-buried.

"But his nature wouldn't allow him to take his own life. He was disgusted by the idea of unnecessary waste. And so he conceived of the museum. I think it was just a project to help keep him busy—he never really expected to have visitors. But his hope was that someday, if civilization arose again, his work might be discovered, and perhaps serve as a warning against folly. 'We must preserve the past,' he would cry. 'Mr. Tines, we must preserve the present. We must never forget.'"

The elevator came to a halt. The door slid open. It was night, and the crystal hall was translucent. Stars were strewn across a clear black sky, and a waning moon illuminated the landscape with silver light.

Samuel stepped out to find Teddy cowering in a corner with the mules.

"Teddy," he shouted.

Teddy looked up and, seeing Samuel, he cried out with joy. He sprang forward and scooped up Samuel in his arms and swung him around. But when Mr. Tines stepped out of the elevator, Teddy stepped backward and shielded Samuel with his body.

"Don't worry," said Samuel, gasping slightly in Teddy's powerful grasp. "This is Mr. Tines. He lives here. He's going to take us to the others. To your brother."

"To Der-Der? Where is he?"

"We have to go in the elevator," said Samuel. "In that room there."

Teddy looked suspiciously at the elevator. "I don't like it," he said, chewing on his lip.

"It's the only way down," said Samuel soothingly. "You're too big for the stairs. It's very safe, and not dark at all, and when we get down we'll see Derek and John and Leggy and Magdalena. And we can bring the animals with us."

Teddy let himself be convinced, though reluctantly. They herded the mules into the elevator, and descended. Teddy nervously bit his lip, and the mules were unhappy to be confined in such a cramped place. But Mr. Tines was delighted. He ran his hands lightly over the beasts.

"Oh, these will do nicely. Yes. Quite nicely. This one is the best specimen, I think," he said, pointing to Minna. "The other seems to have some kind of…mutation."

"True," said Samuel, "but it wasn't all that uncommon where we lived."

"Hmmm," said Tines. "I shall have to weigh the aesthetics and the authenticity. As you know, my master was a stickler for veracity."

The elevator came to a gentle stop. The doors slid open. Mr. Tines exited, followed by Samuel. Teddy coaxed the mules out into the workshop.

"This way," said Tines, heading to a far corner where a large steel cabinet stood. "My subjects will be coming around soon. It's time to administer another soporific."

Samuel and Teddy watched as Mr. Tines opened the steel cabinet. A half dozen shelves contained an impressive array of medical supplies. "My master wasn't sure how long he and his companions might be underground—possibly for several generations. So he planned for just about every conceivable situation. He even stocked embalming fluid. Lucky for me!"

Samuel watched with horror as Tines prepared a sickly green solution in a decanter, and then filled two long syringes with it.

"Is that to embalm them?" he said.

"This? Heavens no. This is another soporific, one the subjects won't wake up from. Once injected, the heart, the lungs, and the other organs will continue to function, but the higher functions of the brain will shut down. Eventually, the bodily mechanisms will cease as well, but this way I will have the time I need to embalm them without worrying about...." The robot mimed holding his nose. "Putrification."

Mr. Tines placed the syringes on a small metal tray, and turned to regard the donkeys. "I'd like to use the same solution for the beasts of burden, but I'm unsure of the dosage. Well, let's worry about that later."

The robot picked up the tray and looked over his shoulder. Its blue eyes glittered cheerily as it addressed Samuel.

"Come then. Let's get to work!"

"Oh. My. God." Leggy's eyes were fixed on the long needle.

Mr. Tines approached the legless old man, who scrambled backward on his hands, until the lascivious robot had walled him into a corner.

Leggy clinched his eyes shut and desperately pushed his thoughts out toward Samuel, unsure if the boy's strange talent worked in reverse, not knowing if Sam could pick up on thoughts directed this way.

SAM DO SOMETHING, Leggy's terrified brain screamed. DON'T LET HIM NEEDLE ME SAMUEL

Samuel looked frantically up at Teddy and Mr. Tines.

"Your companion seems distressed," noticed the robot. "I do believe he has fainted."

"He's afraid of the needle," said Samuel.

"This?" asked Mr. Tines in surprise, looking at the long hypodermic. "But it's not for him." The robot moved closer to Leggy and reached out a hand to the side of his throat, feeling for the old man's thready pulse. "He seems to be convulsing. I believe he needs medical attention."

Leggy clenched his eyes shut as the robot approached. The old man had not had an injection, Hell, he'd not even *seen* a needle, in well over two decades. And for good reason—they tore open deep, painful memories he'd worked hard

SCOTT CHRISTIAN CARR & ANDREW CONRY-MURRAY

to bury, a desperate time of needles and pain that he never wanted to revisit, but now had been exhumed. He remembered the cold leather straps binding his arms and his legs—oh god, his legs!—and he could almost still feel the needles, dozens of them, hundreds it seemed, poking and prying, gouging and sticking and bleeding him until—

Thin, cold metal touched his throat and he screamed. Even the blurry memory of that unspeakable agony was more than he could bear. His heart threatened to burst as adrenalin surged and his brain cramped in singular, atavistic terror. That needle—oh god that sharp, stinging needle, venom-spewing needle—was on his skin. *It was on his skin!* It was searching for his eyes, his veins, the crook of his arm, the soft, sensitive weakness behind his knees. He held his breath in anticipation of the bite and the spreading fire.

"Teddy," he screamed aloud. "Teddy, get him. Don't let him stick me. Kill him, Teddy. Kill him!"

Teddy hit the robot at a full run. Mr. Tines, who'd put a finger to Leggy's neck to feel his pulse, was body-slammed at full-force against the harder than steel nano-crystal window. The cavernous hall echoed with the fury of the impact.

The syringe fell from the automaton's hand and skittered across the floor, stopping at John's feet. Leggy cowered against the wall, whimpering and trembling uncontrollably.

The giant and the mechanical man rebounded from the window and rolled together on the floor. Each desperately groped for a hold, for purchase, for some advantage or weakness in the other. Despite his thin bodice, Mr. Tines proved more than equal to Teddy in strength, easily flipping the gigantic man off him and onto the floor.

Quick as lightning, the robot stood.

He touched a large dent where his head had impacted the floor with a sharp, metallic *clang*. One of his eyes no longer glowed, and the other momentarily flickered before resuming its steady burning light. His immoveable etch grin somehow now evoked an air of menace and mechanical rage.

Teddy sprang to his feet. His fear had turned to anger. He lunged. Wrapping his huge arms around Tines in a bear hug, he lifted the mad robot off the floor.

There was a creaking of metal and Tines moaned. In a slurred mechanical voice, the robot demanded, "You...let...me go! You let...Mr. Tines go... right now!"

Teddy did not let him go. He continued to squeeze.

Mr. Tines slowly raised one mechanical arm. The palm of his hand glowed with a dangerous red energy.

Leggy saw it, but saw it too late. "Teddy," he screamed. "Teddy! His hand...."

The robot pressed his glowing palm to Teddy's temple. The giant screamed in pain and went limp. The robot slipped from his grip. Teddy slumped to the floor, his arms and legs flailing in violent convulsions.

Mr. Tines wobbled on his feet. "Such behavior...is not tolerated...in this museum," he croaked. His one good eye located the syringe at John's feet. The robot reached down, shuffling toward it. "Let us...proceed...with the installation."

Samuel stepped forward. He hoped the panic and desperation he felt wasn't evident in his eyes or voice. "Mr. Tines," the boy began, "it's just occurred to me that something very important is missing. You've left a key display out of your timeline."

The robot stopped. His good eye flickered, grew dim, and then brightened. "Surely, you are in error, young man. Our display is the best, most accurate depiction of the war and the..." his eye briefly dimmed, "and the events leading up to the present day that exists. Anywhere. Period. In the Wasteland or anywhere else. Nothing...is missing."

"Why yes, Mr. Tines, there is. I'm sorry, sir, I don't mean to be critical, but I have studied your display and there most certainly *is* something missing...."

The robot turned and took a step toward Samuel. "You are in error." His voice took on a meaner, impatient edge.

"But the *Dogs of War*—" Samuel started, only to be cut off by Mr. Tines.

"We have three displays depicting the dogs of war, and another *devoted* to them," Tines seemed annoyed. "You really must...pay closer attention."

"Yes, but their power armor and weaponry," Samuel said.

"What of it?" queried the robot.

"Well, where did it come from?"

"What do you mean, where...did it come from? It came from a factory... From...Boeing Industrio-Complex C, to be specific. A subsidiary of the Axel-Fax Corporation."

"Yes," Samuel said. "But who made it? I mean, not who *designed* it, but who specifically mass-produced all the armor and gear for the animals? Who actually *made* it?"

"Well..." the robot stumbled, "factory workers, I suppose. I really don't...have time...for this...." Mr. Tines reached for the syringe.

"Oh," said Samuel. "There were *people* working in the factories? I didn't realize that."

"*Not people!*" snapped Mr. Tines. "Machines. Robots.... Metal workers and automatons at the lower levels...and managerial models and maintenance engineers at the higher levels."

"Like yourself?" asked Samuel.

"No, not like myself. I am...the cutting edge...of robotic AI integration! I...I represent...I rep—" Mr. Tines suddenly stopped speaking. His one blue eye flared impossibly bright—for a moment it seemed as if it would set fire to the inner working of his mechanical head. And then it fluttered, and went dark.

Leggy's eyes were fixed on his reflection in the nano-crystal plate glass window. The scruff of white beard that covered the lower half of his face did little to hide the deep lines that the Wasteland had burrowed in his skin.

The Wasteland, he scoffed. Hell, they'd barely even entered the Wasteland. This strange museum was likely to be the last place even halfway civilized that they'd see for a long, long time. *Civilized*, he thought bitterly. It was that. If nothing else, for all of the robot's flaws, Mr. Tines had, at the very least, conducted himself civilly, with a sense of duty and a respectful, albeit delusional, devotion to his cause.

The robot had had a purpose. The machine had only been trying to do its best under difficult circumstances. That was more than Leggy could say for a lot of the souls he'd encountered in his travels. More than he could say for his own weary band of travelers, if he was to be honest.

The dark memories of needles and pain still lingered in his mind, stirred by the metal curator. Leggy squeezed his eyes shut and tried to force those memories back into the deep well he'd sunk for them all those years ago.

He swallowed and took a deep breath, using his diaphragm, and tried once again with mental palms to push those memories down into calm, unthinking stillness. He felt his body begin to relax as he slowly let the air from his lungs. The bad memories—just balloons floating in his mind, easy to pop or send drifting away on the current of the wind. It was an old trick, something he'd picked up from the Bedouins.

He knew what lay ahead, or at least he had a sense of the vast, growing danger of the deep wastes. And more importantly, he knew that the others did not. Sure, they realized that their road—Ha! Soon enough, there'd be precious few *roads*—was a dangerous one. But did any of them truly understand just how dangerous?

How could they when this had all been their idea, hatched in the paranoid, tormented mind of Derek. It wasn't anymore about *going*, so much as it was about *running away*. And the entire fantastical adventure was really only old Leggy's mission. His *final* mission. His *suicide* mission. They were just along for the ride.

Leggy knew that they would soon see the true madness of post-nuke America—not the bugs and the radiation poisoning and the muties and starving throw-down grovels and shit-towns, but true evil. Only in the deep Wasteland had the mind of man been so utterly corrupted, so maddened by isolation, the sun, and the nuclear fire, that it had actually turned in on itself. Much like the tattoo on the belly of a whore that he'd once seen in Santa Cruz. A serpent swallowing its own tail, eating itself. To Leggy, that image, more than anything else he'd ever laid eyes upon, truly captured the stark, inhuman reality of the Wasteland.

Jesus H. Christ! Leggy shook himself from his morbid thoughts. *That metal fucknut really did a number on me.*

"We done looking?" Derek demanded. "I've had about enough of this crackpot museum."

For once, everyone agreed.

Leggy gazed one last time through his own reflection in the glass. A factory diorama had been constructed in the display case. The rear wall had been painted with the logo of the *Axel-Fax Corporation,* an unclosed circle with an arrow tip bridging the gap.

Kinda like a snake eating itself, thought Leggy.

Inside the circle was the corporate slogan: EXCELLENCE IN EXECUTION!

In the foreground ran a conveyor belt, fed by the museum's enormous supply of spare parts. The parts were attended to by Mr. Tines, who hunched with purpose over the conveyor belt.

The robot's hands moved in a blur of motion, grabbing parts as they came, binding them together with strange, electronic tools. Twisting and screwing, soldering and wiring. The robot, with great attention to detail and authenticity, assembled faux gasmasks and rebreathers, guns, flame-throwers, ammunition. He would do this until the end of time—or until his arms rusted and fell from his body.

Or until his master returned to save him.

CHAPTER TWENTY-SIX

As they passed through the motor pool to the elevator, Samuel pointed to the massive sand crawler. Leggy and Derek looked at the machine, and then at each other.

The two men strode over to investigate. Derek boosted Leggy into the passenger seat then walked around to the driver's side. He climbed in and tentatively put his hands on the steering wheel.

"You ever drive somethin' like this?" asked Derek, eying the control panel.

"Sure," said Leggy. "I mean, not this kind of vehicle exactly, but I think we can figure it out."

"Assuming it still runs," said Derek.

"Right," said Leggy. "Now then. See them pedals at your feet? The right one's probably for go, and the left one's probably for stop."

Derek tentatively pushed down the right pedal. Nothing happened. He looked up at Leggy.

"Well, we got to start her up first." The old man pointed to a green button that stuck out slightly from the steering column. "Try that one."

Derek held down the button. The engine whirred and squealed, a long high note that made his companions clap their hands over their ears. Then it stopped. Derek moved to push the button again but Leggy stayed his hand.

"Hold on," said the old man with a grin. "Feel that?"

Derek sat still. His seat was vibrating almost imperceptibly, as was the steering wheel in his hand.

"What happened?"

Leggy laughed. "It works, that's what. We got juice, boy!"

Samuel started to climb into the back of the sand crawler, but Leggy waved him off. "You all stand back. Let Derek here get a feel for the wheel."

The group moved away from the vehicle, giving Derek a wide berth. He looked at Leggy, who pointed to a lever that stuck up from a panel down by Derek's right leg.

"I'll wager this way is reverse, and this way is probably forward," said Leggy, gesturing to the shifter. "Give it a try."

Derek moved the lever. The sand crawler started to roll forward. Derek, meaning to press the brake, touched the wrong pedal with his foot. The sand crawler lurched forward then jerked to a halt as Derek found the brake. He looked sheepishly at Leggy, who had braced his arms on the dashboard. Derek expected the old man to taunt him.

Leggy just chuckled. "Don't worry, son, you'll get it. Just take it easy for now."

The others watched as Derek grew more confident. Soon the crawler was sweeping through the motor pool, Derek steering with easy grace.

"That'll do," said Leggy as Derek rolled up to their waiting companions. "Hop aboard everybody. Ted, get them donkeys in the back and tie their halters, would ya?"

The bed of the crawler was metal and smooth, with a sand-colored canvas canopy over it to provide shade. Behind the cab was a bench seat that doubled as a storage locker. As Teddy and John struggled to get Minna and Afha into the flatbed, Samuel poked through the locker. It was neatly compartmentalized, and it held a tool set, a first aid kit, rope, a pair of flashlights similar to the battery-less one they'd left at Youslus's cave, a dozen foil-wrapped packages of rations, a ten-liter water jug, and a funny-looking pistol. He hauled out the jug and passed it to John.

"I think there's a spigot over there," said Samuel, pointing to the far wall of the motor pool.

John carried the jug away to fill it up.

Then Samuel picked up the gun and tapped on the back window of the cab.

Leggy turned around.

"What's this, Mr. Nicodemus?" asked Samuel, shouting to be heard through the glass.

"I believe that there is a flare pistol," shouted Leggy. "Shoots a rocket in the sky that makes a big light, so's people can find you if you ever get lost."

Samuel nodded and placed it carefully back in the locker—he wasn't sure who would come to find them, no matter how lost they were.

Derek stuck his head out of the driver's window. "You all loaded up yet?"

"Okee-dokee, Der Der," shouted Teddy, who was simultaneously tying Afha's halter to the rail and giving his brothers a thumbs up.

John returned with the water, which they stowed under the seat.

Derek steered over to the elevator. Teddy hopped down to press the button and then hopped back in.

The group ascended in the miraculous elevator, rising out of the dark hole in the ground and into the bright, glaring sun of the great wastes. They set out on their road again, leaving the Folly of Man behind them.

Through trial and error Derek found that thirty was the top speed he could push from the crawler and still keep it on the road. The old asphalt was cracked and pitted with holes. The first time he'd hit a hole of substantial size, he'd nearly spilled his passengers from the cab. The speedometer had markings up to 100. His foot itched to push the go pedal down to the floor. He contented himself with the twin delights of forward motion and absolute control. Maybe later he'd let John drive—maybe.

The desert sped past, a hard-packed scrubland of pale brown. To his left, he saw the shoulders of a mountain range at the edge of the horizon and to his right a wide-open infinity of hot, dry emptiness. Leggy, fiddling with some controls on the dashboard, figured out a way to make cold air blow on them. It was a magnificent sensation.

His entire upbringing had taught Derek to respect the desert, because otherwise it would kill him. But something about the crawler, about the speed, about the sense of having such a powerful machine at his command infected him with a giddy hubris. He could outrun the Wasteland, outrun the heat and the dryness and the death. Derek flipped the bird at the scrubland outside the window.

For the first time in many, many days, he actually believed that they could make it to New York. Though he would rarely admit it to himself, he'd figured it for a fool's errand from the very beginning—better to try and die in the attempt than to rot away in San Muyamo. But now, with his hands on the controls of this magnificent vehicle, he allowed himself a measure of hope.

He looked over at Leggy. The old man was asleep, his head tipped sideways against the passenger window, his mouth slack and drooling.

Derek turned his attention back to the road, savoring the sensation of movement in silence.

They stopped at dusk. Derek steered the crawler behind a trio of boulders that sat off the shoulder of the road. His passengers were happy to dismount, their bodies cramped and sore from the jarring ride. Sheba ran in circles around the camp, sniffing out a perimeter and barking happily. Minna and Afha nosed around the sagebrush that cropped up around the boulders.

"Goddam, that's what I call travelin'!" said Derek. "If we tried to walk half that far in a day, we'd end up looking like Leggy."

Teddy and John snorted, and even Leggy had to grin at the jibe. "It's true," he said, "ain't no better way to get around."

They set about making camp. John, Teddy, and Magdalena examined a nearby mesquite thicket for brushwood. Derek set out snares. Samuel scrambled up a boulder and surveyed the landscape. Leggy hoisted himself into the bed of the crawler to rummage through the supply trunk.

By nightfall they had a good fire going. After some debate, they decided to eat from the store of supplies they'd brought from Moses Springs and save the strange, foil-wrapped food in the crawler's trunk for later.

"What about them snares?" asked Derek.

"We'll see what's in 'em in the morning," said Leggy. "Wouldn't mind a little skinned hare for breakfast."

After eating, they stayed around the fire. No one spoke—they were weary from the travel and from the ordeal under the ground. Samuel was the first to succumb to sleep, followed quickly by Teddy, then Derek soon after.

Only Leggy was awake to notice when John and Magdalena quietly moved their bedrolls to the crawler's flatbed.

"Good," he thought, laying on his back, watching the magnificent night sky. "Let them have their time. Let's all have an interlude—a bit of rest from our worries." Then he took his own advice, and sank into sleep.

In the morning they checked the snares. Leggy would have to wait for a taste of hare—all they found in the wires was a trio of desert gophers. "Sand rats," said Leggy, rolling his eyes. The old man skinned and cooked them anyway and then shared them out. Samuel took one bite—the flesh was gritty and gamey, little better than a mouthful of sand. He tossed the remainder to Sheba and then rooted around in one of the panniers for a better option.

Derek watched the boy and shook his head. "Goddam, kid. If my dad ever saw me throw meat to a dog and then go look for somethin' better, I wouldn't have teeth to eat with."

Samuel looked up from the supply chest, a hard roll and a dried apple in hand. "It tastes bad," he said.

Derek laughed. John, who was watching carefully, winced at the sound.

"Sure it tastes bad," said Derek. He took a bite off the bone and swallowed it. "It tastes like shit. But you don't ever waste food. Ever. You understand me?"

Samuel looked at Derek for a long moment. The others held their breath. Then Samuel dropped his head. "I'm sorry," he said quietly. "I understand."

"What do you understand?" said Derek.

Samuel glanced at the others, but no one moved to intervene. Then he looked at the ground. "I understand not to waste food."

"Even if it tastes bad?" said Derek, mimicking Samuel's high-pitched voice.

"Yes," said Samuel. He dumped his breakfast back in the panniers and then walked away.

"Fuckin' mutie," muttered Derek. He tossed the bones on the cookfire and stood up. "Well, what're we waitin' for? Let's get this goddam party rolling."

As the crawler rolled on down the road, John moved next to Samuel. They, along with Magdalena, Teddy and the animals, shared the flatbed of the crawler.

The little boy kicked sullenly at the storage locker. The flatbed had a canvas cover to keep off the sun, and Samuel had removed his makeshift turban. John stared at the smooth, veiny skin stretched over the boy's oddly shaped skull.

"Hey, Sam. Maggie said I should come and talk to you." John had to raise his voice to be heard over the noise of their rough passage.

Samuel didn't look up. He continued kicking the locker.

"I mean, in case you were feelin' bad or something."

Samuel turned his head away.

John sighed. He waited a minute and then said, "You grew up in that bunker, right?"

Samuel looked up. That wasn't a question he'd expected. "It wasn't a bunker. It was an underground research center with built-in living facilities."

"But you lived there your whole life?"

"Yes," said Samuel.

"You ever spend any time above ground?"

"A few times. Karen…my caretaker brought me up for a geology lesson. Once, before the war, we camped out for a night."

Before the war? How old was this kid? John wondered. By all accounts, the War proper had been a little more or a little less than a century ago. And Samuel looked like a child—sounded and acted like a child, but…before the bombs fell? Christ! "Did you ever go hungry? Ever miss a meal?"

Samuel looked back down at his feet. "No."

"Ever had to fight someone for your food?"

Samuel shook his head.

John sighed. "Well that's my point. You had it easy back in the...the research center. But nothing's easy out here. If Derek's harsh on you it's because he's right. He's tryin' to teach you."

Now Samuel looked up at John. "But why does he hate me?"

"He don't hate you," said John, though he wasn't sure it was true. "You got things to learn, and he's teachin' you the only way he knows how."

"Bullshit," shouted Samuel, and the expletive surprised them both. "I can feel his hate," said the boy. "If I fell off this crawler he wouldn't even slow down if you and Mr. Nicodemus weren't around."

John pursed his lips. "Listen, Sam. I don't know what you can feel, but I know Derek. I grew up with him. This is just his way with people."

"It's not his way with you. Or Maggie. Or Mr. Nicodemus."

John laughed. "Sam, you think Leggy volunteered for this trip? No sir. Derek up and kidnapped that old man."

"Kidnapped?" said Samuel.

"Put a knife to his throat, tied him up, and pushed him right out of San Muyamo."

"But why?"

"Well, that's a good question," said John. "Sometimes he does stuff just because he gets so angry it makes him crazy. But other times there's a good reason behind the craziness. Like takin' Leggy. It took me a while to figure out, but now I understand. It was for me and Teddy."

Samuel shook his head. "What do you mean?"

John pushed his hair back from his face. "That anger in Derek, it's like this machine. It's powerful. And it drives him. It will drive him from here to New York, even if it means going for days and days without food or shelter. Even if it means crawling a thousand miles on his hands and knees."

"But me and Teddy, we ain't like him. We're baggage. We're draggin' along behind him, lettin' his engine pull us."

"So he wants to get rid of you too?" asked Samuel.

"Nah, nothin' like that," said John. "He wants us to make it. The difference is that if it came down to it, Derek could get to New York by himself. He could do it alone. But not me, and not Teddy. If we were alone out here, we'd be vulture food in about three days. So that's why he took Leggy. The old man knows stuff, stuff that gives me and Teddy a chance, a slim chance, to survive. The old man's here to carry the baggage."

Samuel was quiet for a long while. John let him be. The boy was smart enough to figure out how he fit into the picture.

"And I'm baggage, too," said Samuel. "Another person dragging along behind him."

John nodded. "Derek don't hate you. Hate's too personal. You got to put a lot of thought, a lot of feeling, into hatin' someone."

Samuel thought that, on this point, John was wrong—he was quite certain that Derek hated him, that hating was easy for him.

"But I saved him," whimpered Samuel. "I saved you all.... If it wasn't for me, you'd be museum exhibits."

"Yeah, well, I wouldn't wait around for him to send a thank-you card," said John.

"Maybe next time I'll save everybody *but* him," said the boy.

John laughed, but inside the idea bothered him. He feared that Sam was serious.

CHAPTER TWENTY-SEVEN

On their fourth day from the museum, Derek let John take a turn at the wheel. He rode up front for an hour, keeping an eye on him, but John quickly mastered the basic operations. Once Derek was confident that John wouldn't wreck the crawler, he had him pull over. Derek climbed out and let Maggie and Samuel ride on the bench seat next to John. Sheba also leapt into the front seat with her master.

"Check this out," said Derek, once everyone was settled. He reached across the two passengers and flipped the switch for the cold air blower.

"Praise the Lord!" shouted John as the deliciously chilled air swirled around him. Maggie reached out a hand to feel the current that pushed out from the blower and sighed.

"Merry Christmas," said Derek with a wry grin. He slammed the door and climbed up onto the flatbed, pushing past the mules who sat with their halters tied to the side rail. He squeezed onto the bench seat between Teddy and Leggy then turned around and tapped on the rear window of the cab.

"Fire it up, and let's roll!"

The vehicle lurched forward, and quickly they were on their way again. As the sand crawler rumbled and shook down the road, Leggy grimaced.

"A Hell of a lot more comfortable in there," said the old man, jerking his thumb at the cab.

"Gettin' soft already, huh?" said Derek. But he was glad that the old man had said it first.

Just before noon the road passed between a pair of rocky hills. Shadows fell on the vehicle. Derek poked his head out of the canvas canopy and scanned the hillsides.

"I could use a rest stop," said Leggy, "if that's what you're lookin' for."

"I am," said Derek. "But let's wait till we get through this. I don't like the idea of bein' boxed in between these hills."

"Yeah, I guess you're right," said Leggy. He had to piss bad, and the rattling of the sand crawler wasn't helping matters. But he was pleased to see Derek being cautious, and he certainly wasn't going to discourage it.

Ten minutes later, the hills began to slope gently downward, and soon the crawler emerged onto open road again. Derek turned to tap on the glass and signal a halt when Afha, the donkey, wobbled to his feet and began to bray.

"Probably gotta take a piss as bad as I do," said Leggy. Then he saw the donkey's mutated third eye swirling madly. He looked at Derek. "Do you..."

Suddenly, the ground on both sides of the road erupted in a flurry of segmented legs and clacking mandibles.

"Bugs!" shouted Teddy as the donkey went wild with panic.

"Go go go go go!" screamed Derek, pounding on the rear window of the cab. John had also seen the creatures scuttling up out of the ground. He slammed the go pedal to the floor. The crawler leapt forward. Leggy tumbled down the length of the flatbed and crashed into Afha, knocking the donkey down.

A bug slashed through the canopy, hissing as it scrambled into the flatbed. Teddy struck at it with a wrench that had fallen loose but couldn't get his full force behind a blow, the crawler was jostling so badly.

A second bug skittered up over the tailgate and landed on top of Afha and Leggy, who were still in a tangle. A third leaped onto the canopy above their heads—they could see it writhing, a wormy shadow through the canvas.

Derek skidded down the flatbed to help the old man, who was in as much danger from Afha's hooves as he was from the bug. The crawler bounced once—a high, hard jolt that nearly threw Derek out of the flatbed. John was driving straight over the bugs in his path. Derek grabbed for a railing as the crawler bounced twice more. The impact flipped the giant insect in the flatbed onto its back. Before it could turn over, Derek snatched his knife from his wrist sheath and drove it repeatedly into the creature's soft underbelly.

Leggy wormed free of the donkey. He grabbed the tailgate and pulled himself to his knees. Dozens of bugs were in pursuit, hissing and chattering, but the sand crawler was outpacing them.

Suddenly, the crawler stopped short. Leggy slid up the length of the bed and slammed into the bench seat.

"What the fuck!" shouted Derek, who had also fallen over. "Drive, you asshole, drive!"

The sand crawler lurched forward again—and stalled. Leggy looked up as another bug tumbled through the canopy. It landed upright and raised its claws.

John was pounding on the start button, stomping on the go pedal—frantically trying to get the sand crawler moving.

Leggy flipped up the bench seat and pulled the flare gun from the storage locker. The creature pounced, its mandibles wide. Leggy's arm disappeared inside the bug's maw up to the elbow.

With a start, the crawler's engine roared back to life and the truck lurched forward.

"Gaaahhhh," screamed Leggy and the bug began to bite down on his arm. He pulled the trigger.

The blast knocked the creature back to the tailgate. The flare exploded, dousing the flatbed in burning phosphorus. But still the creature charged. Leggy watched dumbly as burning death descended upon him. Suddenly, strong hands grasped the nightmare insect. Teddy screamed in rage and in pain as he flung the burning monster from the truck. It crashed through the torn canvas out onto the scrubland and moved no more.

Derek looked behind them. The bugs had not given up pursuit but were falling rapidly behind. He could see sunlight glinting off the polished armor of their midsections, and their legs churning up dust in their fury over lost prey.

"Did we outrun 'em? Did we outrun 'em?" John gripped the steering wheel with white-knuckled hands—his eyes locked on the black strip of the road as he sped onward.

"I don't know," said Magdalen, clutching Sheba. "Sam, what's happening back there?"

But the boy said nothing. His eyes were fixed on the windshield. A crack ran straight down the middle of the window, like a jagged flash of lightening captured in glass. A monster had leapt right at them, right at *him*, and had nearly made it through the windshield. Samuel had seen its mandibles, its eager mouth—wet and pulsating and filled with serrated cilia. If John hadn't stomped on the brakes and sent the monster skittering off of the hood, it would've bashed through the glass and...and....

From the back of the crawler had come a sound like a gunshot. Light filled the cabin as the crawler swerved crazily. John fought for control and slowly eased the vehicle to a halt.

"Wait here," he said and leapt from the cab. He ran around to the flatbed. The canopy was shredded, and parts of it were burning.

Teddy was sitting in the back, weeping, his hands held up painfully before him—the skin was red and peeling with blisters. Leggy lay on his stomach, the back of his shirt sliced open, his back riddled with lacerations. He held his bloody hand where the creature had bitten him. Derek had a black eye, and his forearms were streaked with gore.

In the back of the truck Afha sat in a pool of blood, braying softly. Minna shook and trembled.

John noticed that the flatbed was tilted at an odd angle—the rear wheel on the driver's side was a shapeless mass of smoking rubber treads tangled around a crumpled steel rim.

"Holy Jesus," said John. He ran back to the cab. "C'mon, they're hurt!" he shouted.

John's words galvanized Samuel. He remembered the first aid kit under the bench seat. He scuttled around to the flatbed and found the pack. He searched through its contents and began tossing items to John.

Then he turned to Teddy, a small squeeze bottle in one hand.

"Does it hurt, Teddy?" said Samuel.

Teddy nodded, tears streaking his dirty cheeks.

"Try this. I think it's medicine, okay?" said the boy.

Teddy shied away, lifting his hands above Samuel's head. "Don't want medicine. Medicine hurts."

"Not this," said Samuel, spraying bit onto his own tiny finger. "It's a foam. It feels cool, like water. It'll make the pain go away and help your skin grow back."

Teddy shook his head.

"How about if we just try one hand first?" said Samuel. "Just a little bit. If you don't like it, we'll forget it."

Teddy thought. Tentatively he lowered one hand. Samuel sprayed a small amount of pink foam onto the big man's enormous pinky. Teddy winced, then relaxed.

Samuel covered the palms and fingers with a thick layer of the foam. "Here. Now put these on," said Samuel. He pulled another packet out of the medical kit and tore it open. Inside were two gauzy white bandages like mittens. He frowned, realizing there was no way that Teddy's humongous paws would fit inside the mitts. He had to make do with cutting the gloves into strips and taping the material over the worst of Teddy burns.

In the meantime, Derek and Magdalena tended to Afha. Derek shooed Minna out of the flatbed then held Afha still as Magdalena probed his wound.

"It's deep, but I don't think it's fatal," she said. Samuel brought bandages to them, and Magdalena carefully pressed them to the donkey's wound and held them with long strips torn from the canvas and wrapped around the donkey's girth.

Derek hopped out of the truck and examined the damage to the wheel. Leggy limped over on his hands, each swing causing him to wince in pain.

"We can't stop here," said Derek. "Still too close to that bug nest."

197

Leggy nodded.

"We'll have to divide up the gear between us. You can ride Minna. We'll have to put that other donkey down."

Leggy started to speak, but Derek held up a hand. "I know it ain't too bad a wound. If we had two or three days to rest and let it recover, that'd be different. But we don't." Already, in the distant hills, they could see the reflected march of the soldier bugs descending the broken highway.

Now Leggy laughed. Derek turned, a hot flush rising in his cheeks. He knew that laugh: it meant Leggy was about to point out his ignorance.

"You're too quick to give up this here ride," said Leggy. "Ain't you ever heard of a spare?" The old man pointed to the underside of the flatbed.

Derek crouched down and saw it—a pair of balloon tires strapped to the underside by thick canvas webbing.

"But how to do we—?" Derek started and then shut his mouth again. In between the two tires was a metal contraption with a crank handle. He was so pleased to think they might be riding again that he forgot his anger.

"You, me, and Johnny will have to do this," said Leggy. "Ted's out of commission for the time bein'. And we'll have to work fast."

They did work fast. Ten minutes later Derek and John were hot, sweating, and smeared with axle grease. They drank deeply from their canteens and quickly scrubbed off as best they could with a combination of sand and the alkaline juice from a barrel cactus. And then Derek was behind the wheel once again. He drove until well after dark, letting the sand crawler's headlights guide him along the road.

Several days later, Leggy scratched absently at his back, feeling the hard ribbons of scar tissue that had formed where the bug had cut into him. *The Wasteland keeps knockin' us down, and so far we keep gettin' up,* he thought. *So far, at least.*

Teddy seemed all right, though he complained that his hands were still tender. And that old donkey was a tough son of a bitch—they'd taken his bandage off last night, revealing a long angry slash of new pink skin on his flank. The donkey had sniffed it and then brayed defiantly. Derek had re-christened the beast "Scar."

Since the bug attack, the road had been easy and uneventful. No one spoke much, particularly young Samuel. Leggy heard the boy whimpering each night, and once the child had sat up and screamed, a shrill, high sound that cut through Leggy's sleep like a guillotine. He knew why. The boy who could share his thoughts could also share his nightmares. At the same moment the boy had screamed, Leggy saw in his own mind a horrific bug poised to pounce and devour.

The fear was normal, thought Leggy, but Samuel had shared something else—the realization that death could come so suddenly and so easily out here. It was a shock and a reality check for him. The boy knew about death—he was always talkin' about storybooks with battles and great adventures and utmost peril. But now death was real to Samuel, and his mind was tryin' to make room for that fact.

We're all the heroes of our own stories, thought Leggy, and heroes are supposed to live happily ever after, at least in the story books. But the Wasteland keeps its own book, and writes its own endings.

Leggy was stirred from his reverie by a sudden shout from Derek. The sand crawler stopped, and Leggy poked his head around the side of the trailer to see what was going on. That's when he saw the minor miracle.

CHAPTER TWENTY-EIGHT

The only thing stranger than the tree growing in the middle of the barren desert was the man climbing it.

The tree was tall and, unbelievably, full of lush, green leaves. They could see it from nearly a mile off, but it wasn't until they'd gotten within a hundred yards that they saw the small house and tiny shed nearby. And it wasn't until they were almost upon it that they had noticed a man in the tree's upper branches.

Derek stopped the crawler, and they all got out. The sun was setting, and the last rays of the day framed the old black man high above them.

"Hello, I'm Jordan," he called out. He carried a length of frayed rope on his shoulder and was rather frayed himself. His clothes were sun-faded and torn in places. His ebony skin was slick with sweat. And they could smell the rank odor from his armpits wafting down to them.

And he was a *talker*—an ardent and garrulous practitioner of soliloquy. None of the travelers had even been able to introduce themselves, nor had they been asked to.

Jordan worked the rope as he spoke, measuring lengths by holding it between outstretched hands, feet balanced expertly on the thick branches of the tree. He looped one end of the rope over a stout branch and secured it with a strong knot.

"Pleased ta meetcha, I am. That's to be sure! Where're you folks comin' from? Wait, don't tell me, lemme guess. Moses Springs! Ha ha. Where else?

"Me? I'm just throwin' some rope. What else am I gonna do? Got no wife, no kids. Not no more, I don't. Sure! Just me and the tree, me and the tree. I watered this damned thing every single fucking day for fifty fuckin' years and what'd it get me? Do you think this thing ever bore a fruit that wasn't grainy or filled with worms? Nope. Not a one. It's an apple tree, but ya wouldn't know it." The man smacked the trunk with frustrated affection.

"But now why bother? I say, what's the point? Got no wife, got no kids. Not no more, I don't. Yeah, they're dead. You guessed it. Dead and gone. They killed 'em. Ha! An' they'll probably kill you good folks too, if ya keep headin' where you're headin'. Sure! Or if they don't kill ya and eat ya, maybe they'll make pets outta ya. Yeah, they just might, especially the big'un." The man winked at Teddy. "They do that, dontcha know. Eat ya. Kill ya. Make a pet outta ya!"

He laughed. "Keep people as pets. No lie. Don't believe me? You c'mon up here. Ya can just barely see 'em from up here. Yeah, they murdered Ruth and Josh and Mary-Lou, right in my front yard here. I was in the shed, pulling water from the well for this goddamned, accursed, mother-fucker of an apple tree. They didn't know I was here. And I couldn't do a goddamned thing but watch them murder and butcher and slice up my family. For food, ya see. That's what they do. If they don't keep ya as pets, that is."

The man's eyes took on a faraway look. "Well, good day to ya," he called cheerfully, waved, then slipped a loop of rope around his neck and stepped from the branch.

There was a sickening *pop* as the vertebrae of his neck separated, and then the rope creaked on the wood as Jordan's lifeless body swung gently in the still air, the muscles of his legs twitching.

For a long, shocked moment, no one spoke. Samuel pressed his face into Magdalena's side, refusing to look.

Finally, Derek broke the silence. "Well," he said, his voice cracking. He cleared his throat before continuing. "I'm gonna climb up there and see what this crazy old shit was yabbering about."

He started toward the tree and stopped again as Jordan's booted feet swung slowly toward him, and then away again, then toward him, then away, like a compass needle seeking north.

"Maybe ah…maybe we ought to cut him down first," he said. The others nodded.

Teddy boosted Derek onto a branch. Derek reached out and snagged the rope. The taut fibers transmitted the weight of the dead man up to Derek's hand, making his flesh crawl. He sawed through the thick strands, and Teddy lowered the body gently to the ground. Jordan's eyes bulged in their sockets, and his mouth was wide, as if he'd had one last thing to say. Leggy closed the man's eyes.

John rocked back and forth on his feet. "What do we do with him?"

"There's a hole around the other side of the tree," called Derek from his perch. "Dirt looks freshly dug."

Leggy nodded to Teddy and John.

John blanched but did as he was told. They moved gingerly around the wide trunk and returned a few minutes later, their hands and faces smeared with dirt.

"He dug his own grave," said John, wiping his hands repeatedly on his pants. "A grave and a shovel, so we put him in. I said a prayer for him."

"What kinda madman digs himself a grave and then hangs himself all alone?" Leggy wondered aloud. No one answered.

In the meantime Derek had scaled the tree, moving carefully from branch to branch. Though he'd never climbed a tree before, it was remarkably similar to scaling the crane in The Heap back in San Muyamo. He stopped about three quarters of the way to the top. His companions were hidden from view by the leaves, but he guessed he'd come about twenty-five or thirty feet off the ground. A slight wave of vertigo rolled through him. He clutched the trunk more firmly and let his eyes roam across the landscape.

A distant structure caught his attention to the southeast, the direction that the strange man had indicated, the direction that they were heading. He took out his telescope for a closer look.

"Holy shit," Derek muttered, his hands trembling and causing the spyglass to waver. What he saw through it was too bizarre, too disturbing, to relate to the others in shouts and hollers from the top of the impossible tree. He would fill them in once he'd descended. But first, he had to take another look.

A low, concrete building was surrounded by what appeared to be chain-link fence, several miles distant. Standing atop the building—*not a building, a fort*, thought Derek—were three figures dressed entirely in black. Each wore some sort of device over his face, bulging glass eyes with tubes and nozzles trailing down. Rebreathers. Each had a rifle strapped to his back.

But strangest of all were the people down on the ground, within the confines of the fence. Three men and a woman, Derek could see. They were stark naked, and staggered around on all fours as animals would. Collars had been fitted around their necks, and muzzles over their mouths, giving them a disturbing, snout-like appearance. They were staked to the wall of the small building by chains fastened to the collars around their necks. Derek watched as one of the men scratched his own cheek with his foot, and another turned his muzzle to sniff at the groveling woman's buttocks. Derek was ashamed to discover that he had an erection.

After carefully collapsing the spyglass and placing it back in the folds of his clothes where it belonged, Derek descended from the tree and found his companions gone.

Those fuckers abandoned me, was the first thought that flashed into his mind. *Those weirdos got them*, was the second.

But the crawler was still there, and then he heard laughter—the high-pitched giggle of the kid and then Teddy's deep, donkey-like bray. It was coming from around the other side of the house.

Derek walked around and saw everyone stripped to their drawers—excepting Magdalena, who wore a knee-length slip. He cast his eyes away when he saw how the wet fabric clung to her torso.

The group stood on a small patio of flat, neatly laid stone and were splashing each other with water from a big aluminum bucket. They were all soaking wet. Even Sheba the dog had consented to a bath. She stood to one side, vigorously shaking water from her sopping fur.

Teddy emerged from a small shed next to the patio. He carried another bucket, water sloshing over the sides. Then he upended it over John and Magdalena, who were standing close together as Maggie scrubbed John's back with a white cakey substance. Soap!

Teddy saw his brother. "Look, Der-Der. We're havin' bathtime!"

"There's a well in the shed," said John.

"C'mon son," said Leggy, who was soaping up his white hair and grizzled beard. "Feels damn good to be clean again."

Derek hesitated. Teddy put another brimming bucket down in front of him. He reached his hand into the water. It was cool and clean.

What the Hell, he thought. *Guess I can talk and wash at the same time.* He shucked off his boots and then stripped down to his underwear. Then he bent down and plunged his head straight into the bucket. He emerged spluttering and shook his head, spattering droplets across the warm stones of the patio.

"What'd you see up there?" asked Leggy, passing the soap.

Derek was quiet for a moment, and then he began to speak. The group's laughter died away as he described the armed figures and their strange captives.

"Shit," said Leggy after Derek had finished his tale. "I was hoping to spend the night under a roof."

"You think we should move on?" asked John, absently wringing water from his long hair.

"Hell yeah," said Leggy. "I thought that old coot in the tree was just crazy. But it sounds like he was telling the truth."

"We'll have to take a detour," said Derek. "That bunker sits right on the road."

"Which is more dangerous?" asked Magdelena, her blank eyes fixed on Leggy. "Staying here until morning or traveling the Wasteland at night?"

"She's got a point," said John. "What's the chance those gunmen would come back? They already think they killed the folks living here."

Leggy pursed his lips. The sun had gone down and the brightest of the evening stars had already appeared. He looked at the landscape, pointed to the low hills to the north. "We don't have to travel all night. I bet we could put them hills between us and the fort in a couple of hours. Then we hunker down till morning and take the long way 'round."

"Sounds good to me," said Derek. "Anybody else who's got objections should climb that tree and see what I saw."

"All right, let's dry off and get dressed," said Leggy. "It's a damn shame though. I was hopin' to wash these clothes." He looked askance at his dingy shirt and pants.

Derek snorted. "Old man, the only thing holdin' them rags together is the dirt and the stink."

Teddy and Samuel laughed out loud. Leggy shook his head.

When they'd dressed, Leggy suggested topping off their jugs with well water.

John and Teddy drew water and carried buckets to the tank. Samuel and Magdalena tried to coax the mules back aboard the crawler. The beasts had been nibbling green leaves from the lowest branches of Jordan's tree.

Leggy and Derek waited by the driver's seat. "How much longer you think this thing's gonna run?" asked Derek.

"Don't know," said Leggy. "Not forever. I'm not even sure what it runs *on*—not gas. Maybe 'lectricity. I honestly don't know. There's a gauge inside I been keepin' my eye on. When we started it was all the way to the right. Now it's more'n three quarters of the way to the left. I 'spect when it goes all the way left, the crawler will stop. I ain't lookin' forward to gettin' up on the back of a donkey again. But we definitely got enough juice to slide past that bunker you told us about, and for now that's all that concerns me."

"Me too," said Derek. "I—"

"There's men coming," shrieked Samuel, standing in the flatbed. "I can sense men coming!"

"Shit," said Derek. He lifted Leggy off the ground and shoved him inside the cab then jumped into the driver's seat and started the motor.

"Wait," said John. "Teddy's still in the shed drawing water."

"Go and get him," hissed Derek.

John sprinted for the shed.

Magdalena drew her long rifle from a web of netting along the left side of the flatbed's rail. Suddenly Sheba turned toward the shed and started barking.

A group of men emerged from the twilight shadows behind the house. They were armed, and John and Teddy walked ahead of them with their hands laced behind their heads.

The group stopped ten paces from the sand crawler. Derek counted six of them. They wore wide-brimmed hats and long, brown, handwoven ponchos. They carried hunting rifles and shotguns, and one man had what Leggy recognized as a grenade launcher slung across his shoulders.

"Are they the ones from the bunker?" whispered Leggy.

"No," said Derek.

The men's rough faces were exposed beneath the wide brims of their hats. They didn't wear the strange rebreathers that Derek had described on the men of the distant outpost.

John and Teddy were pushed to their knees. Then the tallest of the men stepped forward. He carried a rifle that was, for the time being, pointed toward the ground.

"Where's Jordan?" he asked, his eyes hard. "Where's Ruth and the children?"

Standing in the flatbed, Magdalena trained in on the sound of the man's voice, her rifle at the ready. In turn, three men aimed up at her.

"Who're you?" demanded Derek.

"The name's Burrell," said the tall man. "Captain Burrell. And I'll only ask you one more time—where's Jordan?"

"Dead," said Derek. "Hung himself. The rope's still in the tree, and his body's buried in the roots."

"Ruth? The children?"

"The old man said raiders came for 'em," Leggy called out. "The ones from that bunker down the road."

Burrell tipped his head sideways. One of the men approached, and Burrell whispered to him. The man lit a lantern and went inside the house. Derek watched the light leak through open windows as the man searched the house. He emerged a few minutes later and walked in a slow circle around the tree, squatting for a moment beside the fresh grave. Then he returned to Burrell and spoke quietly into his captain's ear. Burrell listened, nodded, and then turned to face the cab of the sand crawler.

"Step out of the vehicle one at a time. The woman with the rifle will go first. Put your hands behind your heads. Kneel next to your companions here."

"Fuck you," said Derek. "You ain't in charge of us, and we ain't done nothin' wrong."

"Easy, easy," whispered Leggy.

"What you have or haven't done is still to be decided," said Burrell. "But we've got six rifles to your one. We are in charge."

"I'll send you straight to Hell," said Magdalena from the crawler bed, "and then we'll see who's in charge."

"And then it will be five rifles against none and all of you in Hell with me," said Burrell.

"Maggie, put the rifle down," said Leggy.

"No," shouted Derek. "Don't you dare!"

Magdalena stood firm but inside she was wavering.

"John," she called. "Are you all right?"

"Yes, Magdalena," she heard him reply. And then she jumped as a voice rang out inside her heard.

MAGDALENA—I CAN KILL A MAN MAYBE TWO IF YOU TELL ME WHICH ONES—I'M NOT SURE BUT I THINK IF I TRY REALLY HARD I CAN KILL

Magdalena stilled the urge to vomit. She tasted blood in the back of her throat, running from her sinuses. John had told her about Samuel speaking inside his head in the robot's museum, but to experience it herself was unnerving. When he spoke she felt as if her skull were a canyon and his voice a thunder that filled the stillness and echoed off its walls. But even more troubling was the message—that this boy, so much like an innocent lamb who hovered near her skirts, would kill for her. She didn't know how he could do it, or if he could do it, but she didn't doubt his willingness to try. And it was Samuel's willingness to kill that made her decision for her.

"Time grows short," said Burrell. "Decide now."

Magdalena pointed the rifle at the deck of the sand crawler. One of the men climbed in and took it from her hands.

She climbed down from the rear gate and whistled. Sheba leapt down at her side and Magdalena grabbed the dog's harness.

"You're blind?" said the man who took her rifle.

"Yes," said Magdalena. "But I would not have missed your captain's heart. Believe it."

The man stepped away and crossed himself.

Sheba led Magdalena to John. She kneeled down next to him. "I'm sorry," she whispered.

"No," said John. "You did the right thing."

"Now the child," said Burrell.

Samuel walked to the edge of the gate and jumped down. His legs were rubbery and he stumbled. He righted himself and walked slowly toward his companions. His body quivered with adrenaline. He'd been priming himself for a psychic blow, a deadly blast of mental energy that would've burst the brain of his target.

Blood trickled from his nose and ears—a side effect. He felt that it would've been worse if he'd actually tried the attack. A gush of blood and snot and a pain like an ice pick driven through his skull. Great effort was required to overcome the inhibitors that the doctors had instilled in him through his long and careful training. Training that ensured his Terrible Power wasn't used as a reflex. Samuel had to *want* to hurt someone.

Burrell gestured to the two men flanking him. "Now the ones in the cab."

Leggy saw Derek steel himself to resist, so he popped the passenger-side door open. "I'm comin' out," he called. "Nice and slow."

The two men ran around to his door and watched as Leggy eased himself down onto the sand.

"Captain, this one's a cripple," shouted one of the men.

"Name's Leggy."

Burrell shook his head. "A feeb, a blind woman, a crippled old man, and a child, all riding in a machine from the Before Days. You must have strange tales to tell."

"You have no idea," said Leggy. He swung himself on his hands around the front of the crawler. He stopped at the driver's side door and looked up at Derek.

"Come out, son." He could see the cords standing out in Derek's neck, the flush of red blooming on his cheeks. "They're only gonna pry you out anyway. Might as well come out on your own two feet."

For a moment Leggy thought Derek might gun the crawler to life and make a break for the road. Instead the door popped open and Derek stepped down. He took two steps toward Burrell, and then a pair of men intercepted him. There was a brief struggle, and then a third came and bound his wrists behind his back. They led him to the others and forced him to kneel in the sand.

Leggy looked up at his captors. "Now what?" he asked.

"Judgment," said Burrell. "I believe it was Chulo's men who killed Jordan, not you."

"I don't know Chulo," said Leggy. "Does he have somethin' to do with that bunker down the road?"

"Yes," said Burrell.

"So you ain't...you ain't associated with all that?" said Leggy.

Captain Burrell shook his head. "Chulo is a madman. He takes pleasure in the suffering and humiliation of others. He breaks the minds of his captives and turns them into dog-slaves. Pets. Domesticated people. He feeds his soldiers human flesh. If his men had found you, you'd all be in collars by now. Or in the cookpot."

"But you found us instead," said Leggy, holding Burrell's eye. "What do you take pleasure in?"

Burrell pointed to the low hills to the north, the place where Leggy had planned their detour. "Beyond those hills we have our ranches and our homesteads," he said. "I raise goats. These days one in every three kids born has the blood-poison, or strange deformities. I pray that when my son takes my place, it will be only one in five. And when his son comes of age, one in ten. I take pleasure in the hope that the world may heal itself someday."

"But then there's Chulo," said Leggy.

"Yes. Then there's Chulo. Two years ago, he emerged from the wastes. He found a way into that fort, which we'd never before been able to open. Not for lack of trying, mind you. Inside he found weapons the likes of which we'd never seen. And sooner than you'd think possible, he'd gathered a band of wanderers and thieves to him. He set himself up as a king and demanded tribute. Those who resisted were killed. Or worse. And so we did as he demanded. we sent him food and goats."

"At first he seemed satisfied. At least he kept his distance, and his men didn't trouble us too much. But eventually his madness proved even more powerful than his greed. He began demanding more and more from us. Not just livestock—he wanted people—women and children. When we refused, he simply took what he wanted. We defended ourselves as best we could, but our homesteads are far apart. It was too easy for him to take us out, one by one."

"Shit," said Leggy. "Lemme guess. You decided to band together and fight back. So what are you, the scoutin' party?"

The captain smiled. "Scouts are already set. We're the war party. I've got twenty more men beyond that hill, waiting for my command."

"We ain't got nothin' to do with your fight," said Derek. "You let us go, and we'll stay out of your way."

"It's a little more complicated than that," said Burrell. "I doubt you're spies, but maybe you're bandits. Our homesteads are unguarded now, and I can't have you roaming about."

"So what then?" asked Leggy. "Murder us here in the dirt?"

"I'd prefer not to," said Burrell, "so this is what will happen. You will stay inside Jordan's house. I'll leave two guards at the door. They'll shoot you if you try to leave—trust me on that. When morning comes, you're free to go. By then the battle will be over, and either Chulo will be dead or we will."

Burrell beckoned to the man who had searched the house and spoke into his ear. The man climbed into the back of the crawler and tossed out their packs. Then he opened the storage locker and emptied that as well.

"What are you doing?" shouted Derek.

"I'm trading with you," said Burrell. "Your lives for this vehicle. We have a need for it."

"No," shouted Derek. "That's ours!"

"I could just as easily kill you and take it," said Burrell. "I hope you see the generosity of this bargain."

"You fuck," Derek screamed. He tried to stand and run at Burrell but was knocked to the ground as the guard behind him pressed a knee into his back. Another man looped rope around his feet, hog-tying him.

Teddy surged to his feet. "Don't hurt my brother," he roared.

The man guarding Teddy swung the butt of his rifle in a short, vicious arc, connecting with Teddy's temple. The blow spun him around, and he toppled into the sand, moaning.

Derek writhed beneath his captor, flecks of spittle on his lips as he cursed and raged. Now all the captives were on their feet, shouting and scrambling. Rifles were leveled.

"Stop," cried Burrell. He strode forward and ordered two men to carry Teddy inside.

They lifted him clumsily and staggered toward the house, Teddy's feet dragging behind them.

Burrell turned to Leggy. "Take your people inside. Wait until morning. Do it now, or I'll leave you dead in the dirt."

"John, gather the gear and bring Maggie inside," said Leggy. "Sam, tie the mules to the tree and then go tend to Teddy."

They moved to their assigned tasks. The two men who carried Teddy to the house now returned for Derek.

"Will you cut him free?" asked Leggy.

"No. You can do that once we've gone," said Burrell.

The men lifted Derek, who continued to flail like a wild animal, and carried him inside. Derek was in a blind rage, screaming and hissing, his limbs straining against the ropes that bound him. Another man started the crawler, and Burrell's troop climbed up into the trailer bed.

Leggy looked up at the captain.

"I make no apologies," said the man. "Hard decisions are necessary here."

"So much for the world healing itself," said Leggy. "What with men the likes o' you's pourin' salt in her open wounds."

Burrell said nothing. He strode to the crawler and climbed into the passenger side. Then the vehicle pulled away, disappearing into the darkening night. Leggy swung himself toward the house. Two men stood nearby, rifles at the ready. At their feet were the meager weapons of Leggy's band.

"You'll get those back tomorrow, old man," said the guard to the left. "Don't make things any harder than they need to be."

Samuel dragged the last of the gear inside. Leggy glanced once more at the guards and then crossed the threshold.

Jordan's house was neat and spare. The scent of dried herbs and cooked meat flavored the air. Teddy was laid out on a soft mat on the floor, holding his swollen temple and rocking back-and-forth. Magdalena dabbed at the injury with a damp cloth. Derek lay on the flagstone floor near the hearth, still bound. John struggled with the knotted ropes, Derek cursing him for his clumsiness.

Leggy swung himself over to Derek. "I'm gonna unbind you," he said. "But you gotta promise me you ain't gonna make a run for it. I think the captain's as good as his word. Those men outside will shoot you dead if you even poke a toe out that door."

"Just cut the fuckin' ropes," said Derek.

Leggy found a knife in Jordan's small kitchen and slashed the cords. Derek shot to his feet and stripped off the strands tied to his wrists and ankles. He strode over to a pair of wooden shutters and yanked off the bar that held them closed.

"Easy," said Leggy.

Derek opened one shutter and poked his head out. Leggy heard the *snak* of a shotgun being levered. Derek closed the shutter.

"What now?" he said, turning to Leggy.

"We wait."

Hours passed. Teddy complained of a headache. They lit a fire in the fireplace, and John found stores of food in a larder—lamb jerky, a few tubers, onions, dried sage, and a sack of corn. There were half a dozen ratty looking apples, as well, but, remembering Jordan's complaints of graininess and worms, no one dared sample one.

Samuel got permission from the guards to fetch water, and he and Magdalena prepared a meal. Once it was ready, they all ate without speaking.

After supper, Derek peeked through the shutters again. The guards sat with their backs against the apple tree, nearly invisible in the moonlight. One smoked a stubby cheroot, its glowing red eye pointed at the door.

"I still think we could take those guys and get out of here," said Derek.

"What's the point?" asked Leggy. "Maybe we could overpower those two, but how bad are we gonna get hurt doin' it? Besides, there's gonna be a war right on the road we want to take."

"So what then?" said Derek. "Just hole up here?"

Leggy shrugged. He pulled his blanket from his pack and made himself comfortable near the fire.

"But what about the crawler?" demanded Derek.

"What about it? It's been requisitioned, as we used to say."

"But—" began Derek.

Leggy cut him off. "But what? Go steal it back? While it's in the middle of a firefight?"

Derek clenched his fists and stared down at Leggy, but the reality of their predicament overcame his anger.

Leggy fussed with his blankets. "I said I wanted to sleep with a roof over my head tonight. Looks like I get my wish." He lay back and closed his eyes.

Derek snorted. He paced around the darkening cabin as the others shook out their own bedrolls and drifted off to sleep. Eventually he slumped into a wooden chair and joined them.

CHAPTER TWENTY-NINE

They were woken by the sound of distant gunfire. It was nearly dawn, and the sharp crack of rifle shots slashed through the chill air. They were quickly joined by the chatter of automatic weapons.

"Guess they're startin'," said John, rubbing his eyes.

Quickly the individual reports of the weapons blurred into an explosive haze of noise, like constant thunder or the fireworks that Leggy talked about from the Bomb Day festivities in Moses Spring. The fight was getting hot.

Derek got up from his chair and opened the shutter. The moon had set, and the sky was a dark purple, waiting for the sun to rise. The guards weren't there.

"Hey," said Derek. "They're gone." He moved to the door and opened it.

"Slow up," said Leggy, slithering out of his blankets. "Maybe they're around back."

Derek shook his head. "Why would they be around back? This is the only door. I bet they went to help their friends." He stepped out into the yard and walked over to where their own weapons were piled. "Hello? Hello?" he called. "You guys around?"

No response.

Cautiously, the others joined him. They stood in the dooryard in a tight group. The sounds of the battle were clearer out here.

"C'mon," said Derek. "Let's get the fuck out of here."

The others agreed. They moved quickly in the chill morning air, rolling up their bedding, gathering stores that Jordan had left behind, and strapping their packs to Minna. Teddy helped Leggy mount up on Afha.

The gunfire was joined by bigger explosions. They saw flashes of white and red light on the horizon, like distant heat lightning.

"Which way should we go?" asked John.

"We gotta give that firefight a wide berth," said Leggy. "And I mean *wide*."

"We could head north," said John, "toward the place where Burrell said they had their homesteads."

"I don't know that that'd be any safer," said Leggy. "I'll bet they left a rifle or two with the women and children and instructions to shoot first and ask questions later."

"So what then?" asked Derek. "Go south and loop around that bunker?"

"Sounds good to me," said Leggy.

"Then let's roll," said Derek.

Leggy patted Afha the donkey. "I ain't lookin' forward to this," he said. "And I bet you ain't, either. I miss that crawler already."

At that moment a huge explosion lit up the dawn. A few seconds later a blast of air struck them. Afha snorted and reared as Leggy flung his arms around the beast's neck and buried his face in the animal's hide. The others cowered, their hands flung over their heads. A cloud of sandy grit raced past them, slashing at bare skin and coating them in dust. Above them, the leaves of Jordan's tree hissed and rattled.

When the shockwave had passed, John scrambled over to Leggy and the donkey.

"What the Hell was that?" he shouted, steadying Afha.

"Bomb. Musta been a bomb," said Derek, patting dust from his clothes. "A goddamn big one." He pointed to the horizon, where a pillar of fire lit the sky in a false dawn.

They fetched water from the well to clear their mouths and clean the dust from their faces and then stood in the dooryard once more.

"You think we should check it out?" asked Derek. "I'm guessing that blast means the battle's over."

Leggy stroked his chin. "I don't hear no more gunfire, so you're probably right. Still though, we don't know who won. I'd hate to walk right into Chulo's hands."

"The size of that blast," John looked at Leggy, "You really think there's a winner?"

Derek spit. "Well, wait here then."

Once again he shimmied up the tree. The others watched him disappear into the topmost branches. He was down again just as quickly.

"Bunker's gone," he said, tucking his spyglass into his pack. "Just a hole in the ground now. Couldn't make out much else on account of the fire and smoke. But I'll wager that whoever was in that bunker is just a dirty smudge on the ground now."

"Still though," said Leggy.

"C'mon," said Derek. "We'll be careful. We'll approach nice and slow."

"Why are you so eager to go there?" asked John.

"'Cause maybe we can get our crawler back," said Derek. "It's ours and they took it. I want it back."

Derek would not be deterred.

Leggy gave his assent, and the group made their careful way toward the pillar of flame.

"I feel like Moses," said Derek as they walked. "Ain't that in the Good Book, John? Wanderers led by fire out of the desert and into the promised land?"

"That's right," said John. "The Hebrews. A column of smoke by day and a pillar of fire by night."

Derek chuckled. "Now all we need is a sea so I can part it. I got that one all figured out."

"Oh yeah?" asked John.

"Sure," said Derek. "Just load up Teddy with a couple cans o' beans and let him rip. He'll split that sea as neat as you please. Ain't that right, Ted?"

"Fart," yelled Teddy.

Samuel giggled, which spurred Teddy to imitate a long, wet expulsion.

"There it goes," said Derek. "Just follow the dead fish to the other side, you Hebes. But don't forget to hold your noses."

"Pee-yew," shouted Teddy.

"No need to blaspheme," muttered John.

"Take it easy," snapped Leggy. "We're supposed to be on guard here."

"Okay, okay," said Derek. He elbowed his brother, and the two continued to giggle quietly to themselves.

But their laughter stopped as they crested the final rise in the road.

Three quarters of the bunker had been obliterated by the blast—only a skeleton wall remained. It stood precariously on the edge of a crater, out of which rose yellow and orange flames. Bodies lay scattered all around the hole. Above them vultures hovered, ready to descend and gorge.

The group walked on, slowly. Suddenly Samuel cried out and pointed. A head and torso lay in the sand near their feet, flung there by the blast.

"Must've been one of Chulo's men," said Leggy grimly.

What remained of the body was decked out in black armor, rebreather and a helmet—little good it had done for its wearer.

Soon they came upon other body parts, Chulo's and Burrell's men alike, intermingled with chunks of broken concrete and twisted metal. Scraps of burning paper and ash swirled in a feeble breeze. Granules of glass and plastic crunched underfoot.

As they neared the epicenter of the battle they saw other horrors. Burrell's men had been torn apart by bullets and mortar blasts. A yellow powder dusted other corpses. They lay in frozen postures of agony, their hands clawing at their eyes or tearing at their own throats.

Then Teddy shouted. Two men were hobbling along the road toward them. They moved wearily, dragging their rifles on the ground behind them. The men stumbled along, heads down, arms around each other's shoulders, supporting one another. They stopped when they saw the travelers.

Leggy was the first to recognize them—the men that had guarded the house.

"What happened here?" asked Leggy.

"Can't you see?" said the first man. "We won!" Then he began to laugh, a high, hysterical sound.

"Where's the others?" asked Derek.

"They had chemicals," said the man. "And when they saw that we were close to taking their stronghold, they doused us. Hector here was lucky," he said, nodding with his head toward the man he held alongside him. "He only got a small dusting."

The man called Hector lifted his head. His eyes had been burned away, leaving empty sockets. Where his nose had once been were two singed, mucous-filled holes. His lips had been scorched off to reveal nubs of teeth shielding a blistered tongue. The dusted man gurgled his agreement. They'd been lucky indeed. Everyone else was dead.

"Where's Burrell?" asked Leggy, looking away from the ruin of the man's face. "Did he make it?"

"And where's the crawler?" demanded Derek, his grim eyes searching the battlefield.

"Gone. Both gone," said the man. "The captain took it on a suicide mission. He packed it full of manure and moonshine and drove it through the gate, smashed it into the fortress." The man turned and looked at the still smoking hole. "Chulo never knew what hit him. Must've been a Hell of a lot more explosives inside the bunker." He laughed. "Sheep shit and corn liquor don't blow up like that!"

Derek said nothing, but his cheeks flushed red and he clenched his fists.

The men stumbled forward, and the travelers parted.

"Long way home," said the man. "Have to tell the homestead we won." He spit blood in the sand, and then the two victors hobbled away, leaving the travelers to stand amidst the carnage and smoldering ruin.

John leaned heavily against a pile of rubble. Words failed him. All he could do was watch the remains of the fortress smolder. No one else spoke. Samuel sat cross-legged, apart from the others, staring down at the ground. Even the animals seemed unwilling to break the sullen silence. Finally, it was Derek who interrupted the funereal melancholy.

"Goddammit!" He swung his foot hard, kicking at a short length of broken tread—debris which more than likely had come from the sand crawler—sending it hurtling into the air in a plume of ash and sand. "This is bullshit. Fuck this shit!"

Derek was near tears. John wanted to say something, to defuse the rage, but could think of nothing.

Magdalena touched his shoulder and ever so slightly shook her head. "Let him," she whispered. "He needs to let it out."

"Goddamn you!" Derek shook his fists at the sky.

As if in answer, a chill breeze broke the heat and brought the acrid odor of burning fuel and manure from the crater that was once a fortress.

"Fuck you all to Hell!" Derek roared at the Heavens.

The only reply was the wind. Another sandstorm was brewing in the distance, turning the pillars of smoke into odd, twisted forms and thinning them out—covering the violence with dust and sand, burying secrets, and selling the lie of passing time and natural erosion.

Derek felt a wet nuzzling at his hand. "Get away!" He batted angrily at the dog, "Get lost, fleabag."

But it wasn't the dog, or Minna or three-eyed Afha. It was one of Chulo's people-pets, which had miraculously survived the blast. Half-naked and bound in leather straps, shuffling about on all fours and licking his hand. Derek yelped in sheer revulsion of the pathetic thing—it was a man. At least, it had at one time been a man. Its face had been horribly mutilated, its ears trimmed to feral points, teeth sharpened. Scars from beatings or worse covered every exposed inch of flesh. The creature smiled, and tried again to nuzzle Derek.

"Can we keep him, Der? Can we?" Teddy lunged forward and ruffled the creature's patchy skull. "His name's Woofy. Says so on his tag. Leggy says he used ta be a person, but now he's not. Can we keep him?"

"Fuuuuuuck….!" Derek's scream lengthened into a long coughing rattle. He fell to his knees and then slumped resignedly between Leggy and John.

CHAPTER THIRTY

For the longest time, the group sat in silence.

They'd hiked into the night, trying to put as much distance between them and the battlefield as they could, before throwing together a quick haggard camp and surrendering themselves to unconsciousness. They woke with the sun, and Leggy boiled some water, warming the last of their coffee over the embers of the previous night's fire.

The wind rose to a shrill gale and then receded to what, for the Wasteland, might be considered a comfortable zephyr. In the distance, a sandstorm made the grit and dust turn in strange arabesques, but the dance went unnoticed by the sullen band of travelers.

Derek removed his spyglass and scanned the horizon. Endless desert and broken highways as far as the glass eye could see. No signs of life, no signs of civilization. Leggy had called this barren stretch the gateway to the Blasted Lands. Only sand and crumbling tarmac littered the shattered highways, punctuated with distant dust devils, and heat lightning.

Then Derek's glass caught a slight movement to the south. A man. No, two men—the second had been dwarfed by the enormous girth of the first—were scavenging through the rubble of what might once been a small market or a villa, but was now little more than a dry-rotted abutment of broken adobe and rubble.

For a while Derek watched them scavenge. They were at such a distance that he had no fear of being spotted. The larger one might even surpass Teddy in size—surely he was a mutant of some sort. But, strangely, Derek felt no threat from them. Rather, there was a sense of unspoken kinship, a mutual feeling of... *survival* communicated over the empty miles between them.

They might never meet in person, but Derek could sense that they too were survivors. The giant and his skinny little brother—Derek decided with strange certainty that they *were* brothers, not so very different than he and Teddy. Only these two were not lucky enough to have gathered a group around them, or perhaps they simply preferred traveling alone.

Derek shivered, lowering the spyglass to his crossed legs. For the first time since the beginning of this insane quest, he realized that he was indeed grateful for his traveling companions. Though he knew he would never tell them so—any of them—he also knew that without them he and Teddy would never have made it this far. And without them, he might never make it to New York.

He brought the spyglass back up to his eye. The distant travelers had given up on the ruined market, and dejectedly headed out into the wastes, following the cracked path of their own heat-twisted highway. Derek watched as they hiked farther and farther away. He watched until they became mere dots on the horizon. He watched as the distance between the two grew and grew—the small one lagging behind, and the larger, stronger one trudging ever onward. And Derek watched as the little one fell to his knees in exhaustion and hunger, unable to take another step and his brother went back for him. The giant pulled his brother up onto his shoulders, turned, and then marched out of sight trudging with all the weight of his brother on his back, marching directly into the fiery sunset sinking into the blasted horizon.

Tears that Derek couldn't explain suddenly filled his eyes. He hadn't felt a thing when he'd slowly cocked his shotgun and, despite Teddy's tears, put down his brother's infernal half-man, Woofy. But now, thinking of the brothers carrying each other out there in the Wasteland, alone, but *not* alone…. Suddenly, Moses Springs seemed impossibly far behind. And New York? New York had never seemed so far away.

ABOUT THE AUTHORS

Scott Christian Carr lives on a secluded mountaintop deep in New York's Hudson Valley. He spends his time writing novels and stories, producing for film and television, and enjoying the country life with his kids. Carr is the co-creator of The Learning Channel TV series *Dead Tenants*, and has produced television for such networks as MSNBC, Discovery, The Hallmark Channel, A&E, and others. His fiction & nonfiction have appeared in *Shroud Magazine*, *Withersin*, *GUD*, *Horror Quarterly*, *Pulp Eternity*, *Weird N.J.*, and assorted anthologies. His novels *Champion Mountain* and *Hiram Grange & the Twelve Little Hitlers* are currently garnering favorable reviews. His recent accolades include The Hunter S. Thompson Award for Outstanding Journalism, Scriptapalooza TV: 1st Place Best Original Pilot, and a 2009 Bram Stoker Award nomination. He is the author of the upcoming novels *Hiram Grange & The Twelve Steps* and *Matthew's Memories* (illustrated by Danny Evarts).

Andrew Conry-Murray is a technology writer and editor. He is the author of the book *The Symantec Guide to Home Internet Security* and the novella *Fei the Hero*. He lives in Pennsylvania with his wife and two sons.

CPSIA information can be obtained at www.ICGtesting.com
Printed in the USA
LVOW06s1639230414

382933LV00008B/1180/P